PIPPIN'S JOURNAL

ROHAN O'GRADY — — was born in Vancouver, British-American forester and an Lord Byng Secondary School as resident assistant manager after the war she worked in the and married newspaperman would raise three children. She the O'Grady pseudonym: *O'Houlihan's Jest* (—, —), set in 18th-century Ireland and an ode to her own Irish heritage; *Pippin's Journal* (1962), also published as *The Curse of the Montrolfes* and *The Master of Montrolfe Hall*, a historical Gothic novel; *Let's Kill Uncle* (1963), her most famous book, a darkly humorous tale of two children who conspire to murder their wicked uncle that was filmed in 1966 by William Castle; and *Bleak November* (1970), a creepy Gothic novel. She also published *The May Spoon*, a young adult novel, in 1981 under the pseudonym A. Carleon. She died in 2014.

ROHAN O'GRADY

PIPPIN'S JOURNAL

or

ROSEMARY IS FOR REMEMBRANCE

VALANCOURT BOOKS

*Dedication: TO FREDERICK S. SKINNER AND
FREDERIC C. O'GRADY*

Pippin's Journal by Rohan O'Grady
Originally published by Macmillan in 1962
First Valancourt Books edition 2024

Copyright © 1962 by June Skinner, renewed 1990

All rights reserved. In accordance with the U.S. Copyright Act of 1976, the copying, scanning, uploading, and/or electronic sharing of any part of this book without the permission of the publisher constitutes unlawful piracy and theft of the author's intellectual property. If you would like to use material from the book (other than for review purposes), prior written permission must be obtained by contacting the publisher.

Published by Valancourt Books, Richmond, Virginia
http://www.valancourtbooks.com

ISBN 978-1-960241-18-4 (paperback)
Also available as an electronic book.

Set in Dante MT

CHAPTER ONE

Slowly, and not without a certain inexplicable feeling of foreboding, I limped up the weed-grown gravel path to the door of Cliff House.

After a wait of several minutes, the door opened reluctantly in response to my knock, and I found myself looking at the most ancient, wrinkled beldame I had ever seen.

"I am John Montrolfe," I said, extending my hand.

She ignored the gesture, and, lifting her hideous old head, peered at me closely.

"You Mr. Nicholas' nephew?" she asked finally, in a voice that was nearly as hoarse and deep as my own.

I nodded.

"Yer aren't very pretty, are yer?" She rubbed one arthritic, twisted finger under her nose. "Now Mr. Nicholas, he were a handsome one, he were. You be Mr. Phillip's son, I suppose, him what went to South Africa?"

"Canada," I answered. "May I come in?"

She shrugged and, turning her back, walked into the house. I stood on the threshold of my inheritance, hesitant, and then took a deep breath and limped after the old lady.

The house, which was a Georgian mansion of whitewashed brick, had obviously once been a show place, but as I stepped into the main entrance hall, I realized how sadly my family had let the place fall into disrepair.

Not only was the floor covered with dust, the carpet worn to thin shreds and the pictures hanging drunkenly askew, but the main staircase, which curled down one side of the wall, showed occasional treads missing, as conspicuous as newly pulled teeth, and the bannister looked as though some mischievous boy had jerked out every second or third rung.

I stood looking about me in surprise, for my father, on the rare occasions he had spoken to me except to curse me, had led me to believe that I was the last pitiful relic of a mighty line. And Cliff House, for all its substantial exterior, inside resembled nothing so much as a poorly constructed stage setting for second-rate actors in a play without substance. Cobwebs and dust, penury and neglect were everywhere apparent as I followed the old woman from one wretched room to another, until finally we ended up in what appeared, in the dim light, to be the kitchen.

Here the old woman settled herself in a cushioned chair next to the open fireplace, and through the folds of her long skirt she began rubbing her bony knees with her twisted hands.

I stood silent, waiting for her to introduce herself, for, after all, I was the new master of this place, and I had already made one gesture of friendliness which she had chosen to ignore.

She still said nothing, but arose, and, leaning over the fire, began to stir something that bubbled in a black iron pot which hung on a hob. I stared at her, fascinated, for in all the world I had never seen such a perfect embodiment of an old witch; and as the firelight lit up her profile, showing in relief the wispy hair, hooked nose, the pointed chin straining to reach it, the toothless old mouth puckered maliciously and the sunken eyes with sockets as hollow as a skull, I could not but feel how hellish a thing true antiquity in the human frame is, how it twists and distorts, mocking nature for not allowing a leaf to fall from the tree when autumn is over, winter done with, and only a hopeless and barren spring ahead.

The old lady seemed to read my thoughts, for she suddenly turned her head, and in that rusty croak, lisped, "Yer ain't so pretty yerself, young man, like I said. And Nanny Beckett's good for a hundred, she is, for we live long in these parts. My granny, she was a hundred and three when she died, so don't be plannin' on being rid of me for another ten years, for Mr. Nicholas said in his will I was to stay here for the rest of my natural life, if it so pleased me. And two pounds a week I gets, too. Don't be anxious to be rid of Nanny Beckett, for you'll be all alone here when she's gone."

"So you are ninety-three, and your name is Nanny Beckett," I said, seating myself on a bench by the fire.

"And you are John Montrolfe. How old would you be now, Mr. John?"

I made no reply.

"Yer not much like Mr. Phillip," she said, raising the spoon to her mouth and smacking her lips with the repulsive greediness of old age. "He were a handsome one. I remember him when he left. Eighteen he were, and a bonny looking boy, too. Just too full of life to stay in these parts. Had to be off to see the world. And what did he ever do in that there Africa?"

"Canada," I said, lighting a cigarette, the only solace nature allows me.

"Well, I knew it was one of them colonies," she croaked. "Canada, maybe. And so you're his son. Well, well."

She turned her face full to me and I was surprised at the sharpness and brilliance of her black eyes.

"Yer not like yer father."

"You've already said that." I know well enough what I look like, and though her appearance was far from prepossessing, I could never play pots and kettles with her. I loathe peppery old ladies who make uncalled for remarks. Why they think age entitles them to be inexcusably rude is something I can't fathom.

"So you knew my father?" I said abruptly.

"Knew him? Why, I saw him come into this world, I did, upstairs in the master's bedroom there. And his brother Nicholas too, and I helped midwife at your grandfather's birth, and that would be, let me see, seventy-seven years ago. And I waited on your great-grandfather."

"My great-grandfather?" I asked in surprise.

"Aye," she said, ladling out a bowl of slop from the iron pot and seating herself on her cushions. "Aye, I come into this house in service when I was ten years old, and that's eighty-three years ago, and my mother had been here for thirty years then, and her mother and granny before her. Her granny was with the first Mr. Montrolfe, him they called Mr. Guy."

My feeling of repugnance changed to one of wonder; there was something uncanny about those wrinkled, clawlike hands, clutched around a bowl and spoon—hands that had helped guide into the world a newborn infant who would be an old man were he alive today.

"Yes," she said, sipping her gruel, "three generations I seen of them, and you the fourth, and judging from the look of you, the last of them."

I winced and turned my face to the fire. It wasn't fair, it wasn't fair. What had I ever done to deserve the monstrous form nature had seen fit to bestow upon me?

"I suppose you're hungry?" she peered maliciously at me out of the corner of her eye.

I nodded.

"Well," she said, "you won't get no fancy food here. I eats plain. Have to when you reach ninety. All I can stomach is gruel, and I'm not a cook, neither, so if you're hungry, you'll either have to eat gruel or get someone else in to do your cooking."

I felt a surge of something akin to pleasure as I replied to this, for in all things there is some measure of compensation, and I answered truthfully: "Don't look so happy about not waiting on me or cooking, Nanny Beckett. It so happens I have been on a restricted diet from earliest infancy, and all I can digest are milk and egg puddings and gruel, with bread soaked in it, and an occasional bit of broiled meat which I'll be quite content to prepare for myself."

"What!" she said, as surprised as I knew she would be. "Old woman's food for a man your size? Why, you must be six and a half feet tall!"

"Six feet four," I replied.

"And what would you weigh?" she asked in wonder.

"Two hundred and fifty pounds," I replied.

"Bah, you and your foreign ways, how many stone?"

"Nearly eighteen."

"Well, well," she cackled, "well, well." And then she pointed her spoon at my feet and said, "And what's the matter with them?"

I clenched my jaws and stared straight at her.

"I have two club feet, Nanny Beckett. Does that make you happy?"

"Well, well," she clucked, "well, well. The Montrolfe curse truly fell on you, didn't it?"

"Curse?" I said. "Were there other Montrolfes with club feet?"

"No, no, dearie," she answered, in a placating voice, treating me for the first time as though I were a child she had known for years. "No, no. Not club feet, but they has never been a happy lot. Well, well. You needn't worry about your food, dearie, Nanny Beckett will see to you."

"Perhaps I'd prefer to get someone in from the village," I answered stiffly.

"Hah!" she cackled, "you won't find none in Forsham who'll do service in Cliff House."

"Why not?" I asked.

"Why, they're too afraid of *him*."

"Of whom?"

"Why, Mr. Guy, the first Montrolfe, of course."

"And why should they be afraid of him? I should think I would frighten them far more."

"Ah, but at least you're alive, even if you ain't so pretty, my love. And you won't find none in Forsham who'll take a chance of meetin' him, prowling along the cliffs."

"And are you not afraid?" I asked teasingly.

The old lady laughed, an ancient, mirthless, toothless laugh, and stood up. She took two candles from the mantle and lit them at the fire.

"I expect, Mr. John, you'll be wanting to see your room now, and rest after your journey. To be sure, it's a long way from that there Africa."

"Canada," I replied, as I followed her up the dark and broken stairs.

"Aye, Canada," she said. She opened a door and held her candle up for me to see my bedroom. "Aye, Canada, and when you live to be ninety-three, why, there's little in this world or the next that frightens an old body much, Mr. John."

At birth, my father had wanted to destroy me, but my mother, with a woman's perverse instinct, had refused, and weeping, had clutched me to her.

From that minute until her death when I was five, she had never left me alone, always fearful that perhaps he might renege on his promise to let me live.

He kept his promise, but I remained an only child, my father fearful, I suppose, that if the first were as malformed as I, nature might be capable of producing even more dreadful monsters from his loins.

So, like Nanny Beckett, who, at the age of ninety-three, had nothing to fear from either this world or the next, I at the age of thirty-three was unafraid as I walked slowly around my huge bedroom, exploring it with my candle.

The room was magnificently furnished and, considering the state of the chambers I had seen below, it was in a remarkably good state of preservation and cleanliness.

Just as Mr. Nicholas had left it, Nanny Beckett said, except that she had changed the sheets. I drew down the heavy brocade bedspread and fleecy blankets, and there they were: clean, crisp, white linen.

There was, I hoped, a bathroom on the second floor; I set out to find it. It was two doors down the hall, a typical Victorian horror, added about a hundred and fifty years after the house was built.

I returned downstairs and brought up my luggage, two suitcases in all, and unpacked. Then, taking my toothbrush, candle and towel, I went down to the bathroom and brushed my teeth and washed.

Coming out, I had half a mind to explore, but decided against it, for I was very tired, and since the house had no electricity and I could see little by candlelight, I decided to wait until morning.

I was in my pajamas, sitting in bed and ready to blow out the candle when there was a knock on the door and Nanny Beckett walked in.

"Here's your gruel," she said, handing me a porringer such as children use. "And don't think I'm climbin' those stairs every night. It's only because you've traveled so far."

I thanked her and took the bowl, and as I began to spoon it, the old lady went to the fireplace and lit it.

"Why are you doing that?" I asked. "It's summer."

"Bah!" she said, throwing the match into the flames. "First night you're here, don't want you catching your death, straight out from that there Africa."

I finished the gruel and handed her the porringer.

She stood with one hand on the doorknob, an old, old crone, bent double with age.

"Not afraid of Mr. Guy, Mr. John?"

I lit a cigarette and smiled bitterly.

"No, Nanny Beckett. I am beyond fear."

She stood hesitant, then said, "Mr. John, what's the matter with your neck? Why do you walk with your head twisted over to one side that way?"

"Get out," I said.

CHAPTER TWO

For all of my various ailments, most of which doctors lightly classify as hypochondria, not being saddled with them themselves, I have trained myself to do one thing, and that is to sleep soundly.

I awoke refreshed, my slumber completely undisturbed by my ghostly ancestor, and walking to the casement windows, I threw them wide open.

For the first time, in the fragrance of early dawn, I saw the countryside which had bred Montrolfes for two hundred years.

Before me was the ocean, jewel clear and sparkling in the morning sun, and leaning out the window I saw that the house was built within fifteen feet of the cliff's edge.

The house was situated on a bay, flanked on either side by several miles of rolling surf, and across the bay I could see the fishing boats of the village of Forsham, bobbing and tugging at their moorings. By water it would be about a mile to Forsham, but by foot I could see that the route was much longer. The coast line was jagged, and I judged it would be a good five miles by land.

After washing and dressing I found my way down the broken stairs and through dusty corridors to the kitchen. Nanny Beckett was also an early riser; either that or she never slept at all, for I found her as I had seen her the night before, huddled like a featherless old crow on her cushions by the fire, one bright and beady eye on the black pot that bubbled over the fire.

She gave me no greeting, so I ignored her. Going to the dresser,

I got myself a porringer and spoon and ladled out some of the gruel, which she prepared excellently.

I looked up from my food to find that malevolent old eye bent upon me.

"Tea?" she asked.

I shook my head. I have tasted tea and coffee only once in my life, and each made me violently ill.

"Just like Mr. Nicholas," she said contentedly. "All you Montrolfes got weak stomachs. Stop thinking about yourselves so much and your bellies wouldn't bother you."

"Have you any eggs?" I asked.

She looked at me suspiciously.

"I've got some. You want to buy them from me?"

"In the future I shall be buying all the supplies for this house. Your food will cost you nothing. Bring the eggs."

She lifted the top of a stone jar in the corner and brought out four, which she placed before me reluctantly.

"Is this all? I generally eat a dozen for breakfast."

She hobbled back and brought out eight more.

"Give me a bowl," I said.

"Now, now, I'll fix them for you. Just tell me how you like them."

"Beat them in a bowl with a cup of milk and a pinch of salt," I said.

"You eat them raw?"

I nodded.

"Ugh." But she did as I bade her, only mumbling, as she handed me the bowl, that it was no more than she expected from someone brought up among them heathens in Africa.

"Now, Nanny Beckett," I said, when I had finished, "there are going to be some changes made around here."

"Eh?" she said, cupping her hand behind her ear.

"You heard me," I said. "Probably at your age you don't welcome changes, but you'll just have to get used to them. First of all, there's quite a bit of carpentry to be done. I don't intend to break my neck, twisted as it is, on those stairs. All those old carpets must go, and this place is going to be kept free of dust."

"What? This house has over thirty rooms. Do you think at my

age I'm going to get down on my knees and scrub? Mr. Nicholas had some respect for his poor old Nanny, he wouldn't expect a body of over ninety to work like a navvy."

"I don't expect you to do anything," I replied. "I'm going into Forsham today to order lumber and tools, and to hire a couple of servants. The house is far too big for the two of us, but we can keep six or seven rooms habitable and clean with a bit of help and close off the rest."

"You won't find no help in Forsham, like I told you last night. Nor no carpenter to work here, neither."

"Nonsense," I said. "People will work anywhere for a good wage, and that's what I intend to pay. As for the carpentry, I'll do it myself. Tell me, Nanny, how could Nicholas let this place fall into such disrepair? I know he was a very wealthy man, because he left me his entire fortune. Why didn't he use some of his money to restore the house?"

Nanny settled herself in her chair again. "Mr. Nicholas rarely left his room. He had other things on his mind, he did. And you needn't go talking about him that way. You young people think you know everything. Well, you'll find out, dearie. You'll find out, when you've lived here a while, that there's a great deal you don't know. And you won't find no help in Forsham."

"Is there a boat here, or do I have to walk?"

"There's no boat," she said. "Young Tommy Parker rides on his wheel from the village to bring supplies twice a week. I suppose though, with all that money of yours, you could buy a boat."

It took me three hours to walk to Forsham, but then I am a slow walker.

Nanny was right about the people of Forsham. Whether it was my appearance or their superstitious fear of Cliff House, I was treated with suspicion verging on hostility wherever I went.

I managed to buy some supplies and a boat, but no one, man nor woman, would agree to work at Cliff House at any price.

For about a week I worked with a false burst of energy. I repaired the stairs and partially cleared the library of dust and cobwebs. But before the job was half done, I fell away from the crest of energy and in another week I was drowned in a slough of inertia.

There was something enervating about Cliff House; a slow, stealthy ennui seeped into the blood, but so slowly that I was hardly conscious of it. Its influence was so subtle that, like the lost traveler who lies down in the snowstorm, I was lulled by its deceitful comfort almost to sleep.

I cannot quite explain it, but there was a certain timelessness about Cliff House—not as if the clocks had all suddenly stopped, for there was no overt drama about it, but as if they had never started to tick.

It must have been about two weeks after my first night in Cliff House that the two crates of my books and papers arrived from Canada. In Canada these had been to me like beloved children, but here, in the land of the lotus-eaters, I had to force myself to carry them up to my bedroom and unpack them.

Nanny Beckett poked her head in the door and stood watching me.

"Lor," she said finally, "a whole library of books downstairs rotting for want of someone to read 'em, and you have to ship a cartload from Africa."

I sat on the floor, looking up at her, and nodded.

"What are they about?"

"Nuclear physics. I'm a scientist."

The old lady put her head to one side suspiciously, "You have anything to do with that there atom bomb?"

"No," I said wearily. "Bigger and worse things, Nan."

"Trust a Montrolfe to have a hand in dropping misery on innocent people's heads." She went off grumbling, as I picked up a paper and began to read. Very foolishly, as I do everything, I sat on the floor reading by candlelight until midnight, when I looked up, startled to find the old woman standing there with hot milk for me.

I arose and sat on the edge of the bed. As soon as I moved I developed a splitting headache. I put my hands on either side of my head and held it in a vise.

"What's the matter now?"

"Headache," I mumbled.

She hobbled off and returned a few minutes later with a bottle of aspirin, but I waved it away.

"Go on." She pushed it impatiently under my nose.

"I can't take aspirin." Nor can I take any drug, for the simplest, most harmless one blinds and poisons me.

I sat motionless for half an hour, but my head still throbbed painfully. Finally I decided to get up and walk about. I ended up downstairs in the library, pacing back and forth, or rather, I should say, limping back and forth.

Nanny came clomping in, looking more than ever like something loosed on the Eve of St. Walpurgis.

"Now what are you doing down here at this time of night, rattling all the furniture with your feet so a body can't rest?"

"I'm sorry," I said, rubbing my aching eyes.

She disappeared and returned a few minutes later, this time with a bottle of gin and two glasses.

"None of that for me, I can't stomach liquor of any kind."

"Well, there's no harm in me warming my old bones."

I motioned her to sit beside the fireplace, then I lit the fire. I had grown fond of the old Tartar, though I had no intention of letting her know it.

She sat sipping straight gin and smacking her lips, the firelight casting grotesque shadows over her bent form. She became talkative as she drank.

"So yer not afraid of that Mr. Guy?" she said, jerking her thumb at the portrait over the mantel.

"Is that Mr. Guy?" I asked. Though I had noticed the portrait, I had never bothered to examine it.

"Aye, that be him. Handsome gentleman, weren't he?"

I lifted the candle and inspected the painting.

"No," I said finally. "He wasn't. I wonder why he wore a beard? Men were usually clean-shaven in that era. Tell me about him. What was he like? Who did he marry?"

Mr. Guy, complete with powdered wig, sky-blue frock coat, satin weskit and feathery lace jabot, gazed down at me. I had never seen such mournful, terrible eyes.

"Well," said Nan, "nobody knew much about him, Mr. John. He come here about two hundred years ago with a fortune he had made in the Indies, and he built this house. This property originally had an inn on it, but that burned down about five years before Mr. Guy come here.

"He married the Lady Hester Walpole, she was the daughter of an earl. Mr. Guy, he was a strange man.... His wife was very beautiful, but he didn't seem to care for her. He was just like all the Montrolfes, didn't really care for no one but himself.

"At first he wasn't too bad to her, brought her here as a bride and there was merry times when this house was first built. My great-granny told my mother wonderful tales of it. Mr. Guy bought the finest of furniture and silver and rugs and china and horses. And servants, why there must have been two dozen, counting the gardeners, for the place had fine formal gardens then, planned by Mr. Guy himself. And coaches coming all the way from London, and from the houses of all the fine county families, filled to bursting with pretty ladies and gentlemen. Oh, the ladies and their dresses! My great-granny said they was like rainbows, with their silks and satins.

"At first, like I say, he wasn't too bad to Lady Hester; he give parties for her, masquerades and garden parties, dinner parties and sailing parties on his yacht, which he kept anchored in the bay, and there was balls and pageants.

"But after a few months, he began acting strange. He'd give the parties, but he wouldn't go to them. He'd just walk alone on the cliffs, leaving his guests to entertain themselves. And just like he tired of the parties and guests, he got tired of his bride, and he was moody and cruel to her, just when she needed kindness, for she was expecting a child. Her being an earl's daughter, and a lady, she wasn't used to that kind of treatment, but there was nothing she could do, and five months before the child was to be born, he got so he couldn't stand the sight of her.

"He used to tell her he detested her, and if she didn't keep out of his way, he'd kick her clear over to Forsham. Finally she got so frightened of him that she left and went back to her father's estate. After her son was born she tried to come to Cliff House to reason with him, but he just told her to keep her high-born brat and if she valued its or her own life to stay out of his sight. So she never did come back."

Old Nan sat sipping and staring into the fire. Five minutes passed and still she did not speak.

"What happened then, Nanny?"

The old lady started.

"Happened? Oh, nobody really knows. But one day Mr. Guy sent everybody away. He dismissed all the servants except my great-granny, who stayed on as housekeeper. Then he closed the house and took to living in a few dark rooms, and saw nobody. He walked the cliffs of a night, weeping and wringing his hands and calling, 'Pippin, Pippin!'"

"Pippin? What does that mean?"

"Why, that's what we calls rosy apples in these parts."

"Now why should he walk the cliffs, weeping and calling for apples?" I asked, amused by the story.

"I expect," said Nanny, sipping, "that he had went mad, poor fellow. My great-gran said he was that unhappy it was enough to make a body shudder just to walk into a room where he was."

"And finally?"

"Well, one night a great storm come up, and when my great-granny went up to his room, the same one you have now, to take him his dinner, he wasn't there. She opened the casement and over the noise of the storm, she heard him screamin', 'Pippin, Pippin, take it all, take the house, the jewels, take anything, take everything, but come back! Come back!'

"My great-granny, she was the only one who could ever do anything with him, even when his wife was here, and thinking he'd be safer in bed, she ran out to the cliffs to bring him back. Like I say, he was never fond of anyone, but he always treated her decent, so she wasn't afraid to go out after him. She saw him, standing on the cliff's edge, still screamin', 'Pippin, Pippin!' He turned, saw my great-granny, then he jumped over the cliff. She had no way, during a storm, of getting help, so she just had to wait until morning, and when the dawn broke, there he was, floating against the rocks below, with his neck broke, and his head all twisted horrible to one side."

"And is that all?"

"No. Clutched in his hand, in a death grip, they found a little card, and on it was printed, 'Virtue is its own reward.'"

I turned away, wearied with Nanny's meanderings.

"Aye, you might well hide your face, for from that day to this, there's never been a happy Montrolfe."

My headache had gone, but I felt very tired.

"Good night, Nanny Beckett."

CHAPTER THREE

I spent my days in bed until noon, then I stumbled through the weed-grown gardens after my infant's lunch, kicking turf absently from the hidden brick paths and tripping over broken urns, chipped statues and overturned marble benches.

Occasionally I wished I had enough energy to do something about the garden, and half a dozen times I thought of getting down to work and cleaning the place up. Lying in my bed in the evening, I had visions of it as it must have been—formal gardens, clipped box hedges, dark cypresses and green cedars, with lawns like velvet, bordered with all the sweet old English flowers, hollyhock, marigold, sweet William and lavender, and a dozen different kinds of roses perfuming the air like the hanging baskets of Babylon.

But when morning came, I was as weary as an invalid, and merely continued my aimless meanderings, ending up at the edge of the cliff, watching the milky waves, as purposeless as I, advancing and retreating.

One day, when I had been at Cliff House several months, I walked into the library and found, to my surprise, a woman standing beneath Guy Montrolfe's portrait.

She turned when she heard me enter, and we stood looking blankly at each other.

Then, "Good morning," she said, with a cheerfulness that chilled me.

I nodded and stared at my feet. It is agony for me to meet strangers, and I am completely without social graces.

She said nothing more, and when I looked up at her again, I found her gazing intently at me.

"You startled me," she said. "Not by coming in, but by your resemblance to him." She indicated the portrait.

What a handsome creature she was. She fairly radiated health and beauty, with her glowing skin, toothpaste ad teeth and blond hair.

"If you had a beard, you'd look like twins! But of course, you're a relative of his. You must be Mr. Montrolfe."

I nodded and stared down again at my cursed feet.

"I'm Beatrice Beckett," she announced heartily. "I'm Nanny Beckett's great-granddaughter."

"How do you do." I wished she would go.

Nan, who could hear a pin drop when she chose, must have caught the sound of our voices, for she came hobbling in.

"What're you doing here?" she shrieked at the girl, ignoring me. "Mr. Nicholas don't like visitors. You get to the kitchen where you belong!"

Her great-granddaughter was obviously not easily abashed.

"Oh, come off it, Gram. Nicholas has been dead for ages, and you know it. I've brought you some medicine for your arthritis. Ted drove me over."

She turned to me.

"Ted's my fiancé." She flashed a large diamond ring under my nose. "He's the local medico, Dr. Forbes. I'm his nurse."

I couldn't have cared less. Why didn't she go? Her strength and wholesomeness appalled me.

"Well then, gimme it!" It was old Nan, as graceless as myself.

"Oh, the medicine. Here. Take two pills, three times a day. Now have you got that straight, Gram?"

Nan snatched the bottle and dropped it in her apron pocket, where it clanked ominously.

A shadow of irritation passed over Beatrice Beckett's glowing countenance.

"For God's sake, Gram, why don't you wear your teeth? What was the point of me going to all that trouble to make you get them, if you just cart them around in your apron pocket?"

"Very high and mighty, aren't yer, since you been carrying on with that Forbes? Yer just like Hanner, and you'll come to no good, just like Hanner didn't!"

Nan clamped her toothless gums together and flounced out.

"I'm not carrying on!" shouted her great-granddaughter after the retreating figure. "We're engaged to be married."

A disdainful sniff was the only answer she received, and the kitchen door banged loudly.

The girl turned to me.

"You have no idea what a problem she is to me." Then she laughed, a big, hearty, farmer's wife kind of laugh. "Hannah was her daughter, my grandmother. She bore a child out of wedlock. That was nearly sixty years ago. Gram hasn't got over it yet."

I stood gazing at this Beatrice, fascinated in spite of myself. She was too alive, too vital. She woke the house up, and strangely, I felt that she, not I, was completely at home here. She belonged here, and the house needed her; there were no cobwebs or complications in Beatrice Beckett's life.

"Nan suits me," I said, dropping my eyes. "We get along very well together. I'm afraid, Miss Beckett, that both she and I are hopeless misanthropes."

"Oh really?" said this great glowing girl. If she understood, she gave no indication. "Well, I must be going. Ted's out in the car, he wouldn't come in. I shouldn't keep him waiting."

She extended her hand, so I took it.

"Well, cheerio!" she said heartily.

She paused in the doorway and her eyes rested momentarily on my feet. She gave me a pitying glance, and then like a breath of spring she was gone. I heard the roar of a high-powered sports car on the gravel driveway, and I was alone again, oddly disturbed, as if the bricks of my grave had been rudely kicked apart.

I shrugged at Guy Montrolfe, who gazed down at me with his frozen, agonized face.

"Well," I said, "there's somebody who isn't afraid of either of us."

So she pitied me, did she? It so happens I think pity is the most condescending of the virtues and I detest it. I may have been singularly unfortunate since birth, but I have never pitied myself. I don't know the meaning of either pity or remorse.

I don't want her pity. I refuse to tolerate her pity. I would rather spend the rest of my life pitiless with old Nan than accept one minute of her precious pity!

Nanny came in. "Did you call?"

"You know damned well I didn't. I was talking to myself, you old witch."

She cackled with delight and poured herself a glass of gin.

"Nasty baggage, that one. But you put her in her place, comin' here like she owned the house. Just like Hanner. Can't leave the men alone."

"Oh, never mind about her." I felt restless and bored. I stood looking up at Guy Montrolfe.

"Nan, what happened to his son?"

"Oh," said Nanny, "he come a cropper, like all the other Montrolfes did."

"What did he do?"

"Ran through all his mother's money, broke her heart. Finally he come and lived here. Died here too. Died of the drink, ravin' mad. My grandmother, she was his housekeeper.

"Now, his son Gregory, he died of the drink too. My grandmother was his housekeeper as well. When he died the doctors cut him open to find out what killed him. It was his liver; it was so hard the surgeons rang guineas on it. And *his* son—"

"Wait," I said, but she went right on; the only thing she really enjoyed talking about was Montrolfes.

"*His* son, now let me see, that would of been George—yes, George—he only lived to be twenty, got killed by the Duke of Angelsey in a duel, so his brother got the house. That was James, and my mother was his housekeeper. He never married until he was sixty-eight. He was your great-grandfather. His bride was sixteen. He—"

"Don't tell me," I interrupted, "I know. He either died of the drink or ravin' mad."

"He did not!" said Nanny indignantly. "That was his wife what done that. Not the drink, mind you, the madness. Poor James, he was thrown into a ditch by his horse when he was hunting, had his back broke and lay there a week before he was found. He was eighty-seven at the time. Died of a cold in the lungs.

"I midwifed at the birth of his son Simon, and become his housekeeper. Come here in service when I was ten, been here ever since. Simon was your grandfather, and his son Phillip was your father, and Phillip's brother was my poor Mr. Nicholas.

There was one other son, young James. He got shot in France in the war. His own men shot him, poor boy. Desertion in the field, they called it. Just plain murder, if you ask me.

"Now, then, your father—"

"Not another word!" I said. "God! What a family!" I arose, and having nothing better to do, went to bed.

CHAPTER FOUR

Autumn passed all too quickly and the long winter began. Storms became frequent and it was dark by five. The cold and mighty winds that swept from the icy sea battered uselessly at Cliff House, for it was built to last a thousand years.

How long the evenings became, and how I pined for spring! But yet, I could not have left the house were it always winter, and in my heart I knew I loved it best when the gales whistled and shrieked, and the waves pounded unceasingly on the cliffs, as reassuring as a heartbeat.

And gradually, as the weeks passed, the strange spell of lethargy fell deeper and deeper upon me, as though I lived in a world of shadows, and I could hardly wait for the darkness to fall so that in the warmth and comfort of my bedroom, with the fire crackling in the fireplace and the candlelight glimmering on the mahogany furniture, I could sit up in bed, drinking my hot milk, smoking cigarettes and studying my scientific papers. There was something strange and wonderfully comforting about my room that made me feel like a bear in its den, or a bird in its nest, a feeling that I had come home, and I began to realize why my Uncle Nicholas had spent thirty years in there. For the first time in my life, I was content. And I began to dread spring, for I knew I would, like a hibernating bear, have to come out, and it would be cold, and all manner of things would be springing to life, growing, flourishing, while I— I would be the same.

It must have been in late November, the first time I dreamed of her. I had been sitting up in bed, reading *Alice in Wonderland*, for I had found a mildewed, rust-spotted first edition in the library, and I was studying the Tenniel drawings.

The fragrant hot milk was steaming in my cup, the dark velvet hangings of the room were warm and comforting, and the brass fire irons gleamed in the half-darkness like Homeric armor. I fell asleep with the book in my hands, and when I awoke, it was no longer there, and I looked about for it.

And there she was, sitting cross-legged before the fire.

The firelight glimmered on her long yellow curls, and I saw that on her lap, held by her rosy little fingertips, was my book.

She seemed unaware of my presence, so avidly was she reading, and I arose noiselessly, putting my hands over my face, lest my appearance frighten her. I approached to within five feet of her, then she heard me, and closing the book, sprang to her feet.

Slowly, and with dread, I took my hands from my face, praying she would not scream and leave me.

She stood, looking up at me, a pretty little maid in her early teens, and the fire had flushed her cheeks so that in contrast the skin of her brow and throat was like white silk. No, for that is too dense, and her skin had a transparency like white rose petals. And about that snowy brow floated golden tendrils of hair, as soft as burnished gossamer.

She smiled. What is it about dreams, that they distill our emotions so? Why is it that a grape, sweet and mild, when distilled, becomes its own essence in a liqueur? For a smile is only a smile when we are awake, but in a dream it can carry all the weight of the dearest embrace, the softest words, or the loveliest thoughts. What is there about a dream that in a smile alone, it can convey the sweetest essence of paradise?

Once, during my student days, I read some verse in which an Elizabethan poet wrote of his lady, lips and teeth like cherries and snow.

Suddenly she put one dimpled hand across those lips, as though she feared her laughter was too merry to be seemly in my presence, but her eyes, which were the color of gentian, sparkled with mirth, and she handed me the book.

How can I explain it? How can I convey what it meant to one like myself, to have that lovely maiden smile at me, even in a dream? For you see, she was not afraid of me; she had looked upon me and she was not afraid. And somehow, as we know in dreams, I knew that behind her merry laughter and mischievous eyes, she loved me.

She loved me. Can I explain what that means? Even if she were only a dream, when in conscious life do we feel as we feel in dreams?

To be loved in a dream is infinitely sweeter than to be loved in life. Is not terror in a dream more terrible than any terror felt in life? Is not horror more horrible? Is not awe more awesome? Is not wonder more wonderful? And so it follows, that without so much as a spoken word or a handclasp between us, love was infinitely more lovable.

Every night I dreamed of her, and what a charming, merry companion she was. She never spoke, but by her gestures and smiles, she told me what she wanted.

She loved to have me read to her, and dancing impatiently about me she would hand me *Alice in Wonderland*. Sitting on the floor, with her hands clasped about her knees and her eyes dreaming in the firelight, she listened with an intensity that only lonely children have.

I often tried to question her.

"What is your name?" I whispered, but she only shook her flaxen head saucily.

"How old are you? Sixteen?" She shook her head, no. "Seventeen?" No again. "Fifteen?" She nodded and smiled that radiant smile.

But she would not let me touch her, and I loved her so dearly I would not have jeopardized losing her for a caress, however much I longed for it.

Once, unthinking, I stretched my hand to touch that golden glory, her hair, but she sprang back from me, and the roses faded from her cheeks and her eyes were filled with the terror of a dying fawn.

"I won't hurt you," I whispered. "Do not fear me. I wouldn't hurt you for all the riches of this world."

But something in my words displeased her, and in a twinkling she had disappeared, and for two nights I did not see her.

I was very careful after that, for I had no way of recalling her when she was gone.

She was as restless as a hummingbird and did not always wish to stay indoors. Beckoning me to follow, she danced down the stairs and out to the cliffs, and I, with that strange illogic of dreams, followed her without limping.

As light as eiderdown she floated along the path on the cliff top, stopping now to pick a wild flower, then jumping up to chase a butterfly. Always, luring me on.

She loved flowers, and had a way of bringing them to me, looking up at me inquiringly, wanting to know the names of all of them, and she seemed puzzled and indignant when I could not tell her. She would throw them at me disdainfully and dance away, but she always looked back to make certain I followed, for she loved me too, and hated to be parted from me.

She loved me, and her moods were like the sea, forever changing and forever the same. When I did not please her or could not understand her, she was haughty and teasing. But oh! when I did please her! How sweet and wild were the wind-blown kisses she tossed me, mischievously leading me on.

I lived only for her, and sought only to please her, and what times we had! She could be difficult, and childishly imperious, for she could not speak, and I was stupid and earthbound in the manner of mortals, and strangely, it was she, the sprite, who was so keenly attuned to all the senses—of love, of excitement, of life itself.

She was as airy as thistledown and fragrant as a breeze, completely unafraid of the heights or the water. How charming she was, my dream companion in a dream world. And so my life became completely inverted. I existed during the day only to sleep again so I would dream of her at night.

Who was she? What was she? She was certainly not an angel, for she sulked outrageously when crossed and flirted deliciously when pleased. I never thought of her as a ghost or a fairy; she was too real for that. Indeed, our roles were changed; it was I who had never lived and she who was alive and knew the true exhilaration of life, never hesitating to savor every second, teaching me to do likewise.

Life and love were so precious to her I should have known our time together was limited, limited by an earth-clock, the physical, palpable heart that beat and beat and beat in my breast, and it was I, grievingly, who was left a mortal, alone, and in my own terrible fashion, alive.

It was during December that it happened. In that horror which is infinitely more horrible in a dream than it can possibly be in life, I lost her.

She was tripping lightly along the cliff edge when suddenly she stopped, swaying perilously above the pounding waves and rocks.

Without a thought I ran to her side, drawing her away from the edge and to my chest. And then—oh God—it happened.

She gave a terrible cry, and her head, her pretty little head, swayed like a flower on a broken stalk. And before my eyes, it drooped, drooped to one side, until it was as hideously twisted as my own, and in my arms, in my very arms, she closed her eyes and died.

I awoke, tears streaming down my cheeks, to find Nanny bending over me and shaking me.

"Wake up, wake up!"

"Oh God!" I cried. "Her neck, Nan, it was twisted all to one side, as horribly as mine."

The old woman crooned and petted me as if I were a baby, stroking my hair and murmuring words of nursery endearment as I wept.

"Who was she? Who was she? You must know, Nanny, you've been here for over eighty years. Who was she? Was she a relative of mine, that her neck was like mine? I touched her, and then I saw her neck twist down, until it was just like mine. Who was she, Nan?"

But the old woman merely shook her head.

"I do not know, Mr. John. Three generations of them I seen, grown men, waking up, weeping, crying like babies, and calling for their old Nan."

"They saw her? Which ones, Nan? Who?"

"Why, any Montrolfe who ever slept in this room."

"And will she come back, Nan? Will she come back?"

"Mr. Nicholas walked those cliffs for thirty years, waiting for her, watching for her. He was sure she would come back. Even as he lay on this bed, dying, he said, 'Nanny, I can't understand it. She must know I'm dying. Why doesn't she come, Nan? What did I do to drive her away, Nan?'"

I turned my face to the pillow, weeping for the first time in twenty years.

I shall never go to a zoo again, to see those animals, maddened by their confinement, so that they pad the same sinister pattern, back and forth, back and forth, every step measured, only to face the walls, a turn, the bars, a turn, the walls, a turn, the bars.

Why had it happened to me? Why should the most hideous, lonely creature on earth be given a glimpse of love only to be tortured for all eternity because it has been snatched back? Had nature not jested enough, merely allowing me to be conceived? If there were a Supreme Being, what terrible whim made It take pleasure in letting my weak twisted brain form such dreams? Had It no compassion that It chose the most pitiful and hopeless of Its creatures on which to play Its monstrous jokes?

And looking down at my twisted, clubbed feet, I wondered what I had done to deserve this, to be a misshapen, grotesque clown in whose veins ran the same blood that had once coursed through the heart of that unhappy shade, Guy Montrolfe. What had I done to be the last of his cursed race?

I searched my brain, my memory and my soul, but there was no answer, and my scientific training was a farce, untimely and almost obscene in its uselessness.

How little I know of anything and everything. The infinite, which I have spent my adult years probing, is frightening, and I know nothing of it. I am a child.

"Why don't you go for a holiday? You're becoming just like my poor Mr. Nicholas."

But I shook my head wearily—she might come back and I couldn't risk missing her.

Nan nagged and nagged for me to at least go for a walk, and I was unwillingly prevailed upon to take some air. Walking is no pleasure to me and with the angle of my neck what it is, far from enjoying the beauties of nature, I seldom observe much except my poor misshapen feet, which I would prefer to forget.

However, *she* had loved the twisted dwarf oaks that faced the sea and were bent by generations of winds, and I stumbled along, my head painfully lifted so I could see them.

I heard human laughter, an unseemly sound, and I came face to face with Beatrice, Nan's great-granddaughter.

She was not alone. Behind her I saw a slender blond man of about thirty. He was getting out of a powerful red sports car, which was parked on the private road that runs through the estate of Cliff House.

Beatrice came forward immediately with her disturbing lack of either self-consciousness or aplomb.

"Hello! I didn't know you took walks."

I suppose I am unduly sensitive, but I might have known she'd say just that.

She motioned to her companion, who had not bothered to open the door of his car, but sat upon it, one leg on the seat, the other dangling over the side.

"I'd like you to meet my fiancé, Dr. Forbes."

The young man straightened up, smiled pleasantly and extended his hand.

"This is Mr. Montrolfe, Ted."

What happened next was so extraordinary, that even I, unmannerly as I am, could hardly credit it.

Dr. Forbes's hand froze in midair and his pleasant smile faded, to be replaced by a look of the most unmistakable distaste. Flinging himself back into the driver's seat, he put the car in gear with a roar that shook the very trees and shot down the road, leaving myself and a scarlet-faced Beatrice looking at each other in bewilderment.

I had the dubious gratification of seeing that she could feel embarrassment.

I turned on my heel toward the house.

"Wait!" She was by my side and clutching at my arm. "Really, I don't know what's got into him. He's never behaved this way before. I know he's always hated Cliff House but— Well, I'm sorry."

There was nothing much else she could say. I shook her hand off and continued walking to the house.

Needless to say, that finished my morning strolls.

God knows I am well aware that I am not pleasant to behold, but this was too much, even for me. If I horrified him, a doctor, what must I have done to *her?*

I was back in my living grave, and gradually my feverish brain devised a plan to lure that sweetest of maidens. I wired to the city and had thousands of hothouse flowers sent out, and I decked the bedroom with them, bank on bank of gardenias, roses, orchids and night-blooming jasmine, for she loved flowers.

But oh! It was the simple wild flowers which had drawn her like the honey bee, and I sat alone, watching the exotic blooms fade and droop and die, until their scent became so overpowering that it poisoned the air.

I opened the casements, weeping, and flung them far out, to the sea below, where they were swept away, dead funereal offerings to a departed maiden.

But I could not give her up; she was in my blood and heart and soul. And then I remembered the book. She loved to have me read to her. She would hear me read her favorite book, and creep silently and happily to my side, as she used to do, that fairest of faces glowing in the firelight.

That delightful book about Alice, how she loved it. But where was it? The room was littered with hundreds of my scientific books, thrown carelessly about.

In desperation I began tossing my books aside hoping to find the lost favorite. With the viciousness of a vandal I ripped open bureau drawers and turned the contents on the floor.

I wheeled to the drum-shaped bedside table and, wrenching open the doors, swept out a motley collection of medicine bottles left from Nicholas' illness.

It was not there. In a transport of rage, I smashed my fist against the table.

There was a click, then a grating, and what I had taken to be ornamental wood beading under the top of the table suddenly moved. I clawed at it. Lifting the candle over the table, I peered into the hidden drawer and saw a book.

Not *Alice in Wonderland* but an old, black, hard-cover ledger, such as is still used for keeping accounts.

Slowly I sat on the edge of the bed, holding the slender black book in shaking hands.

Then I opened it and began to read.

MY JOURNAL

My name is Catherine Barton, and I am thirteen years old, and until a short time ago I lived with my Aunt Tillie, who is owner of an inn.

The Reverend Mr. Peterson, with whom I was in service for two years, and who taught me my letters in his leisure hours, says that we should all keep journals of the more important events in our lives. This I have not done until now, but because I am what one person, whom I shall describe in my journal, calls more than ordinarily advanced for my age, I shall begin to set down, as near as true as I can, what has happened to me in the last fortnight.

Aunt Tillie went across the bay to Mr. Thompson's funeral, taking our dory to get there, and as she left she said, "Kate, you will have no visitors tonight, the weather is too inclement for the fishermen to be out in on open water and the bay is deserted. So lock the door at eight and go to bed, and do not touch my preserves, and bank the fire carefully, and there is cold mutton in the larder for your supper, and I shall be back before noon tomorrow. Wash the parlor windows and sweep and dust the two front bedrooms, and be a good girl, for remember, God is watching you."

My Aunt Tillie dearly loves a funeral. She put on her best black bonnet and I watched her climb down the steep path from the inn to where the dory was beached below. The waves were high with great white crests, and I knew a storm would be up by evening, and Aunt Tillie knew it too, but she would get to Mr. Thompson's funeral if she had to swim.

I watched Aunt row across the bay, and then I went back to the inn. It was early spring, too soon for the summer visitors, and as Aunt had said, too rough for the fishermen to leave their own coves. From the parlor window I could see their boats moored at Forsham across the bay. And I could see Aunt's little dory approaching the village. And when I saw her nearly there, I went and poured myself a glass of port and built up the fire.

As the clock struck six, the storm broke loose and a heavy rain began to fall. Suddenly it was nearly dark, so I lit a candle and ate my mutton on the settle before the fire. Then I went to draw the curtains and looking down into the bay, I saw a barque, and in the dim light, I saw the ship's boat launched. I drew the curtains and went back to the fire.

When the clock struck eight there was a knock on the door, which I expected, for there was no other place for the ship's boat to go except to Forsham or here and I wondered why it had taken her men so long to row to our jetty.

When I opened the door the wind nearly blew out my candle, and there was a very tall gentleman standing there with a black greatcoat flapping around him, so I said, "Will you come in, sir?" and I wondered where the rest were.

He stepped inside, shut the door, and he says to me, "Where is your mistress, my pretty maid?"

"She's gone to Mr. Thompson's funeral across the bay, sir."

"Well, let me speak to your master then, for I want lodgings for the night," he says.

"There is none. Just Aunt and I live here."

"What?" he says sharply. "Gone and left a snippet like you in charge of her establishment?"

"We were not expecting guests, sir," I says, "because of the weather and the season."

"And what is your name, my dear?" he asks.

"Catherine Barton."

"Very well, Catherine, go fix me some meat and bread and bring me a glass of whisky."

"We have no whisky, sir."

"What? No whisky? Then bring me a glass of rum and hot water."

"We have no rum either, sir. My aunt does not hold with strong spirits and will have nothing but wine in the place."

"Damn your aunt," says he, taking off his greatcoat and shaking it before the fire. "Small wonder she has so few guests. However, it suits my purposes, so bring me some food and wine, pretty Catherine."

He sat on the settle and stretched his legs before the fire, and I saw he was booted and spurred.

"Well, my pet," says he, "did you never see a man before?"

"I did not know sailors wore spurs," says I.

"Why, you are a most observant young lady," he says, not smiling, and I saw there was a deep dimple in his cheek, although he was not smiling. "And how do you know I am a sailor?"

"Why," I answered, "I saw the barque in the bay and the ship's boat launched from her."

"A barque?" says he. "Are you sure she was not a full rigged ship, my pretty?"

"No," says I, "she was a barque, not a ship, for her mizzen rigging was fore and aft."

"Why, you are a clever girl as well as a pretty one, Catherine." He sat up and reached over and touched my face with his hand. "And you have, I swear, the rosiest cheeks I have ever seen. Bright as a pippin." He sat back, lit his pipe and says, "Fetch me my food and drink, Catherine."

I fetched him the rest of the cold mutton and a bottle of port, and I stood watching him while he ate.

"Well, Catherine," he says, "am I handsome?"

"Why," I answered, "you are either the handsomest gentleman I have ever seen, or the ugliest. I cannot make up my mind as to which."

"What, my Pippin," says he, still not smiling, "no doubt you think I am an old man because my hair is gray?"

I looked at his hair. It was cropped short, and very curly, and all gray, but his face was young and very smooth, no marks but the deep dimple in one cheek, and I still could not decide if he were handsome or ugly, for his features were large, but not too large, and irregular, but not too irregular.

"Why," he says, "Catherine, I shall tell you the truth, which I rarely tell to ladies, and inform you that I celebrated my thirty-third birthday not a fortnight ago, and while to a slip of twelve that may seem old, it is not."

"I am thirteen," I replied.

"Thirteen? Do not lie to me, Catherine. You are not one whit over eleven, and I shall ask your mother tomorrow to prove it."

He stopped and said, "And where is your mother?"

"In Forsham, sir," I lied, "with my little sisters."

"And how is it, my pretty, that your mother lives in Forsham with your little sisters and you live here with your aunt?"

"Because, sir," I says, "my daddy died two years ago, and I must earn my own keep, and Aunt pays me to work here, while my mother works in Forsham to keep my little sisters."

"And how many little sisters have you?" asks he.

"Five."

"And of course you are a good girl and turn all the monies your aunt gives you over to your mother?"

"Of course, sir."

"What a commendable little trick you are, Catherine," he says, and reaching into his vest, brought out a gold coin and held it between his fingers in front of my nose.

"And how would you like this, on top of what I shall pay you for my lodgings, my pretty Pippin?"

I reached for the coin, but he laughed for the first time.

"No, no, Catherine. First we must have a small understanding. I shall give you this, but only if you will promise me something."

I did not answer him and his smile disappeared, leaving only the deep dimple.

"Catherine, what would you think if I told you you saw no barque in the bay tonight and you had no guest at the inn?"

"Why sir," I says, "I would think that my aunt would beat me when she returns tomorrow for being a glutton and eating all the meat and drinking a full bottle of port."

"Come now, my pet," he says, "you had been tippling before I arrived, there's your glass on the mantel."

I took the coin from his fingers and placed it in my pocket.

"See that you observe our bargain, little Pippin," says he, pinching my cheek, "for you will not be the first female who has rued the day she crossed my ways, should you not."

He stood up and stretched and his spurs rang on the flagged hearth.

"And now, Catherine, you will show me to my room, and then you will tuck yourself into your own little bed, to sleep soundly until morning, for the clock says nearly nine."

I took my candle, lit another from it, handed it to him and led him up to the front bedroom.

"And where do you sleep, my pretty?"

"Downstairs, sir, behind the kitchen."

He walked across the passage, looked in the other front bedroom and said, "Tonight, Catherine, you will sleep in here."

He took my elbow and led me in and closed the door. He pointed to the bed.

"Sleep there, Catherine, and do not leave this room tonight, for it makes me very nervous to have children prowling about."

With that he went, closing the door behind him. I listened carefully, but he did not go into the other front bedroom, for I heard him go down the stairs, through the parlor and out the front door, which faced the path that led down the cliff.

I waited a few minutes, then opened the casement, and slid down the twisted old vine that crept from my window to the ground. But I was not quick enough and could not follow him, for the night was very dark. I walked up and down the path and then returned to the inn and was about to go in when I heard men's voices.

"This must be it," said one voice, "there ain't another place around here for miles."

"Eh, and if this is it, then where is he?"

There were two men, and they walked to the inn door.

"Should we knock?" asked the first.

"Why not?" says the second, who beat on the door until it shook.

In the dark I quickly climbed my vine, crept through my room, lit a candle, and ran downstairs.

When I opened the door, they both stepped back.

"Why, it's a lass," says the first, a big fair man.

But the second pushed him aside and stepped forward. "Is there a gentleman here called Mr. Fabian?" he asks, and I did not like his face, for he looked like a scoundrel.

I stood back and said nothing, and the fair man took a step toward me. "Hold it, Dozer," he says, "you've frighted a little maid near out of her wits, in the middle of the night." Then he leans down in a friendly way and says, "We won't hurt you, my dear. Is there no one about but you?"

I shook my head.

"He can't be here yet," says the one I did not like, "or else this is the wrong place. Let's get out of here."

"Patience," says the big fair man, and turning to me, "Have you had no guests tonight, miss?"

But before I could answer, the scoundrel says, "Don't be blowing your gaff in front of strangers. I say we go."

The fair man stood silent for a minute and then followed his ugly companion.

I shut the door and raced upstairs and then climbed quickly out my window again. This time I would not lose them. And as I knew the cliffs like the nose on my face, and they stumbled and cursed their way along them, I knew I should have little difficulty following them.

They stopped and the tall fair man lit his pipe, while his companion said, "Now then, Davy, let's put our cards on the table. Do you really think Fabian will split four ways? Because I don't think he will. He's an oily devil and once he gets his hands on that money, who's to say if we gets a penny?"

"Nay," says the tall man. "He'll split."

"If you and me now, was to just go there first and get our share, why, sure, then there'd be no trouble, would there? And no chance of us being left out."

"No," says the tall man, "we'll work according to plan, as he willed it, and, Dozer, he's a clever one. Yorek will be here soon, as was our plans, and then the four of us will get going and split as we agreed."

"Yorek!" says the scoundrel. "I tell you, Davy, I know Yorek, and he's a spineless rat. If Fabian decides to cross us up, you may be sure Yorek won't dare to stand up to him."

"Fabian won't cross us," says the tall one. "Why should he? This is a business, Dozer, and a man must have some decency, or else even his own mates won't work with him."

"Dead men tell no tales," says Dozer, "and what's to stop Fabian, him being so smart, doing us in and taking the lot?"

The tall man spat over the edge of the cliff and did not answer him.

"Come on, Davy," says the Dozer, "where is it stacked? We'll get our share and skip, and who'll be the wiser?"

"No," says Davy.

"Why, mate," says Dozer, "you know me, you can trust me. Why, Davy, to risk hanging only to be done out of our lot—now that's not right."

"No," says Davy again.

"Have you got your instructions in writing, Davy, mate?" asks the Dozer.

"I have 'em here," says Davy, and in the wan moonlight I saw him pat his breast pocket. And then I saw steel flash in the moonlight, the Dozer moving quick as an adder, and Davy lurched over the cliff.

The Dozer scrambled down the cliff path, and I hid behind a scrub oak in the dark, watching.

He was gone five or six minutes, and then I heard him climb to the top again, cursing and grunting, and he headed for the inn.

Then I crept down the cliff path.

The man Davy was lying across a rock at the bottom of a drop of fifteen feet, and even in the near dark I could see a darker line run from his mouth, and I put my hand down and felt the warm, sticky blood.

He groaned and turned his head.

"Are you much hurt?" I whispered, but he did not answer me. I sat down beside him and lifted his head onto my lap. The moon came out again, and his long yellow hair gleamed.

"Are you sore hurt?" I whispered again, and he nodded, and I saw the dark spot on his jersey where the knife had pierced him.

"Why," he says in a clear voice, of a sudden, "it's the little maid from the inn. How did you get here?"

"I followed you and the one you called the Dozer," says I.

"Ah," he says, and suddenly there was a great dark stream from his mouth and he lay still, and I stroked his golden hair.

"Listen, my dearie," he gasped slowly, "I want you to give a message to Fabian, Max Fabian. You'll know him when you see him, for he has a dimple in his cheek, though he seldom smiles."

"Yes," says I, leaning over to hear him the better, but he suddenly coughed and more blood spurted from his mouth. I wiped it clean with the hem of my gown.

"Listen, my dearie," says he, gasping terribly, "tell Max, tell him our plans is changed. Tell him things is backwards and to turn the mill upside down. Tell him to change an eye to an ee."

"Yes," says I.

"Have you got it straight?"

I repeated it, and he says, "That's right, my pretty lass. Now tell no one except Max Fabian."

I heard voices at the top of the cliff, and then Davy gagged terribly.

"Perhaps you'll feel better if you sit up," says I.

"No, dearie, I'm done for, let me lie." And he breathed as if knives were in his throat.

I used my whole strength and lifted him to a sitting position, and he died so.

I laid him down, crept back to the inn, up my vine and into my room, and I was none too soon, for shortly after there was a thunderous knock on my door, and I heard the voice of my first guest shout, "Wake up!" He opened the door and I saw him standing there, a candle in his hand.

"Wake up, Catherine," he says in his way, as if he could order kings about. "Up with you. There are more guests, and I want glasses and wine before the fire below, and build the fire up well."

"Blow out your candle, sir," I said, "before I arise." For I still had my day gown on and did not wish to let him know that I had just jumped under the covers.

He threw back his head and roared. "Why Catherine," he said, blowing out the candle, "I had no idea you country wenches commenced coyness at so early an age."

And with his spurs clinking, he walked downstairs.

I went down to the parlor, and there, besides Fabian and that scoundrel Dozer, was a solidly built, quiet-looking fellow who sat in the shadow of the settle.

I fetched clean glasses and poured port for them all, and built up the fire, while Max Fabian strode up and down the room, every so often looking outside.

"Well, Yorek," he says finally, turning to the quiet man in the settle, "you've done me proud, for I must confess I chose you for your honest face, and I had qualms about you. A man who's familiar with oakum and the treadmill is rarely only a poacher, but you have done me proud, Yorek."

I looked at Yorek, but he only turned his face to the fire at Fabian's words, and I must say, he did not look like a convict, for he had the fresh-cheeked look of our own fishermen and farmers.

The Dozer sat, cracking his great knuckles and swilling vast quantities of wine, every so often shaking his head as if to keep awake.

Fabian suddenly noticed me. "Off to bed, lass," he says, as if I were a dog.

But before I could leave, the clock struck ten, and the man Yorek glanced around nervously.

"Davy's taking his time," he says.

The Dozer arose, but said nothing, his ugly face glaring at me.

"If he's a tall fair man," says I, speaking up for the first time, "he won't be here tonight."

"What, my pretty?" Fabian turned to me, grabbing my arm. "What do you know about this?"

"He stabbed him with his knife," I said, pointing to the Dozer, "and the other fell over the cliff. I saw him." Fabian let loose of my arm and drew a pistol from his pocket. The Dozer stepped back, but not quick enough, for the barrel was against his temple.

"I think I shall kill you, Dozer," Fabian says, very cool.

"Now Max," says the Dozer, "Davy was not to be trusted. Why, mate, I stabbed him because he said to me, only a minute before, let's do in Fabian, he says, he wants it all for himself."

"You lie," I said. "I heard you ask him for to tell you where the money was stacked, and you said you and he would get yours first because Fabian could not be trusted."

The Dozer glared at me as if he would give his share of the money to turn my head full compass on my shoulders.

"Thank you, my angel," says Fabian to me. "And what else did they say?"

"Why," says I, "the man called Davy pats his chest and says he has the instructions here, and then he—" and I pointed to the Dozer—"he stabs him, and Davy fell."

They all stood looking at me.

"Have you anything else to say?" asks Fabian.

"Only what Aunt has told me," I says, "that he who lives by the sword shall die by the sword, and I think you are a pack of rogues."

"Shut your mouth, you little toad," says Fabian, and turning to the others, "Now we are in a pretty fix, for Davy had the fourth cipher. Only he knew it, and he committed it to memory, not on paper. And this fool," and he jabbed his pistol against the Dozer's temple, "has killed him without finding it out first."

"What!" says Yorek. "Do you take us for such fools, Fabian, as to think that you did not know the fourth and most important cipher, where the loot was hid, when it was you who was behind the whole plan?"

"Yes," says Fabian, "I was the brain, and I made one mistake. I shall not make it again. I chose me an honest assistant, not like that dog of yours, Edward. I would shoot this rogue if I knew the third cipher."

"No, you shall not shoot him, Max," says Yorek. "Our plans have gone astray badly enough because of him, but one more killing will not solve matters. You told me when I went in on this that there would be no bloodshed."

"And who has shed it? Your own man, you puling coward," says Fabian, his dimple twitching.

"Now mate," says the Dozer, "let us all be reasonable. The third cipher was mine and only I know where the horses is hid, and you, as a gentleman, Fabian, must grant me some measure of good will, or you won't get them. And you, Yorek, must pledge to see Fabian don't do me in, for I swear to both of you, Davy was against us. You especially, Fabian. That brat lies."

"That I can believe," says Fabian, turning his eyes but not his pistol from the Dozer's head to me.

"I do not!" I says.

"Be silent!" says Fabian. "Or I'll blow your head off too."

"Well, Max," says Yorek, "if the Dozer leads us to the third cipher, then it will be up to you from then on, for I have done the first and second, and the Dozer will the third, but you must the fourth."

Fabian sat back and put his pistol in his pocket. He tapped his forefinger on his lips as he sat thinking.

"None of us will get none," says the Dozer, "if you don't. And if you does, then we all gets a third."

Fabian looked at him in his unsmiling way.

"It's true, Max," says Yorek.

"Very well," says Fabian, "but I can only take you to the place of the fourth cipher. Where Davy hid the gold I do not know, and you know this to be true, because I have not seen him since the job was done, and we all decided before that the final hiding place would only be known by Davy, and that Yorek would meet up with the Dozer, and they would both meet up with Davy, and we should all meet here for Dozer to lead us to the horses, and then ride to the money."

"Come now, Fabian, where was Davy going to lead us?"

"To a deserted mill, and when the Dozer takes us to the horses, then I will lead you to the mill, but I shall not tell any of you where it is, you must follow me."

"And what's to stop you two from slitting my gullet, once I takes you to the horses?" says the Dozer.

"I give you my word," says Yorek.

"And I mine," says Fabian, "for you know by my speech and actions I am a gentleman. And you, Dozer, are the scoundrel amongst us who has scotched our plans, and if you do not trust us, why, it is because you are not to be trusted yourself."

"So I'm not, aye? And where was you when Davy and I got here? You should of been here first."

"I was, but I went out to get the lay of the land and to see what was keeping you fools, taking damn good care no one saw me, too."

"She seen you, that brat. And what's to be done with her now?"

"So she did, Dozer, so she did," says Max Fabian, "and what's to be done with her now? Why, you footpad, thanks to your bungling, there's a deal to be done. First of all, you and Yorek go down to the foot of the cliff and bring Davy's body back here."

He stopped, and I saw the dimple in his cheek deepen, and he was looking at my feet. I looked down, and there was blood on the hem of my gown, where I had wiped Davy's mouth.

"And then what?" asks the Dozer.

"Why then," he says, looking into my eyes, "why then, Dozer, we fire this inn, with Davy's body in it, to a heap of ashes."

"And what about her?" says the Dozer, jerking his thumb at me.

"Well, my pretty," says Fabian, and the dimple in his cheek twitched, "what about you?"

But Yorek stood up.

"I'll have no part of this, Fabian," he says. "Robbing is one thing, but murdering babes goes against me."

Max Fabian said nothing, tapping his forefinger against his lips.

"What!" says the Dozer. "Leave her on the loose to blab? Not likely."

"Listen to me, Max," says Yorek, "my missus and me has a little lass, nor a head shorter than this one, and I'd never rest easy in my grave if harm comes to her."

"Ned," says Fabian, "you are a lily-livered fool." He turned to me. "Come here, my Pippin, sit on Fabian's knee." And he put his arm about me and kissed my cheek. "Is she not a beauty? Look at those cheeks, Edward, and her hair like corn silk, so fair and soft."

"Max," says Yorek, "you wouldn't harm an innocent child, would you, Max?"

"Harm her?" says Max. "Why bless you, Edward, I've become uncommon fond of this little maid, I have. I wouldn't harm a hair of her pretty head." He kissed my cheek again. "You are my Pippin," he says, "and you shall leave here tonight with me and Yorek and the Dozer."

He turned to the two of them. "And now, bring back the body. We haven't all night."

Taking a lantern from the mantel, they left, and Fabian lifted me from his lap.

"Catherine," he says, very grave, "did I not tell you to stay in your room?"

I said nothing, hanging my head.

"And yet, my pretty, I left the inn for not more than a quarter of an hour, and when I return, I find you pretending to snore in your trundle bed. The Dozer went down the cliff, after he stabbed Davy, did he not?"

I nodded.

"And then he went on to the inn?"

"Yes, sir."

"And then you climbed down to Davy, did you not, my pretty Catherine?"

I shook my head.

"Do not lie to me, Kate," he says, very soft, "for I don't like dishonest little girls. There's blood and sand on the hem of your gown. Now then, my darling," and he pulled me onto his knee again, "was Davy dead when you reached him?"

I nodded.

"Do not lie to me, Catherine," he whispers, his lips against my throat, "for I have ways of making little girls tell the truth."

He rubbed his stubbled chin against my cheek. It was like a rasp, and I turned my head away. "What did Davy say?"

"Why," I says, turning to him, and this time it was I who kissed his cheek, "what could the poor man say, lying there as dead as a mackerel?"

"Catherine, my pretty Pippin," he says, very gentle and sweet, "what do you intend to get out of this?"

I put my hand in my pocket and handed him a Sunday-school card, for the Reverend Mr. Peterson had given me many when I was in his service, and Fabian took it.

"Virtue is its own reward," he read aloud, and then he leaned over and whispered, "Catherine, you are a serpent of a child."

I kissed his cheek again and jumped down from his lap.

I went to my room behind the kitchen, hid the coin he had given me and then changed into my other gown, which was heavier, and when I returned to the parlor, there was the Dozer with the body of Davy slung across his shoulder.

"God's truth!" says Fabian. "You are a brute, Dozer, for Davy must weigh sixteen stone."

He walked over and grabbed Davy's legs.

"Let him down easy, Dozer, for I wish to have a careful look at him." And he opened Davy's bloody mouth and pushed up one of his eyelids and peered at his eyeball and I had to turn my head away.

"After you stabbed him and you first went down the cliff, was he dead when you got to him then, Dozer?"

"Nar," growls Dozer, "but nigh on it, breathin' like a set of pipes."

Fabian stood up.

"Very well," he says, "we'll fire this place, for it should go up like tinder."

The Dozer took a candle and moved to the cellar, but Yorek stood staring at Fabian.

"Damn your bloody eyes, you craven milk-sop," roared Fabian, "what did you expect this venture to be, a meeting of Quakers?"

"I shall wait for you outside," says Yorek, very quiet.

"You," says Fabian to me, "go with him, and you, Ned, if she gives you the slip, I'll cut the living heart out of you."

Yorek took my wrist firmly and we walked out to the edge of the cliff.

"You're in rough company, lass," he says. "Do what I say and I'll see if I can't find a time and a place for you to slip away. And if the authorities questions you, my dear, tell them the one called Edward Yorek never bargained for murder, nor did he have any hand in violence done."

I nodded and looked around. The inside of the inn began to glow with a cherry light.

"Don't look, lass," says Yorek, "and bear in mind what I say. Keep close to me and steer clear of Fabian, for no matter how soft he may speak, he's a hard, cruel man at heart. And above all, my lass, never, at no time, let yourself be alone with the Dozer, for Fabian hurts none who can be of service to him, but after you spilling about Davy, why the Dozer will kill you for the sport of it, and he won't kill you quick-like neither, my poor lass, so mind you do as I say."

"Yes, sir," says I, and I meant to take his advice, for, truth to tell, I feared that Dozer a hundred times more than I did Fabian.

Dozer and Fabian joined us.

"How long do you figure, Dozer, till we get to the horses?" asks Fabian. "We'll have eight hours before dawn."

Dozer scratched his shaven poll. "Well," says he, slow, "we'll have to stick to the fields and woods, and we daren't be seen by day. 'Twill be two nights hard walking, Fabian."

"Lead on," says Fabian, and so we began our march.

When the moon had risen full, I began to tire, and I dragged on Yorek's hand.

"Bear up, lass, we've a long way yet," he whispered, so I did. But as we walked on and on and the ground was uneven and rough, I stumbled and began to weep.

We had all been silent, none speaking except for Yorek to whisper to me, and Fabian stopped in his tracks and says, "Catherine, you must cease this sniveling, for it does not please me."

"I can go no farther," I says. "I am so tired I want to die."

"And that's what ye'll do," says the Dozer, "if yer don't shut yer mouth."

"Please," I says to Fabian, "let me sit just for the space of a few minutes, for I have never been so weary."

"Fabian," says the Dozer, "shall I wring this brat's neck now and throw her in a ditch?"

"No," says Fabian, "you'll do no such thing, Dozer. When I want her neck wrung I'll say so, and I am very particular about not wanting her neck wrung now, do you understand, Dozer? And if you scotch my plans further, my bison, it will be Thomas Parr and not Catherine Barton who lies face downwards in a ditch. Have you taken all this to heart, Dozer?"

"It were only a thought, mate," says the Dozer.

"All right, Catherine, climb on Dozer's shoulders, for he is to carry you if you cannot walk farther."

"What?" says I. "Never, Mr. Fabian. I do not like him."

"I do not care what you like," he says, "and furthermore, my maid, I'm not at all sure yet how you fit in my plans, so do not tempt me."

"Go on, Catherine," says Yorek, "I shall walk right beside you."

So I climbed on the Dozer's shoulders and it was like sitting astride a horse. As soon as I got my wind and was fair rested, I says, "Let me down, I can walk again."

Dozer did so, and as he led the party, I took good care to walk between Yorek and Fabian,

When dawn began to break we hid in a wood, and Fabian wrapped his greatcoat about me and says, "You have done well, Catherine. Now sleep." And sleep I did, for that day's sun was setting when I awoke. Yorek sat a few paces away, and Fabian lay by my side.

"Well, my Pippin, how do you feel? Are you rested?"

"I'm hungry," I says.

Fabian sat up and handed me a lump of bread and a piece of cheese, which I ate.

"And has your hunger abated, my love?"

"Now I'm thirsty."

He handed me a flask and I drank the cool sweet water in it.

"On your feet, the lot of you," says Fabian, "for we are on the march again."

I arose and looked around, and the Dozer was sitting with his back against a tree. Fabian walked over and dug him with his spur.

"Up, Dozer." But the Dozer never moved, and I understood why he was called the Dozer, for Fabian had to kick him like a stubborn mule before he so much as opened his eyes. And when he did get up, I swear he walked for ten minutes before he knew it.

Our second night was like the first, except I took no rides on the Dozer. When the first light of morning showed them up, the men were a sorry and wicked-looking pack, for they had not shaved.

I had my second wind by that time, and had no difficulty keeping pace, but strangely enough both Dozer and Fabian were tired, and it was only Yorek and I who had good spirits when we all lay down to sleep. But still Fabian wrapped me in his greatcoat, and ten seconds later was sleeping by my side like a dead man.

But I did not sleep so readily, and lay awake for half an hour, trying to calculate my position, for I remembered our sailors from my own harbor, counseling the young lads, telling them to know their stars and their compass and their tides and rips, but that all the knowledge of the universe would do them no good if they knew not the hidden rock.

And so I lay there, trying to fathom the depth of the hidden rock.

We all slept until midafternoon, and when we awoke, Fabian was in a foul humor, for Dozer had promised us we should reach the horses that morning.

We were camped by a small brook and I arose and went to it

and bathed, and then I plucked a willow branch and brushed my teeth well.

Fabian joined me and he was like a bear who has stuck his head in a honey pot and found only wasps, so I did not waste words on him.

Later he gathered watercress and mushrooms, for our diet had begun to pall on us. By then his temper was better. The lot of us ate our dinner in silence around a tiny fire, Dozer and Yorek looking at Fabian and me curiously, for they were afraid to eat the mushrooms for fear they were poisonous. So we enjoyed the cress and toasted mushrooms as well as their plain fare of bread and cheese, although I sorely missed the tartness of vinegar and salt.

Later, as we sat waiting for the dusk to fall, Fabian became restless, and rising, he says to me, "Come, lass, we'll have a stroll through these woods, for I am weary of sitting and your company cheers me."

I arose and followed him. I knew the question of Davy plagued him mightily, and I wondered how he would broach it.

As soon as we were out of sight of the others, he sat on a fallen log and drew me on his knee.

"What a pretty trick you are, my Pippin, and what a pity you are not five years older."

I said nothing and allowed him to kiss my cheek.

"And your hair is like sunshine, Catherine. No, 'tis more the hue of new minted gold." And he stroked my head and then he says, very soft and sweet, "And how would it suit your fancy to have pearls to twine in your hair, my love?"

"It would suit my fancy well, Mr. Fabian."

"Bah! Don't call me Mr. Fabian, but Max, or Fabian if you will. Let us be less formal, for though my hair be gray 'tis misfortune and not age which has made it so, as I told you, and I wish us to be friends. Think of me not as your senior in years, but as a comrade, or if you will, a playmate. I am a lonely man, Kate, without kith or kin, and few tears would be shed should Fabian leave his mortal state."

And with that, much to my surprise, he kissed my cheek and led me back to the others without further ado.

At about eleven that night, the Dozer says, as we walked through a field, "The horses should be tied to a grove of oaks about a mile from here."

Fabian nodded and patted my head in a pleased way.

A half an hour later we came to the grove, and there were the horses, tethered together—a great black stallion, a bay gelding, and a sorry-looking farm nag, heavily laden with packs.

"What!" says Yorek, standing back. "Something's amiss here, Fabian. Two riding horses for what should have been four men?"

Fabian looked very wroth, and turning to the Dozer says, "Have you fallen short of your orders, sir? Why are there only two riding horses?"

Dozer looks at Fabian queer-like for a minute and then smiles and says very smooth, "I dare say, Max, some o' them scoundrels I trusted has got their orders mixed, for to be sure, I followed mine."

"Do better next time, Dozer," says Fabian sourly. "Remember, you made a grievous error doing in honest Jenkin Davy, and Yorek and I may not be pleased to forget it."

Dozer made as if to mount the stallion, but Fabian says, "Do not touch him, Dozer, for I've marked him for my own."

Dozer, looking sullen, turned to the gelding, but Max says, "Leave that one be, you fool. Do you think we shall be such numbskulls as to ride the highways by night and so draw attention to ourselves? Tomorrow morning, well shaven and clean, we'll ride abroad like honest men, and not before. We'll rest in this glade tonight."

"They're a fair piece of horse-flesh," says Dozer admiringly, "especially that stallion. You must allow I have good taste." He plucked a handful of grass and offered it to the gelding, and then he stroked the beast's head, and I was surprised, for he seemed genuine in his fondness of the animals.

"Unsaddle the black and the gelding, for we want them in good shape for the morrow," says Fabian.

"What?" says Yorek, "and leave yon poor beast standing all night laden with packs?"

Fabian shrugged, so Yorek began to unload the farm horse, and rubbed his hide with grass, and then started to lead him off to water, but the Dozer snatched the halter from him jealously.

Fabian and I sat together on the grass. Neither of us was tired, having slept all day.

"Are you warm, my Pippin?"

I nodded.

"The night dews are chilly," says he, "and I do not want my darling to catch her death, so come close to me."

And he draped his coat about my shoulder and sat with his arm about me.

"Have you settled your mind on whether I am the ugliest or the handsomest gentleman you have ever seen, Kate?"

"You are the handsomest," says I, and indeed, I spoke the truth, for he had a way of growing on one, and even the deep dimple in his cheek, which made him different from other men, was like a beauty mark on a woman.

"And you like it when Fabian kisses you, don't you, my sweetheart?"

I lied and shook my head.

"Do not lie to me, Pippin, for Fabian always knows when you do not speak the truth. And Fabian likes to have his pretty girl kiss him, too. So kiss me, Catherine."

I kissed his cheek, but he says, "Oh no, Kate, you are of an age when you should learn to kiss properly. Kiss my lips."

I leaned over and kissed his lips very soft, and he said nothing for a minute, then he whispers, "Catherine, my darling, are you quite sure Davy was dead when you reached him?"

"Quite sure, Max," says I.

"'Tis odd," says Fabian. "I have seen men stabbed just as Davy was, and they lived sometimes for as long as half an hour."

"Ah, but did they fall over cliffs in the bargain?" says I.

"You are a sharp one, aren't you, Kate? Why, that never struck me before this moment. You are indeed a clever Pippin, Catherine."

And he sat musing for a while, and then he says, "Davy was alive when the Dozer reached him, and you followed not three minutes upon him. It is strange to me, my darling, that Davy took exactly that length of time to die."

I said nothing.

"Davy was a rare one," says he. "An honest thief. And I know for sure, Catherine—" he paused, and his voice took on a hard tone, "—I know for sure that Jenkin Davy wouldn't die with a maid bending over him, without first giving that maid a message for Fabian."

Then he says, very cool, "What was that message, Catherine?"

"Why," says I, "Davy, who had just been stabbed by his own mate, did have a message, and not a pleasant one either, Max. Bend your ear toward me and I'll give it to you."

I felt his heart beat like a hammer as he pressed me to him and leaned his head down, and then I nipped his ear with my teeth as hard as I could.

He threw me from him and sprang to his feet.

"Why, you little snake," says he, "I'll spur you like an adder."

He raised his boot and I saw his spur flash in the moonlight, but he changed his mind halfway, and instead kicked me in the ribs with the toe of his boot.

The Dozer walked up and joined us at this moment and says, "Here mate, let me give you a hand, for I said before, this one'll live to see us hanged if we don't do her in."

And he raised his foot, but Fabian pushed him aside, saying, "Lay off, Dozer, I give the orders here." Then he says to me, "Get up, but do not speak, for you have tried me so sorely I do not trust myself."

And he drew his kerchief from his sleeve and held it to his bleeding ear.

"Be off," he says to the Dozer. "I want to speak to this one alone."

He said nothing for the space of five minutes, only staring at my face in the moonlight, while I rubbed my aching rib.

Finally he says, "By God, if you're thirteen, I'm a babe in arms. You're a witch in the body of a pretty child, that's what you are."

I could feel my anger rising and I knew I would be a fool to let it master me, but I could not forbear saying, "Aye, Mr. Fabian, and should the humor be upon you to use your spur on me again, then I may tell to Mr. Dozer what you so sorely wish to hear."

"Ah," he says, very soft again, "you have given yourself away, Miss. Then Davy *did* speak!"

I sat chewing a blade of grass, thinking that for all of being kidnaped by such rough company, it was a stroke of rare luck for the likes of me to be on a treasure hunt, with part of the puzzle in my head—me, who might live a lifetime in service with no more nor a sixpence a month and my keep.

And I knew that if I wanted any part of that fortune, I needed Max Fabian.

"Catherine," says he, "I did you an injustice, for I took you for a foolish child, which you are not." But he was still very angry with me.

He plucked a blade of grass too, and sat chewing it, and then he says with his grim smile, "Do you know, I don't think you are a child at all, but a goblin."

"Bah!" says I, rubbing my side again, and I got up and took his coat to go off to sleep, and he did not stop me, and I knew then how valuable I was to him.

The next morning Fabian took a razor from one of the packs and the three of them shaved clean. Then he gave the orders for the day.

"Yorek and you, Dozer, will take turns riding the gelding and leading the pack horse. I shall go ahead with the stallion, and you, my pretty," and he turned to me, "you shall come with me, but you shan't ride. You shall walk every step of the way, until your poor little feet are in ribbons, for last night you bit Max Fabian's ear."

"What!" says Dozer. "You go ahead on a fast stallion so you can reach the loot and give us the slip? Not likely, Max, we sticks together."

"Shut your loutish mouth," says Fabian, "you shall do as I say. I shall go ahead, no more than a mile afront of you, so as not to excite suspicion by a gentleman riding with two ruffians, and keep my eyes peeled in case there should be any too interested in our actions."

"No yer don't," says the Dozer. "'Tis not that I don't trust you, mate, but we're in this together, and there's none but you knows where the mill is, and should harm befall you, why, we would be too far behind to aid you."

"Harm befall me?" says Fabian, cocking his pistol. "Do not fret your kind heart over me, Master Dozer."

Yorek looked at him and then at me, and I knew he feared Fabian would murder me, for Yorek knew nothing of Davy's message.

"Leave the lass with us as a pledge," says he.

"Aye," says the Dozer, "leave the lass as a pledge, for you seem uncommon fond of her, Max, and it ain't like you."

"What?" says Fabian. "Be parted from my darling? Never, gentlemen, I would die first."

The four of us stood looking at one another and then Fabian says, "Are you fools? What good is buried treasure to me if I must dig it up with my bare hands, on an empty stomach, not even knowing for sure where in that deserted mill Davy hid it. And you are left with the pack full of shovels and axes and ropes and picks and victuals and drink."

This seemed to strike them as reasonable enough, though had I been them, I would not have been so trusting.

"Well, lads," says Fabian, "I keep a mile ahead of you on the highway, and we head straight inland. We meet at nightfall. Pippin and I shall wait for you by the roadside, and I shall seemingly be examining my horse's shoe, while my little sister watches, and you shall offer aid, and then we all move on to the first secluded spot to spend the night. And, mates, we stay away from inns, and from ale, and country wenches. And if you two are questioned or should you stop to water your horses at an inn and are forced to make pleasant speech with the stableboy, why then, you Yorek, are a farmer, going north to a fair to buy horses, and the Dozer is your groom. You are a farmer by trade, Yorek, so act yourself but say little, and you, Dozer, keep your bloody trap shut all the time or you'll hang the lot of us."

Fabian and I started out, with the others to follow in a half an hour, and Fabian was as good as his word, keeping me trotting at a wicked pace and touching me lightly with his whip when I lagged.

After a mile, I says, "I'm done in Max, and can go no farther."

"What, done in so soon? Why, we've just started, Kate!" And he flicked the whip in the dust at my feet and cut the earth a full two inches. "Hurry, my darling, for I've no time to squander on naughty girls."

And so he kept me going for another quarter of a mile; then he drew in the stallion's head.

"I can bear willfulness in neither a woman nor a beast," says he, "and when I ride a horse, Kate, he soon learns to gratify my least whim, for he knows what's in store for him if he does not."

I said nothing, pressing my hand to my bruised rib, for the running made it very sore.

"And I shall teach you to be civil, if I must break you like a horse," says he, snapping his whip. "On you go, Catherine."

I started again, but a moment later I fell, and I knew I could run no farther.

"Get up," says he, and I felt the whip lightly on my shoulder, so I got up.

"Have you had enough of this marathon, my Pippin?"

"Yes," says I.

"Very well," says he, and slipping his foot from the stirrup, he offered me the toe of his boot and his hand and swung me before him on the saddle. "And I hope you have profited from this lesson, Catherine."

I leaned back against his chest, for I was so spent I could not sit up by myself.

"Did you hear me, Catherine?"

I nodded.

"And are you going to be a good girl henceforth, my Pippin?"

"As good as I can be," says I.

"Now what sort of an answer is that?" he says. "When I ask a question, I want a straight reply, miss."

I had my breath back now, and I says, "You have me now, for the reason that you are stronger than I, but bear in mind, Max Fabian, 'tis I who have the bait, and you who'll be the hungry fish should your rough ways be the end of me."

"What?" says he. "Do you want to go over the side again, miss, with my whip for your tutor?"

"Leave me be," says I, "for I was brought up on a diet of your tutor, and he does not frighten me, no more nor my aunt's broom."

"Why, damn your eyes," says he, "you are a bold one." And he kissed my cheek and we rode on with no more ado.

At noon we stopped for bread and cheese and wine in the shade of some trees by the roadside, and he says, "And what name do you think I should christen the black, my Pippin?"

"Why," says I, "to be sure, sir, name him for his master and call him Satan."

"You're a rare one, Kate," says he, laughing and kissing my hand gallantly, "and we shall do famous together, bless me if we shan't, and Satan it shall be."

We camped in a grove that night. Yorek unpacked the sack that held the food supply, and there was naught but bacon and oatmeal and salt, plus a good quantity of rum and port. I wanted to cook the oatmeal and the bacon, for I was weary of bread and cheese, but Fabian forbade me to light a fire, saying that in another day we should be at the mill and then I could make porridge around the clock for all he cared.

The Dozer uncorked a bottle of rum, and Fabian took his wrist.

"Three tots a night," says he, "for you are an ugly dog at the best of times, but the drink makes a mad dog of you, and when mad dogs snap at me I kill them, Dozer. You wouldn't want Max to do you in, would you now, mate?"

Dozer took three huge gulps from the bottle and handed it grudgingly back to Fabian, who corked it and in turn handed it to Yorek.

"Yorek," says he, "I charge you to see that the Dozer drinks no more than three tots a night, for remember, Edward, it was you who chose him, and he's done full damage to our plans already."

The next day we traveled without incident, and as dusk began to fall, we entered a forest, and for the next two hours our pace was slow on the rough path, for the dark made it dangerous for the horses.

"What manner of country is this?" I asked Fabian, for I had never been inland before, and never seen a true forest.

"Why," says Fabian, "this is part of the estate of a great lord, and we are his guests, though he does not know it."

"And will he be angry if he learns of us?"

"He won't learn of us, my Pippin, for he is in a far country, having a gay time, and his chief keeper has been given a pretty penny to put his underlings to building a road three leagues from here."

A great jagged pile loomed before us. It was the mill. But it was so dark that Fabian decided we should camp beside it for the night.

When dawn broke I awoke, and sat looking at the mill. Then I shook Fabian.

"Max," says I, "that's the strangest mill I have ever seen," and indeed it was, for the top was square except that one great corner had fallen away, and the stones were three feet thick.

"Aye, my pet," says Fabian, "but it was not always a mill. Once, many hundreds of years ago, it was a keep, and it has not been even a mill for nigh a century."

Then Yorek and the Dozer awoke. All four of us were anxious to go inside—I to see if I could fathom the cipher Davy had told me, and the others, I suppose, hoping the loot would be piled in a neat heap before their eyes.

We entered, Fabian leading, and the Dozer following, and me keeping close to Yorek.

One vast room of the mill was still habitable, by which I mean it had a roof over it, for the rest of the place had fallen into ruins.

"Well," says the Dozer to Max, "where do we look?"

"I do not know," says Max, "but we must use our wits and not waste our strength. We shall start by going over it inch by inch and looking for any evidence of change that seems recent. Then we shall make a list of all the spots that seem like reasonable hiding places and start to work systematically on the first that merits our attention."

He paused and looked around, then says, "And since we do not know how long it will take us, why then we shall be comfortable in the meanwhile, and make ourselves at home, for I see there is a usable fireplace in the main room, and that shall be our headquarters. So, Dozer, bring in those packs."

He turned to me. "Catherine, go and fetch some firewood, and mind you don't wander afield, for this forest is haunted by an ogre whose favourite dish is tender young maidens. Yorek, water the horses in the stream, which is fifty paces to the north, and then bring more water back here."

"What shall I bring it in?" asks Yorek.

"Is there no bucket in one of the packs?"

"None," says Yorek. "I've been through the lot."

"Well, surely there must be a pot for cooking?"

"Yes," says Yorek, "there is a large iron pot."

"Use that. And Kate, do not stand there woolgathering. I told you to fetch wood."

And indeed, I had been standing lost in thought, gnawing my knuckles, trying to fathom the cipher. But it meant not a thing to me, so I left for the wood.

I did not wander far, for there were broken branches lying about, but I could have walked a whole day, the forest was so pretty. It was not all heavily wooded; I came across pretty little glens and clearings, bright with wild flowers.

When I returned, Max started the fire and he had some trouble, as the chimbley did not draw well, owing to disuse. But finally a small fire was crackling cheerily, and I made us a breakfast, cooking the bacon in the iron pot after first emptying out the water Yorek had brought. Then I asked him to half fill it again, so he brought me more, and I made porridge.

After breakfast the three men began exploring, and as there was a winding stone staircase leading to a sort of attic, or loft, above our heads, Fabian decided it was there they would start.

Up they went, and when Fabian was halfway up the stairs, he stopped and called down, "Come, Catherine, and join us, for they say children's eyes are very sharp."

But I knew he wanted me within his sight, fearful that I might be poking about on my own with Davy's clew, and find the loot.

On the loft above were stored ancient barrels, a trestle table and benches, old timber, parts of a plow, and moldering bits of harness.

Dozer and Yorek were busy pulling things apart and emptying barrels, but Fabian found a wooden chest with a lock on it, and I saw him glance around to see if the others had noticed, and indeed his very gesture gave him away, for they both dropped what they held in their hands and ran to him.

"Well, now," says Fabian, "we must find some way to open it."

But Dozer, looking at the ancient and rusted lock says, "Don't look for no crowbars, Max. You need none."

And with that he grabbed the top of the chest and ripped it off with his bare hands, and I confess I felt my spine chill to think what those same hands could do to my neck.

The three crowded around it, and since I came past the shoulders of none of them I could not see, but in two seconds they fell back in disappointment. The chest contained nothing but ancient bills and papers, and Dozer turned the whole lot on the floor and kicked it.

Leaning down, I picked up a bound book, such as is used for keeping accounts, but Fabian says, "Hand that here, miss, and prompt," so I did.

He thumbed through it and handed it back to me, and I looked and saw the pages were blank all through.

"May I keep it, Max?" I asked, for the Reverend Mr. Peterson had taught me (as well as my letters) to respect paper and books.

"Yes, yes," says he, impatient, giving me no further thought. "Dozer, take one end of that table and you, Yorek, the other and carry it down stairs before the fire. And when you are through, take down the benches."

They followed his instructions without argument, for I suppose they were used to being ordered about, and indeed, Fabian always acted as though he was used to ordering.

He saw me standing idly by and it seemed to annoy him, for he says, "Go, lass, and along the edge of the stream fifty yards up, you'll find a clump of willows. Cut some branches and make a broom and sweep out the room below."

"What shall I cut them with?" I asked.

"Why," says he, "you shall cut them with a knife, but not mine, for I won't have its edge dulled."

Looking down the stairs he shouted, "Dozer, give the maid your knife, and not in her ribs, you rogue. Hand it to her pretty, still in its sheath."

I went down and the Dozer handed me his knife as Max ordered, but he licked his lips as he did, in a way that made my blood run cold, and I renewed my vow never to be found alone with him.

I swept busily for a long while, and the men worked unceasing, and finally I joined them and said, "Max, I'm tired of sweeping. What shall I do next?"

"Sit on your hands and be silent," says he, staring at a mighty stone wall with a crack in it.

"I do not want to sit on my hands," I says. "I want to go for a walk and see the flowers in the forest. I saw them while I gathered wood, and they are so pretty."

He looked at me without seeing me, and then says, vague-like, still staring at the wall, "Very well, my darling, go and smell the pretty flowers."

I started out and suddenly he gathered his wits and says, "And Pippin, if you wander too far, then it's the Dozer I'll send to bring you back. You wouldn't want to be alone in the forest with the Dozer, would you, my love?"

"No," says I.

And I had a pretty walk, for the forest was so little like my own wild, barren coast that it caught my fancy mightily.

There was a pretty wandering stream which had once turned the wheel of the mill, and I could see how it had changed its course over the years, now a hundred feet from the mill and narrow, whereas the dry pebble bed where it had once been was broad and deep.

Then I came to what seemed to be a very ancient well, the lip of which was only a foot or so above the ground, with a rotting wooden cover, half overgrown with vines, and I wondered why anyone would dig a well so near a stream.

I walked further and saw many sweet flowers, for it was spring, and some were yellow and some orange and some red and some blue, but I knew the names of only a few, such as violet and woodbine and dandelion.

And then I had a thought, for I had brought the account book Max had said I could have, and I decided I would keep a journal. I sat beneath a yew tree, trying to solve the problem of what to write with, for I had little trouble deciding what to write about.

A pen would be easy, I decided, for in a forest there must be birds, and I had only to keep my eyes open and I should be bound to find me a few quills if I looked carefully.

But ink was a problem I could not solve so easily. Finally I concluded that port wine would be a good base, mixed with soot, and I would seek in the forest to see if I could find any root or berry that had a dye in it.

That solved, I knew I should have to find a hiding place, for I wanted to be able to speak free to my journal, and that meant that Max Fabian should never set eyes on it.

I walked again past the well, and of a sudden decided to lift the lid. I pushed aside the vines and tugged, but I could not move it. Then I spied a sharp branch, and using it as a lever pried the lid off for the space of a few inches. A foot below was a ledge, half a foot deep. I smiled, for I had found my hiding place.

Then I went back to the mill and found all three men covered with dust and cobwebs and sweating, trying to clear a passage to a small back room which was plugged with great blocks of stone.

"Make dinner, Pippin," says Fabian. And turning to Yorek, "Fetch water for me; I wish to bathe."

"If you bathe, you do not eat," says I, "for we have but one pot, and I am not eating out of it after you have bathed in it."

Fabian turned on the Dozer.

"Hell's bloody teeth, you fool. Why did you not have enough wits to pack a bucket?"

"Bathe in the stream," says I. "It's no deeper than your waist."

"Be silent, you little bitch," says he. "I hate running water like a cat. If I wasn't born to be hanged, it was to be drowned."

He strode off in a high dudgeon, but he did bathe in the stream, for when he returned he was clean and shining, if in a bad temper.

Yorek went out and bathed and when he sat down at the table his honest country face glowed from the cold water, so that Max said, "You two could be father and daughter, or brother and sister, so alike are your rosy cheeks. Tell me, what is the secret of your rude health?"

"Hard work," says Yorek, and closed his mouth, for he was not given to small talk.

"Methinks I shall never have a rosy countenance," says Max.

The Dozer shambled up to the table like a huge, dirty stable dog.

"Upon my soul," says Fabian, "it is that lovely youth, Ganeymede, cupbearer of the gods, scented with musk and attar of roses."

"What?" says the Dozer, suspicious. "I stink and my name's Thomas Parr, so what are you talking about, Fabian?"

When I served dinner, Fabian sighed and says, "Bacon and porridge again?" And I understood his feelings, for I had been born and raised on the ocean and was used to fresh fish and oysters and lobsters and shrimp, and a good red roast with pudding of a Sunday, and a diet without seafood and meat was pale to me.

"We shall be coming down with blackleg if we keep to this diet," says Fabian peevishly.

Yorek nodded. "Yes," says he, "I had a touch of it, and some of my mates, they died of it, and before they did they pulled their teeth from their gums like they was bedded in cream cheese."

Fabian winced and tucked his dirty sleeve ruff up into his coat in a dainty manner.

"Well," says the Dozer, amiably picking his teeth with his knife, "there's no cause for a man to get scurvy. Meat and rum's the cure, but only fresh meat, mind you, salt pork won't do it, and don't I know it. I done a stretch where four of five was done in by scurvy. But not the Dozer."

"How did you avoid it?" asks Fabian.

"I et rats," says the Dozer, belching and rubbing his huge chest.

"Jesus!" says Fabian, and then, turning to me, "Well, chuck, don't stand there with your mouth open, you'll swallow a fly. Here, get me some more slop to fill my stomach, I'm still hungry."

I said nothing and stood staring at the Dozer.

"Come now, Catherine," says Yorek, "the Dozer is only joking. Fetch me more food."

And he winked at me and pinched my cheek, but I knew the Dozer spoke the truth, and Fabian knew it too.

After our meal Fabian bade Yorek go and cut boughs for a bed, saying a dead man could not rest in comfort on the cold stone floor.

"Enough for all of us?" asked Yorek.

Fabian raised his head and says, "What care I, you fool, so long as you cut enough for me."

Yorek returned a while later, his arms piled high with feathery green boughs, which Fabian took from him and made into a bed in the corner, then Yorek went out again for more.

"Come here," says Fabian to me. "You shall sleep by my side, as usual."

I lay beside him and he covered me with his greatcoat, and then he whispered, "And have you anything to say to me?"

"Why yes," says I, kissing his cheek. "Good night, Max."

"Ah," says he, "my darling has no more to say to me? Perhaps she would prefer to share the Dozer's bed rather than Fabian's, eh?"

But he did not fright me, so I laughed and replied, "Oh, I pray not, Mr. Fabian. I might speak in my sleep and tell secrets to the Dozer."

The dimple in his cheek twitched and he turned his back to me.

Directly after breakfast in the morning, the three began the task of clearing away the great stones again, so when I had cleaned the pot, washed the plates and swept the floor, I said, "May I walk in the forest again?"

"Aye," says Max, never turning his head toward me. "And see if you can snare us a quail."

But I found nothing in the way of food in the forest, though not looking very diligently, for I was more anxious to find me some bird feathers to fashion a quill from. I found about half a dozen all told, but only two were strong enough to be of use. They would have to be baked in sand for hardening.

I wandered for five hours in the forest, the time going like minutes, for never had I seen such beauty, so free and untouched, as though I were the first ever to walk there.

And I found a bower, a shaded bower where the willows laced out the sun and the stream bubbled by, and the floor of the bower was thick green, green grass winking with forest flowers, and I knew I had found just the spot for me to work on my journal. I sat me down in the grass with my journal on my knee and opened the pages and felt with my finger tips the paper, smooth as silk, and I turned the empty pages one by one, and planned in my mind what I would write on them: the truth, in every detail. And as I sat listening to the stream sing and heard all about me the soft wonder of the forest, I could have wept because I had no ink, and the empty pages cried out to be written upon.

After a while I arose and put my journal in its hiding place and walked slowly back to the mill, thinking hard about the cipher. I knew it as I knew my own name: "Tell Max, tell him our plans is changed. Tell him things is backwards and to turn the mill upside down. Tell him to change an eye to an ee." But the more I thought of it, the less sense it made, and I could not fathom one whit of it.

When I entered the mill, I found Fabian and Yorek and the Dozer working like horses to raise a great block of stone, which they had rigged with ropes and stayed with bars of iron for levers, and Yorek says, "Fabian, it stands to reason, no one man could lift this, so how could Davy have hid it here?"

"I do not know, Edward," says Fabian, sighing wearily. "Nor do I know where else to look, but we must get this passage cleared to the room beyond, and there's a deal more work when that is done; if we have to tear this pile apart, stone by stone, I'll find that fortune. Methinks the open part of the mill too likely a place for Davy to leave the loot lying about, so if there were a clear passage leading to a room beyond, and Davy hid it there, why, one man might, with a crowbar and ropes, work out the base stones of these walls, leaving the top ones to fall in and block the way."

"Aye, and he'd be squashed like a bug under them," says Dozer.

"Not so," says Fabian. "Perhaps, unlike us, he used his head, and had a knowledge of engineering. And do not forget, Master Dozer, Davy was a sailor, and ropes and weights were his trade."

But even as he spoke, I had a strange feeling Mr. Fabian was playing for time, and merely keeping them busy.

"Well," says Dozer, "I don't mind work myself, when it's in a good cause, and, lads, I never knew a better cause than someone else's money, so I'm all for moving it stone by stone, Fabian, if that's your fancy. So it's off with my shirt, boys, and to work with a will."

And he unbuttoned his shirt and threw it over a stone and began to heave on a crowbar.

A fright went through me when I saw the Dozer stripped to the waist, for though both Fabian and Yorek were strongly enough built, stacked together they did not equal the Dozer's chest. He seemed to have no neck, his ears sitting upon his shoulders, the muscles of which stood out as big as my fist, and he had coarse hair, even upon his back. I felt sick with fright, for though he seemed like an animal, I would far sooner be rent asunder by an angry bear than the Dozer, for at least a bear was not of my own kind. The Dozer was like those monsters I had heard of in old tales, with fins and claws for hands, and only one eye, and sinews like a sea serpent. He was truly fearsome, and I crept humbled and quiet between Yorek and Fabian, for they seemed so clean and slight next to him.

"Well," says Fabian, looking down at me, "it's the Pippin back."

The Dozer turned his head toward me, and his eyebrows were so heavy his eyes could not be seen clear like the eyes of ordinary folks, but were like dark sea caves which no one dare enter lest the tide catch them, and I moved nearer to Fabian.

"In truth," says Max, "the child adores me and cannot bear to be from my side. Why, it would break her little heart to be parted from her Fabian, would it not, my darling?"

"I've been parted from you for nigh on six hours and I feel uncommon hale at the present moment, Mr. Fabian," says I, for he had a way of mocking one that provoked me mightily, which was why he did it, I suppose.

But the Dozer turned to me full. "And if it ain't Fabian you loves, why it must be me or Yorek," says he. "For you would have shewed a clean pair of heels, being allowed free to wander about, if it were not so."

I could have bitten my tongue for speaking saucily to Fabian and so making the Dozer suspicious, so I took Fabian's hand in mine and said very quiet, "No, Mr. Dozer, it is not you, nor is it Yorek, but only Fabian, and I jest when I say I did not miss him, for I did truly."

Yorek and Dozer stared at me curiously and then at Fabian, who shrugged and said, "It seems to be my unhappy lot, gentlemen, wherever I go, to have the fair sex hanging on my nether lip like leeches. Why I am so blessed with this singular charm I do not know, but it is so, and much misfortune it has caused me. So when I meet an innocent, guileless damsel like my Pippin, she is a thousand times dearer to me than a painted court beauty, for high-born ladies are too cunning and wily for my taste."

"I likes little girls too," says Dozer, grinning.

"For supper, Catherine, so beware of him."

The Dozer guffawed, showing his huge teeth, which were like a horse's but as white as milk, and he winked at Fabian and went back to work. Yorek stood staring at Fabian and at me, still looking puzzled, and then he shook his head and put his shoulder to a lever with Dozer.

"Off with you," whispered Fabian to me, "and be more careful next time."

So I went to prepare dinner, which was, as usual, porridge and bacon, and when the three of them sat down to eat, Fabian says, "Curse your black heart, Dozer, you could not have chosen any food less likely to tickle my palate than this evil swill. Because you are an animal and prefer an animal's fare, what made you think your mates would?"

"Why," says Dozer, shoveling porridge into his maw, "what ails this for food? And I never give no mind to food when I'm thinkin' of money, Fabian, which is what I'm thinkin' of all hours of the day here, and so should you, for if you does, why you'll find this fare as pleasing as any you'd eat in a gentleman's hall."

I pushed my dish away from me, for I had little appetite, and Fabian says, "You see? My pretty does not fancy it either." And then he turned to Yorek, saying, "Edward, tomorrow you shall go hunting in the forest for a nice fat pheasant or hare. You should have little difficulty in finding one, for I do believe it was your chosen profession to be a poacher, was it not?"

Yorek flushed and did not answer him.

"What, Ned?" says Fabian, in his bantering way, "so modest? Why, I thought you would spring to your feet and declare yourself the best poacher in the land, for so you should have been, my boy, having done a spell at the prisoner's oar for your skill in that fine art."

Yorek raised his head and looked straight at Fabian.

"Be silent, Fabian," says he, very quiet. "You tread on dangerous ground."

Whatever it was that ate at Yorek and made Fabian enjoy

plaguing him, I did not learn at that time, for Fabian just laughed and said no more.

The next morning, at dawn, Yorek went out hunting, and did not return until late afternoon, when he took a pheasant from his pocket and threw it on the table.

"What, one paltry bird?" says Fabian.

Yorek nodded sourly and said nothing.

"Bah!" says Fabian, and then, "Well, we must make do with it. Clean and pluck the bird, Catherine."

So I did, and when I put the tail feathers carefully away in my pocket, Fabian says, "Do you intend, my love, to gnaw those later when the bird is eaten, and so make us envious?"

"No, Max," says I, "I intend to place them in my hair, and tomorrow when I play in the forest, I shall pretend I am a savage from the colonies."

Fabian gave one of his rare smiles. "Why," says he, kissing my hand, "I used to play that game when I was a lad, Catherine. How I would love to join you and be as carefree as I was wont to be then. How I envy you, my Pippin, how I envy you, and what I would not give to share in your childish fancies."

And even Yorek smiled at me, saying that he too once played so, and he turned to Fabian, saying that he had been absent from women and children so long that it gave him rare pleasure just to look at me.

"Aye," says Fabian, ruffling my hair, "in truth, Ned, this one is full of surprises, for I credited her with being too old for her years and thought she had put away childish things and had entered man's estate."

"Woman's estate," corrects Yorek, smiling and going outside.

"No," says Fabian very soft to the absent Yorek, "no, I meant man's, for my Pippin plays a dangerous game with dangerous men."

He said no more, and also went outside. When he returned he had his pockets filled with water cress and mushrooms, and he stuffed the bird with them and fashioned a spit from an iron bar and roasted the bird over the fire, basting it with wine, and though it was but the size of a small chicken, it made my mouth water, it smelled so good.

Yorek and Dozer and I sat at the table waiting for the bird to be cooked, and when it was, Fabian put it on the table and drew his knife from its sheath and split the bird in three sections. He put steaming pieces of breast and wings and legs on three plates. Then he handed one to the Dozer and one to Yorek and took the third himself.

"What," says Yorek, "none for Catherine?"

"No," says Fabian, beginning to eat, and the Dozer gnawed his portion like a wolf.

I felt my lips begin to tremble and my eyes to smart, but I did not wish to weep before them.

Yorek smiled and said, "Sit beside me, Catherine, and you shall have some of mine, for I could not enjoy it with you watching me, all eyes."

"No," says Fabian, "for fowl is very bad for children, and Catherine shall have none."

I tried very hard not to cry and says to Yorek, "I do not want your food, thank you, Edward, but it is kind of you to offer it me." And I gritted my teeth so I should not weep.

"Do not tease the child, Max," says Yorek, laughing at me and my pent tears.

"Tease her?" says Fabian, very serious. "Why, Yorek, I do this for her own sake. God's teeth, once I knew a little lady, enough like this one to be her twin, and a naughty girl she was, too, always telling falsehoods. Well, Edward, one day this young lady partook of some fowl, and do you know what happened? Why, Edward, she was taken with a fit, and was never the same again, poor little thing. She took fits on the hour, all day long, as the clock struck, for the rest of her life, and I could not bear for that to happen to my Pippin. So you see, Edward, you must not give my pretty any of your meal, for I could not bear it, on my soul, I could not bear it if the same fate befell her."

Yorek laughed, and I let out a great sob, I could not help it, and the Dozer took time out from his chewing to laugh. Then Fabian laughed too, and I let out another boo-hoo, though I cursed myself for it and rose to leave the table, but Fabian grabbed me and drew me to him, whispering, "Catherine, what did you want with those feathers? Do not lie to me, Catherine."

I hit him with my fist and sobbed harder. "I want them for my hair, as I said, and I hate you, I hate you more than the Dozer."

I tried to get away from him and he roared with laughter and offered me a plump drumstick, saying, "Why, Catherine, you did not let me finish my story about the other little girl. Once, after many years, she told the truth and her fits stopped and she ate all the fowl she wanted."

Yorek and the Dozer were still laughing, for men like to see badgering, and I think they all felt a victory that Fabian had made me weep so, and I said, "I would not eat your food if I were starving. Let me go."

But he would not, and held me to his chest still laughing, and then he says very serious, "Come Catherine, I'm done with teasing and I deserve to be sent supperless to bed myself for plaguing you. I am as naughty as you, so eat well."

"No," says I, "I will not." And I pushed myself away from him and stood up, but Yorek took my wrist and says, "In truth, Catherine, it was a cruel jest, one I've played on my own children, but it is only a jest, and Fabian has had his fun, so sit and eat."

"No," says I. "Let go my wrist."

"No, no," says Yorek. "Come, child, sit down, and you needn't eat Fabian's portion. I shall give you part of mine."

"No," says I, still crying, "for you laughed at me, Edward Yorek, and you are as cruel as Fabian." And I pulled my arm away and ran out to my bower and wept until I was exhausted.

And when I returned Fabian sat by the fire waiting, but I went straight to the bed of boughs and threw myself down, so he came over and says, "Sit up, Catherine, for I wish to speak to you."

I would not answer him, so he says, "Catherine, I am not so cruel as you think. It was only a jest."

Still I would not answer him, so he pulled me to my feet and dragged me to the bench by the fire. Sitting me beside him, he drew the drumstick from his pocket, saying, "Here, Catherine, you did not speak the truth, but even so I have saved this for you."

Still I would not speak to him, and his voice became soft as he spoke, saying, "It was a jest, Catherine, one of ill taste, and

I regret it now. I beg you to forgive me, Catherine. For all that I may be harsh in some ways, my darling, that is not one of them, and truly, I am very sorry."

"I do not believe you, and I hate you," says I, very calm.

"Oh no, you do not, Catherine," says he in my own tone. "Whether you know it or not, you love me more than you have ever loved anyone before, and you shall continue to do so."

And as he spoke, I had a heavy feeling in my heart, for I knew he spoke the truth.

"And for all I may tease and curse you, I am no more fortunate than you, Catherine, for I love you, and I do not wish to. For love is a weakness, Catherine, and you and I are two fools who have snared each other in our own traps, through being so uncommon clever. And listen to me, my dear; if I thought it would remedy the situation and set me free of you, I would break your neck, for there's no room for love in Max Fabian's plans. But there's not another like you in the world, Pippin. I've met my match, so God help the two of us, for if there is a solution to this, I do not know it."

He sat unsmiling, staring into the fire, and the flames lit up his profile and I saw how strong and harsh his face was, and I knew I loved him.

"Give me the drumstick," says I, and he handed it to me, not turning his head but still staring into the flames.

I cleaned it to the bone, which I threw in the fire, and then I arose.

"Good night, Max Fabian."

He stood up and bowed.

"Good night, Catherine Barton," says he, still unsmiling. "I salute you, for you are a formidable enemy, and it's a dangerous game when enemies love each other. One of us will break the other's heart, and I hope with all my soul, Catherine, that I break yours, for I would not wish to be at your mercy. And do not weep if I do, Pippin, for I've given you fair warning."

"You made me weep tonight," says I, "and someday, I shall see you cry."

He turned his face to me full, and it was the most unhappy face I had ever seen, and he says, very gentle, "Nay, my child, pray that you never see that day, for do you not know the one thing that could make Fabian weep?"

If he slept at all that night, I do not know, for when I closed my eyes he was back by the fire, staring into the flames, and when I opened my eyes in the morning he was seated at the table shaving, and he turned to me in his usual bantering manner, saying, "Good morning, my darling. I trust you slept well?"

"Aye," says I, wary.

"No," says he, "you did not, Catherine, for whether you remember it or not, you had a dream, in which you fancied Max Fabian said strange things, and you spoke them aloud in your sleep, and I heard them, and I say, forget them, Catherine, forget them entirely. For when you were off, sobbing your little heart out, Max Fabian drank half a bottle of rum, and Fabian had strange dreams too, my dear."

I said nothing and began to walk outside, but he called me, saying, "It was that cursed fowl which gave you those night fancies, my pretty. I knew you should not have eaten it."

His eyes were twinkling, and I could not help laughing.

The men worked steadily that day until afternoon, when Fabian put on his coat and said he had had enough of it and would take a walk.

"And leave us with all this work?" says Dozer.

"Bah!" says Fabian. "Why do you think the good Lord fashioned you like a beast of burden if it was not to labor like one? As for me, I am a gentleman and I work when I please, and it does not please me to do so now."

Dozer and Yorek did not argue with him, for, whoever he was, they put great store on his claims to gentility and accepted his superior airs as right and proper, seemingly finding it quite fit that he should not toil and they should.

"Come, Pippin," says Fabian to me, taking my hand, "we shall walk together."

And as we went through the forest, he pointed out a great number of flowers to me, telling me their names in both English and Latin and explaining to me ways to classify them, and showing me mosses and ferns and trees, and saying why some grew so well in certain spots, so that I said, "How do you know so much of this, Max?"

"Oh," says he, almost as if to himself, "these things have always caught my fancy, Pippin, and I have read whatever I could of them."

Finally we stopped by the stream and sat down. We looked at each other a long moment.

"Well?" says Fabian.

I shrugged and looked away, and he sat silently staring at the water.

"Max," says I after a time, "who are you and where do you come from, and how did you get a dimple in but one cheek? I have never seen a man with but one dimple, nor so deep."

"Aye," says he, "mark you well the dimple in Fabian's cheek, miss. Is it not a wonder of nature for a man to have but one such deep dimple?"

"Well?" says I.

"Why, you goose," says he, "it is not a dimple, but a scar, from a pistol ball."

I stared at his face again.

"But how did you get shot, Max? In a duel?"

"Yes," says he.

"Ah," says I. "That proves something."

"What, Miss Muffett?"

"That you are a gentleman, of course," says I, "for poor people do not have duels, only the gentry. Tell me about it, Max."

"Well," says he, "there was a fair young damsel, who was insulted by a blackguard. Mind you, he was a gentlemanly blackguard, not like the Dozer, so I challenged him."

"But Max," says I, looking at him out of the corner of my eye and laughing, "the pistol ball caught you broadside on the cheek, did it not?"

"It did," says he, "and knocked a hind tooth clean out of its socket. Look." And he opened his mouth, and there was a gap in the back of his strong white teeth.

"But Max," says I again, pinching his ear, "I thought duelists faced each other in combat. How is it that you were caught broadside, Max?"

"Why, my darling," says he, smiling, "it was not precisely that sort of a duel."

"No?" says I.

"No," says he, "for you see, Pippin, I did not have a pistol in my hand at the time."

"That was very careless of you, Max," says I. "I hope it taught you a good lesson."

"Oh, my pet, it did. Two days later, I challenged my opponent to another duel, and by a strange coincidence, he had no pistol in his hand this time, and, Catherine, he learned *his* lesson too late, poor fellow, for my shot caught him in the back of the head, right between the ears, which is, you know, a mighty sore place to be wounded."

"'Tis mortal," says I.

"Yes," says he, very sad, "mortal it was, my darling."

"And what happened to the fair damsel, Max?" asks I, laughing.

"Fair damsel?" says he. "Oh yes, the fair damsel. Why, she married a fairy prince and lived happily ever after."

And we both began to laugh and Fabian says, "You are a rare one, Pippin, by God you are."

And he kissed my cheek saying, "Someday I shall tell you another secret about that dimple, my love."

"Tell me now," says I.

"No," says he, "for you have secrets from Fabian, too."

"Very well," says I, "I shall tell you a secret, Max."

His eyes, which were dark and slightly tilted like a sprite's, sparkled as he leaned toward me, and I saw his hair cropped to half an inch of his skull and curled like a lamb's, and his rugged face with the dimple beginning to twitch as his head neared my own.

"Yes?"

"Max," says I, "I lied to you, for I am not thirteen, but fifteen. And this is the truth."

His dimple twitched and his eyelids dropped like hoods over his strange eyes, and he says very soft, "You are uncommon small and slight for your years, miss."

"Yes," says I, taking his hand and pulling him to his feet. "There are times when I am glad of it and times when I am sorry."

"Not so fast, Pippin," says he, "for I must tell you something. Things would not be one whit different were you fifteen or fifty, for at either age you would be the same."

He arose, and as we walked back to the mill, I says, "And when the treasure is found, you will take a fine lady to wife, I suppose."

"Do you?"

"And what will you do if *she* bites your ear, Max Fabian?"

"Kick her arse from here to Hades," says my gentle companion without hesitation. When we reached the mill, he looked down at me, mocking and laughing.

"You know, I do believe you are fifteen, my little Helen of Troy, and it's a pity, for that other Helen was only thirteen when she caused the topless towers of Ilium to be burned for her. Truly, it's a shame you are so slow for your years, Pippin, having had only an inn burned for you."

That night we dined on porridge and bacon again and spirits were low, for already they had labored five days and, having moved a great deal of stone, had accomplished nothing else.

After the meal, when the Dozer slept soundly, Yorek says, "Hand me the rum, Fabian, I could do with a drop."

"What, losing heart, mate?" says Fabian.

Yorek grunted and took a deep drink.

"Go slow, Ned," says Fabian. "That's the last of the rum."

But Yorek tilted the bottle to his lips again, and, in truth, it was near full.

"Here, give me a swig," says Fabian, and in turn he took a deep drink.

The two of them sat moody and quiet by the fire, drinking occasionally, Fabian raising his head every so often to see if I was by his side.

"Edward," he says finally, "you shall go hunting again tomorrow, for we cannot live on this swill."

"I shall not go hunting," says Yorek, his face flushed and surly from the drink.

"What?" says Fabian, and he turned to me, stroking my hair. "Do you hear that, my Pippin? This great hulk fears to go out and catch a hare."

I looked from him to Yorek, puzzled.

"If I had your knowledge of snares, I would go myself," says Fabian. "But I have not, so you will go, and no argument, Edward."

Yorek turned his head sharp. "I will not. I'll work like a dog, digging and lifting here, but I shall not hunt."

"Why?" asks I.

Yorek looked at me for a minute, then he smiled in a sad fashion and says, "Leave Fabian, and sit by me for a spell, lass."

So I sat beside him, saying, "Why will you not hunt, Edward?"

"Because it brings me bad luck, lass," says he. "Curse the day I first set a trap or a snare, for I would not be the man I am now, had I not."

Fabian's face looked weary and tired, and he says, "What poor, honest Edward is trying to tell you, Kate, is that he fell afoul of the law through poaching."

"Aye," says Yorek, "my life ruined for a partridge, my head shaven for a partridge. I picked oakum for a partridge, I walked the treadmill for a partridge."

"Aye," says Fabian, mocking, "and do not forget how they transferred you to a spell at the prisoner's oar, too, for that same partridge, Ned."

"What!" says I. "They sent you for to pick oakum and to walk the treadmill for the killing of one paltry partridge?"

"Yes," says Yorek, "and my missus left with four little ones to feed."

"Bah!" says Fabian. "If you had poached on my preserves, I would have seen you hanged in chains. You set yourself above the law by killing one bird, which you knew to be unlawful, Edward, so do not whine like a cur when you are punished, but bear your chastisement like a man when you are found out."

Yorek again drank deeply, saying nothing and staring into the fire, but after a while he turned to Fabian, his face morose and even more deeply flushed.

"You, Fabian, what do you know of poor folk? You who was brought up a gentleman, with your fine linens and your blooded horses and your fancy ways. Why, if you don't eat, the law don't bother you, and you'll snatch the food from another's mouth. And you have not walked the treadmill and had your head shaven because you have had the good fortune not to be caught by the law. Nor would you care so much if you were, for you have no wife nor babes, and if you had, methinks you would not care overmuch about them. But I will say this, Fabian, this land has come to ruin when honest yeomen are turned into rogues for the sake of a single bird."

"For the sake of a bird!" says Fabian. "Our country is based on such laws, and they have held her together, though ones such as you do try to pull her apart at the seams. 'Tis the men of strength and breeding, the landowners, who murder off your paltry sort, which makes us English the breed we are."

"Aye," says Yorek slow, "the ones like you and the Dozer."

"You go too far, Edward," says Fabian. "I've put up with your milksop ways, for in some things you have the discretion of a gentleman, but do not, I pray you, mention me in the same breath with the Dozer, for it makes me long to kill you both, and I am in my cups as well as you, my rosy-cheeked, honest farmer's lad, and irresponsible."

Yorek stood up, squaring his shoulders, but before he could answer, Fabian went on: "You are a fool, and I have no pity for you. You had not the wits to commit a true crime, only a fiddling misdemeanor, and you are not man enough to accept your punishment."

Yorek sprang for him and knocked him down, and they both rolled over and over on the floor, trying to get a hold on each other.

They were evenly matched for strength, and commonly I would not have cared if they blackened each other's eyes, but both were drunk and angry and both had knives in their belts, and I would not see murder done. And oh! If they killed each other off, I would be alone with the Dozer!

I ran over to the Dozer, and after kicking him in the ribs half a dozen times I managed to rouse him and pointed to the two men, twisting and cursing on the floor.

Dozer shook his head sleepily a few times, and I wondered if I should kick him again, when suddenly he came fully awake, and with a speed that surprised me he leaped for the two of them, grabbed them both by their collars, dragged them to their feet as if they were children and held them at arm's length.

"What in hell," says he, shaking Yorek, "you fool, you know better than to try to kill gentlemen, for if you kills them you hangs, and if you don't kill them, they make sure you hangs."

He turned to Fabian, throwing him roughly against the stones of the fireplace.

"And Yorek here is my mate, what got me in on this job, and he's done me no harm, so lay off him, unless you wants a few rounds with the Dozer."

He stomped back to his bed of boughs and was snoring again in two minutes, while Yorek and Fabian stood panting and glowering at each other.

"Finish what you had to say," says Yorek, sober now, "for I mean to hear it, and there will be no more fighting."

"It is this," says Fabian, spitting on the floor in disdain. "You are an honest man and in the wrong service. And there is nothing which distresses and provokes me so as honest men or folk out of their proper service. I admire the Dozer more than you, and if I ever do another job, why, I'd sooner have the Pippin here, for my accomplice. For that girl has larceny in her soul, and I know what to expect, and when I brought the whip down on her shoulders, there were no tears of self-pity or whining such as yours, only a bold statement that she knew my tutor the whip well. The only tears she sheds are tears of anger, and I love her for them. You are put to shame by a maid in her teens. Well, you are a fool, and I do not like fools. Nor do I forget any man who has raised his hand against me, so beware, Yorek."

Fabian lurched off to sleep and Yorek bowed his head to the table and wept like a child.

I stood by his side, not knowing what to do or say, and finally I put my hand on his shoulder and says, "Do not weep, Edward, you will soon be home with your wife and children, and they love you. Edward, do not weep, I pray you."

But he did not answer me, only put his hands over his face and sobbed the more, so I went and sat on the bench by the fire.

What Fabian had said of Yorek was true, and at times his unmanliness aggravated me, for even I knew it was no light matter we were engaged in, and mildness has no place in a business where one man had already been killed. Yet at times Fabian had an unnecessary harshness about him, and I would not sleep by his side that night, but sat up instead, dozing on the bench.

And I wished Yorck had not raised his hand to Fabian, for I knew Fabian's heart like my own, dark and filled with dreadful fears.

When morning came, Yorek did not appear to remember a great deal of the happenings of the night before, for after soaking his head in the stream, he came in dripping wet and picked up the empty rum bottle.

"God," says he, "my head hurts and my mouth tastes like an almshouse. Did we quarrel last night, Fabian?"

Fabian removed the cold kerchief he had placed on his brow, sat up and nodded.

"What about?" says Yorek.

Fabian shrugged.

"No more of this stuff for me," says Yorek. "It makes me ugly. I seem to remember hitting you, Max, though I cannot fathom why. What did we fall out about?"

"Gentlemen," says Fabian, smiling wryly. "It seems you do not like them, Yorek. And I was maudlin myself, which was foolish of me. We must have no more quarreling like that again, Yorek. It is in my nature to vex people, and I am sorry, but there is no harm in it while we are both sober."

He scrubbed his hands wearily over his face, then he said, "I could do with a hair of the dog, but I see the bottle is empty. Which is as well, I suppose. If I tease you when I am sober, Edward, ignore me, and if I taunt you when I am drunk, for God's sake leave me, for we have enough on our hands without murdering each other in drunken rages."

He offered Yorek his hand, which Yorek took, much to my surprise, and then they sat down to breakfast and no more was said. And I wondered, as I served them, if a handclasp was really the end of last night's falling out, for I have known others like Yorek, who always see themselves as righteous, and who hold a grudge from one year to the next. And as for Fabian, well. . . . No more, I am young and perhaps too harsh and final in my judgments, without the benefits of experience to guide me confidently.

Things went well until the afternoon, when they quarreled again, this time over me, Yorek saying it sickened him to see a man of Fabian's years kissing a young girl, and Fabian saying

Yorek was a foul-minded bumpkin and that Catherine would be deflowered no sooner by him than by Yorek.

"Well, why don't you leave her alone then?" says Yorek.

Fabian ran his hand over his curly head and looked nonplused, for he could not very well tell Yorek he would beguile me into telling him a secret he did not wish to share with Yorek.

He had to content himself in telling Yorek that he loved me in a way Yorek could not comprehend, but Yorek shook his head, and turning to me says, "Beware, Catherine, I do not think he is such a villain as to dishonor you, but mark my words, no man ever loved a woman without wanting something from her."

But I only said blandly that if I knew what it was Fabian wanted, I should be glad to give it him, for I loved him truly, so that Edward turned to Fabian saying, "You see? She is such a child she does not even comprehend our words."

And Fabian hid a smile and said, aye, it was that very artlessness that made me so dear to him, and I need not fear from him on that account. Then he says, "But it would be another matter with the Dozer, so see that you stay close to my side, Catherine."

And Yorek nodded and says, aye, youth and innocence would mean nothing to that man. As if I did not already know it and was not appalled by the mere thought of him. Then Fabian says if I cannot stay by his side, to be by Yorek, and patted my head, and Yorek patted my head too, and they smiled at each other as if they had not been cursing each other five minutes before. Men!

Then Fabian went off, and I stood watching Yorek water the horses, and suddenly he sat down, scratched his head, looking puzzled, and says he did not trust Fabian for all his fine words. And when he saw my expression, he says, "Nay, not on your account, lass, for I do believe he is genuinely fond of you and would not hurt you. But I do not trust him, Catherine. And you would be best to stay beside me rather than either him or the Dozer."

"I would be better without the lot of you," says I, leaving him and going to my bower.

The fire burned brightly that evening and we looked a cozy lot, if we were not, for the drink was all gone.

Edward sat carving a boat for one of his children, Max and I were side by side before the fire, and the Dozer slumped on the bench with his head on his arms at the table, asleep.

"Well, Pippin, talk to me, for it's dull company here when you are silent." And in truth, he could not bear his own company, and Yorek and the Dozer wearied him.

"What shall I say?" says I, poking the fire.

"Say what you please."

"No."

"And why not?" asks Fabian. "Are you not happy here?"

"No," says I, for in truth that day I had, for the first time, missed the sea and my cliffs and the smell of salt in the air, and I was not used to this inland living for all that the forest was beautiful.

Yorek raised his head from his carving. "Are you homesick, lass?"

I nodded, but Fabian only laughed and turning to Yorek says, "Poor Kate, she pines for her five little sisters and her mother in Forsham."

"Do not jest, Fabian," says Yorek, very grave, "for I know what it is to long for your own field and folk."

And he patted my cheek and went off to his bed.

"Well, Catherine, what are the names of your little sisters," says Fabian, lifting me on his knee.

"Why," says I, "there's Abigail and Beatrice and Charlotte and Dorothea and Eleanor and Fanny."

"Why, my darling," says Fabian, his eyes sparkling, "you have six little sisters, can you not count? And I'll warrant the seventh, the baby, is called Gertrude, is she not?"

I could not forbear from smiling, he was such a rare sharp one, for I have no little sisters. But I wanted some to amuse me, for I am often lonely. I began with just Abigail and when she wearied me, I moved on to Beatrice, and now I seem to have six.

The Dozer suddenly raised his head and says, "What, six little sisters in Forsham? The next time I pass through there, I shall creep into their bedroom at night, and wring all their little necks." With that, he put his head on the table again and closed his piggish little eyes.

"You are too late, Dozer, for they are all dead and buried in the churchyard, poor little things, and Catherine was wont, of a Sunday, to sit upon their tombstones and pray and weep for them, were you not, my Pippin? You are such a pious child.

"And the Reverend Mr. Peterson, him who taught you your letters.... That was uncommon kind of him, Kate, was it not? A busy gentleman such as he."

I nodded.

"Now why should he do that?"

"Why, because he perceived I had a clever mind and it was a pity to waste it," says I.

"Aye, that would be a pity. And I'll warrant you sat on that good gentleman's lap and kissed his cheek too, did you not, Kate?"

"Yes," says I, "and I did not like it, but it was the price of my lessons, and he was so anxious to save my soul. Indeed, Fabian, I have never met a man so concerned with souls. Do you know, I do believe he would walk a hundred miles to save a soul, and two hundred for mine. To be sure, it is very puzzling to come upon a person like that."

"Not so," says Fabian, "for he was a preacher, and souls are his business, as beeves and steaks are a butcher's, and tallow and wax a chandler's."

"Perhaps that is so," said I, thinking back on that good gentleman.

"And to what purpose do you intend to use this hard-won education, my darling?"

"For to be a lady," says I. "A grand lady, somehow, someday."

"And so you shall, my darling, so you shall, and Max Fabian will teach you every trick you need know. But back to our reverend gentleman. You did not like his caresses, Kate?"

"Ugh!" says I. "No, for his breath was like rancid cheese, but it was worth it to me, for now there is not a book in the English language I cannot read if I put my mind to it."

"Well," says he, letting his breath out slowly, "I am glad you did not like his kisses, of that I am very glad. You are a clever girl. But what caused you to leave the service of that good gentleman?"

"Why," says I, sighing, "one day, his lady, who had eyes like gimlets and a long red nose like a poker, walks into his study unannounced and says, 'So, Mr. Peterson, this is your charity to teach this fisher's brat, to learn her to read so she may know her Scriptures and improve her soul. And you, you lecher, have been kissing her behind my back. Begone out of here, you hussy,' she says to me, 'back to your aunt, for I will not have you in this house.' So," says I, "I went back to my aunt, who was very wroth and beat me and told me it was what I could expect, but I did not care so much, for by that time I knew history and reading and writing and geography and a bit of mathematics and Latin. It is a pity I could not have remained another six months, though, for he was going to start me on French, and that is a very fashionable language for ladies."

"Upon my soul, Pippin," says Fabian, "upon my soul, I have never met your like. As I live and breathe, I would not have believed such guile could hide behind so innocent and sweet a face. Why, my pet, you are a true mate for Max Fabian, bless me if you ain't."

He looked into my eyes, and says, firm and soft, "And now that we understand each other, my jewel, tell me what Davy said to you as he lay a-dying, for, in truth, you cannot find the money yourself. You would have by now if you could read the cipher, and even if you could, what good would all that money do you? It would look wondrous strange, a lass of your years with a pocket full of gold and no way to account for it to the authorities. You need Fabian to tutor you on these matters, my little sweetheart."

But before I could say aught, I saw the Dozer open his eyes, and stare at me, dazed-like, for a second, and then he closed his eyes again and slept. A great fright went through me, for those eyes were the eyes of a dreaming beast, crafty and sly, and I did not know whether he had taken in Fabian's words or not.

Fabian, too, had noticed the Dozer, and he placed his finger across my lips and shook his head and says in the same tone he spoke before. "Why, you and I could amuse each other all evening with our foolish tales, my darling, but it is late, and you must have your beauty sleep, or else your pretty cheeks will fade."

He wrapped his cloak about me and drew me down beside him in the corner and whispered, "Sleep with your head close to Fabian's heart tonight, my love, for the Dozer is not so thick between the ears as he appears to be, and it will go ill with all of us, should he think you have a clue. I tell you, Catherine, if he suspects, he'll torture the truth from you and then murder both of us, and Edward too."

And he kissed my lips. "So tell Max, my pretty, what Jenkin Davy said, as he lay a-dying, for Max Fabian will guard you with his life, and you shall be his lady."

I lay thinking for a long while.

"Well, my darling?"

"Why," says I, "Jenkin Davy, as he lay a-dying, says, 'The moon is made of green cheese,' which I thought a strange thing for a dying man to say."

Fabian said nothing for a while, then he leaned over me and kissed me again, saying, "Sleep sound, my pretty. I shall not let the Dozer harm you."

"Are you not going to sleep?"

"No," says he. "I wish to think, Catherine."

The next morning Fabian says, "This wretched diet palls on me. We need meat if we are to toss these stones about." And he turns to Yorek: "Yorek, there is a town called Handley six miles from the forest, and this is their market day, and methinks it would be a wise step for you to take the pack horse there, and sell him, and buy fresh supplies, for we may be here another fortnight."

"What, sell the beast?" says Dozer. "You are a gentleman, Max, and must have some gold upon you."

"Yes, you fool," says Fabian, "and Edward here, a farmer, would look true to form, throwing gold about in a village like Handley, where the folk haven't seen a sovereign since the time of the Stuarts, and pay their debts with vegetables and chickens."

"You are right, Max," says Yorek, "and we do need many things—candles, and meat, and a bucket."

"And onions," says I, "and fresh cheese, and carrots to cook in a stew, and a bottle of vinegar to pour on chopped raw cabbage, and sweet butter and eggs."

"Why, you know how to market, my darling. You shall go with Yorek."

"And more rum," says the Dozer, "for I would as soon drink water as port, and whisky's a drink for them heathen Irish and Scots, but a man needs rum to drink."

"And a bottle of rum for the Dozer," says Fabian.

And he walked back and forth, his spurs jangling on the stone floor, as he tapped his finger against his lips, thinking.

"Yorek," he says, "we must use great caution. Now, you shall be a farmer, newly widowed, and Kate here is your daughter, and you are taking her north, to live with your married sister, for they are very curious in these country parts. And you have never traveled so far afoot before, and the journey costs you more than you bargained, for you feared to carry much money, as you have heard of cutthroats who watch at inns for honest people with fat purses, so you needs must sell the horse, which is from your farm, that you brought along for the little one to ride, and so you must both walk now.

"And you, Catherine, should any speak to you, why you shall put your finger in your mouth so, and make your eyes wide as saucers, and should they persist in speaking to you, why, you shall weep and hide behind Yorek, who shall say you still grieve for the mother you have so recently lost."

I laughed, but Yorek took Max's instructions to heart and nodded, very serious.

Just before we left, Fabian took me aside and says, "For your sake, lass, I want you away from the mill for a time, while I sound out the Dozer, for I fear he will do you some harm, my dear."

"And you would not have that," says I. "At least, not until you unlock the cipher."

"You are a clever girl," says he gravely. "And I should miss you sore, should ill befall you. For all you may jest, my darling, Fabian has been a lonely man, and few are the women who have given him much happiness. But with you, Kate, whether I will it or not, I am as a lad again."

He stood staring down at me, and his face looked neither sad nor happy.

"Max," says I, "you do not smile often."

"Do I not, miss?" says he. "Well, that can be remedied, for I shall show you a secret that none but we shall know." And he looked at me, very searching.

"Well," says I, slow and wondering.

"Now my darling," says he, "give me your hand."

And he took my hand and pressed my finger against his dimpled cheek, and lo, it was like drawing a curtain aside and letting in the sun, for his face lit up, and he laughed, and when he saw my surprise, he laughed even more and rubbed his cheek against mine, saying, "Aye, my pretty, you are the only one in the world who can make Fabian smile. I'll laugh only for my Pippin, and it shall be our secret, Kate, shared by no one in the world."

And then he says in his ordinary tone, "And now off to market, my dear, and see Yorek drives a hard bargain, for between you and me, my pretty, our stalwart farmer friend is too honest to suit my fancy."

I nodded and he squeezed my hand and says, "I cannot bear honest stalwarts, for they have a way of doing in rogues like me. And since you are a rogue yourself, if a small one, why, Kate, watch that Yorek well and see he follows my words."

"Fabian!" called Yorek from the doorway. "Leave that girl be, and Catherine, get out here if you wish to go with me."

Fabian took my hand and led me out and I says, "Why, Yorek, that beast looks handsome. He should draw a good price." (And the animal did, for his coat was glossy and shining.) Yorek says in a gloomy way, "Aye, the Dozer has groomed him well, and he knows more ways of cheating honest farmers than I would have thought."

"Bah! you cowdung!" says Dozer, "I likes horses, I does, and it gives me pleasure to see 'em lookin' smart, and if I touched up yon beast a bit, why 'twas for his own sake, so he'll find him a rich farmer who will feed him well."

And he put his ugly face against the horse's head and kissed him. "Well, curse my black heart!" says Fabian. "Thank God I am not a horse, for I do believe you speak the truth, and Dozer, it turns my blood to vinegar to think that had nature not been so clement as to fashion me a man, I might have lived to be a poor dumb beast and felt those lips upon my brow."

Yorek offered me the toe of his boot, saying, "Mount the beast, Catherine."

"If you please," says I, "I wish to walk, Edward."

"You shall ride," says Yorek, "for 'tis a long day ahead of us, and it is not my shoulders you will ride home upon if you are foolish enough to tire yourself early." And his tone was so surly that I looked at him in surprise, but Fabian's dimple twitched, and he lifted me on the horse, saying, "Poor honest Edward prefers a beast to me, Catherine, and it goes against him that I claim to be a man and better than an animal. Is that not so, Yorek?"

"Yes," says Yorek, in his stolid country way, and led the horse off to the forest.

The dew hung like tiny baubles on the trees, and the grass shone like new-caught fish. The birds piped saucily at us and the flowers were opening their petals, and I said, "Let me walk, I pray you, Yorek, for indeed, this is the prettiest time of the day, and within the hour it will all be changed and ordinary, and everything will seem tired, as if it has known a million days, but for this space in the morning it is like magic. So let me walk and run as I please." He looked up at me, still surly, and then his face softened, and he says, "Aye, lass, walk if you will, for none but plain folk know of the beauties of the morning, them that is rich being too sodden from drink to see God's realm. But you are like my own people, Catherine, for all you come of fishing folk rather than farmers."

And he held out his hand as I slid from the horse's back. But his good mood did not last long. I plucked some violets and showed them to him, saying, "Look, Edward, I should not have picked them, for now they cannot open their little eyes full to the sun, for I have broke their stalks."

He took them from my hand and threw them roughly aside. "Aye, lass, that's what you've done, and you perceive it only after doing it. You are like Fabian in that, and like him you can speak naturally in pretty ways as well as plain, for it comes to you like some women can cure fever and some men divine water, it's in your heart, and why that should be, I do not know."

And he slung me astride the horse again and stomped along in front, holding the halter.

Moving without haste, we reached the village of Handley by late morning, and the farmers from all the countryside were gathered there to trade their produce.

Yorek and I passed through the small square where stout farmers' wives sat offering cheese and butter and vegetables. Yorek lifted me from the horse and pointed to a stone by a huge cart. "Sit there, Catherine, while I see what price I can fetch for the horse."

"Can I not come with you?"

Yorek looked at me in a strange way.

"Goodbye, Catherine." And he walked away, leading the horse.

"Wait, Yorek," cried I, and he stopped and turned.

"Give me a penny to buy a ribband for my hair."

He put his hand in his pocket and handed me sixpence. Noticing my surprise, he hesitated and said, "It's all I have, Catherine."

Then he moved on, so I sat on the rock and looked about me. A fat farm wife leaned from the huge cart next to me and says, "Well, dearie, I don't think I have seen you before. What parts are you from?"

I pointed south.

"And that was your dad, was it, my dear?"

I nodded again.

"And what would your dad be doing so far from home, my dearie?"

"My father is selling our horse," says I.

"Ah," says she, "and why does he wish to sell his horse, my dearie, for it seemed like a good sound beast?"

But she asked too many questions, so I jumped to my feet and ran away.

I came to a booth where an old lady sat selling apples, and I asked her how much one would cost.

"One?" says she, smiling. "Why, my pretty, I never sold but one apple before, and I do not know." She polished one and handed it to me, saying, "There, you may have it for nought, to match your cheeks."

I thanked her, and looking over my shoulder saw the farm wife standing on tiptoe to watch me. I waved and moved on till I came to a common where the livestock was, and farmers offered sheep and beef and geese and chickens, and in the center of a group of farmers I saw Yorek and the horse. I walked on past them.

Finally I came to a clump of trees among which was camped a band of gypsies. As I walked among them, they all raised their eyes and stared at me curiously, and spoke to each other in their heathen tongue.

Then a tall black man spoke to me, saying, "Will you have your fortune told, Miss?"

"How much will it cost me?" I asked.

"A penny," says he, and he pointed to a woman sitting on the ground by a small fire. I turned to her and she motioned me to sit before her.

"So you would like to know the future?" she says, taking my hand, but I drew it back from her.

"No," says I, "for I shall see to that. I want to buy a dye, and I will pay you a penny for it."

"Dye?" says she, and ran her dirty fingers through her greasy locks. "And what would a pretty little maid want with dye, and why would she ask me for it?"

"I want it for to make ink, to write in a book," says I, "and I ask you because I have been told your people know much about herbs and roots and dyes."

She turned laughing to the man, and in my life I have never seen such white teeth.

"Hah!" she says. "They ask the Johnny Fahs for strange things, but never have I been asked for a dye before, and she does not want her fortune told, and she writes in a book."

The man sat beside me and they both sat staring at me as if I were a fish with two heads.

"Well," says I, "do you want my penny or no?"

They looked at each other and laughed, and his teeth were as white as hers.

"No, my pretty," says she, "I have no dyes for sale."

"Do you know where I can get some, or can you tell me where in a forest I might find some? For I will give you a penny if you will but tell me."

She turned to the man, speaking to him in their strange language, but he shook his head.

"No, my dearie," she says to me, "for they have not hanged a Johnny Fah in these parts in a lifetime. And if I gave you a dye, and you misused it, and poisoned your mistress or your master, why, it's the Johnny Fahs who'll swing for it."

"But," says I, "I have no mistress or master to poison, and I spoke the truth; I want it only to write in my journal, and I shall give you my silver sixpence if you will sell me dye," and I held the sixpence before her.

The man took it, tested it with his sharp white teeth, rang it against a stone, and spoke to the woman in the strange tongue.

"You shall have the dye, my dearie," says the gypsy woman, "but my man says, if you tell where you got it, a curse will fall upon you. Remember, the curse will fall on you if ever you say you got it from a Johnny Fah. He says, if you tell, false kisses and pretty words will turn your head. Beware now, dearie, for we've warned you."

"What do I care for your curses?" I said. "I was born with one on me. I said I would use it to make ink and I give you my word I shall tell no one of it, so give it me."

She led me to a covered cart where dusky gypsy children and babes rolled on the floor playing, and she pushed them aside with her naked foot and opened a carved chest. From it she took some gnarled roots and handed me three.

"Boil these in four gills of water," she says, "for the space of half an hour, then put the juice in a bottle with a cork in it, and you will have a dye that will be bright for a hundred years. But wash the pot well, the one you boil the dye in, for it won't improve your health should you swallow any of it. Half a wineglass of this would kill you deader than those chickens hanging by their necks at the butcher's cart!"

I took the herbs and put them in my pocket, and as I left their camp, she called to me, "Do not forget the curse, dearie, for if you say you found the dye from a Johnny Fah, the curse will be upon you for sure, and you don't want your pretty head turned, do you?"

"Fiddle," says I, laughing, and I left.

I went back to the stone beside the big cart, and the motherly, inquisitive woman was not there, so I sat down to wait for Yorek.

He walked past, half an hour later, and he started with surprise when he saw me.

"Catherine," says he, "you waited."

"Yes," says I, surprised in my turn.

"Oh, Catherine," he says, and put his hand upon my head, "I left you for to give you a chance of escape, to go back to your own people, for I told you that night at the inn that I would help you to get away from Dozer and Fabian the first chance I had. Why did you not go, child?"

"Go back to Forsham? Go back to scrub pots and sweep floors and run with beer and ale and be looked down upon for the rest of my life?" says I. "No, Yorek. I would sooner be at the mill with you and Fabian."

"You foolish child," says he, "why should the people of Forsham look down on you? You only fancy it. And what do you think the Dozer will do when the loot is found? Why, he'll do you in for sure, if Fabian don't do it first."

"Fabian won't do me in because ..." I stopped. I could not very well say that they would find no loot until it suited me to tell Fabian the real cipher.

Poor Yorek, who knew nothing of Davy's words, looked as if he would weep.

"Catherine, go. This may be your last chance. Go, lass, and remember it was Yorek who helped you, should you be questioned."

"Yorek," says I, "you *are* a fool." And I shrugged his hand off my shoulder. "If you set me free, and I make my way back to Forsham, and tell them where I have been, why, it won't matter if you have helped me or no, for they'll get you for being in on the crime of the money."

"But not the murder, Catherine, not the murder of Jenkin Davy, for I had no part of that. And lass, if you go back to Forsham, you won't have to wash pots and pans and run with ale, for the inn burned down. So go, Catherine, while you may."

"Not wash pots and pans!" says I. "Why, Yorek, you are a poor man yourself, and you know what chance I have, and if the inn is burned down, why, that dragon of an aunt of mine will find another place for me with more pots and pans to wash, and more floors to scrub, and I won't have it. I could have escaped before, had I wanted, but I do not. Yorek, I have cast my lot with the crew of you, and I shall share your fortune."

"Or misfortune," says he, looking grave. "You need not work

so hard for the rest of your days, Catherine, for in three years' time you will be of an age to marry, and you will find yourself an honest fisherman and have your own cottage."

"Bah!" says I. "So I can raise a dozen brats and live like an animal. I would sooner scrub pots. Yorek, I can read and write, and that is my undoing, for now I know how much there is in the world, and I cannot and will not forswear it."

Yorek sat down on the grass and rubbed his hands over his face for a long while, and finally he turned his head to me and says, "Catherine, you say I am a fool to offer you escape, but in truth I have given it a deal of thought. And Catherine, I have no stomach for this business I am in, and I feel in my bones that only ill will come of it, and I wish with all my heart that Fabian had not beguiled me into it. Go, Catherine, and tell the law what you will, so long as it be the truth, that they may come and take Fabian and Dozer and me. Fabian said I could not take my punishment like a man. Yes, I remember the cause of our quarrel now. Well, I can, and I would, before more ill can come of it. Now, for God's sake go, Catherine."

"No," says I.

"Why not?"

"Well, truth to tell, Yorek, I have grown uncommon fond of Fabian and cannot bear to leave him."

Yorek boxed my ear so hard my head rang.

"You are a wicked, unnatural child," says he, his face scarlet with anger, "and were you mine, I'd use my whip on you."

"What!" says I, rubbing my ear and beginning to weep. "And you chide Fabian for his rough ways! For shame to hit one weaker than you, Edward Yorek."

"It is not meet," says he, "it is not meet for any woman, let alone a little maid, to love a man like Fabian. I am sorry I struck you, Catherine, for it was wrong, but it sets my teeth on edge to think of one so like my own daughter near a man like Fabian."

"In three years' time, you say I shall be of an age to marry. Well, it is not so long, and I shall wait and marry Fabian, for we are two of a kind. We both know what we want."

Yorek stared at me strangely.

"Yes," he says slowly. "Yes, in truth I must confess I have never seen Fabian tender to any but you, and in God's name, it is true you are a strange one."

He chewed a blade of grass, then spat it out. "I am glad you are not my daughter."

He stood up and so did I.

"Come," he says, "I have the supplies to buy."

The fat goodwife came lumbering up and climbed into her cart, where she stood gazing at us curiously.

"Well," she says to me, "I see your dad has sold his horse. I trust, sir, that you got a good price for the beast?"

"Yes," says Yorek, blushing.

"And perhaps you would like to buy some nice fresh produce, for I have eggs and cheese, cheese that is the best made in this country, and fine sweet butter."

Yorek looked at me, and I poked him in the back and nodded.

"Aye," he says slow, and the woman began handing down the food.

"Give me your kerchief, my dear," says she to me, "for to wrap the eggs in, for men are clumsy when it comes to eggs."

I took the eggs and stood idly by Yorek's side while he paid her.

"And where are you bound, sir, with your young one?"

"North to my sister," says Yorek, his cheeks scarlet.

"Ah," she says, and turning to me, "And do you like traveling, my dear?"

I put my finger in my mouth and turned my eyes to Yorek.

"Why, what ails the child?" says she. "Is she ill?"

So I began to weep and hid behind Yorek.

"Oh," says Yorek, "she has just recently been bereaved of her mother and weeps constantly, so I am taking her north to her aunt."

"Ah, poor little thing," says the fat goodwife. "And you are right to do so, sir, for young ones, especially maids, should be brought up around women, for it has a softening influence and fathers have heavy hands at times, do they not, my dear?"

She reached around Yorek and patted my head. "Do not weep, my child, your aunt will be good to you, and you will be happy with her, though you may feel strange for a while, away from your daddy."

Yorek thanked her hurriedly, and, clutching my hand, dragged me off to where fresh butchered meat was offered for sale, and when we were out of hearing of the goody, he wiped the sweat from his brow and says, "My God, Kate, I am not much of an actor, but you do tolerable well for a beginner."

I laughed, for it pleased me to play games on simple country folk, and I reached on my toes and kissed his cheek, saying, "Why Yorek, you are the nicest daddy, I swear, in the world. Now give me a penny."

"Try none of your wiles on me, miss," says he, "for I am not Fabian. What did you do with the sixpence I gave you?"

"I lost it in the grass while I was running," says I.

"Then you shall have no more for being so careless. When I was a little fellow your size, I never so much as held a sixpence in my hand, let alone having one given me for naught. You are a very careless girl."

So I began to weep again, saying I wanted a ribband for my hair, for I did, and looking around I saw the fat farmer's wife approaching. She stared at us very curious and finally walked up and says to Yorek, "And what ails your lass now? From my cart I saw her laughing, only a minute ago."

"Why," says Yorek, blushing again, "I gave her a sixpence, which she lost in the grass, and now she weeps because she cannot have a penny to buy a ribband for her hair."

"Oh, sir," says the goody, "do not be so harsh on a little one who has so recently lost her mother." And she opened the purse at her waist and took out a farthing. "Here, my dearie, I cannot afford a penny, but you shall have a farthing."

I put out my hand, but Yorek struck my wrist and says, "Thank you, mistress, but you can ill afford it, and perhaps this will teach her to be more careful."

"Ah," she says, sighing, and putting the coin back, "you are a hard man, sir, a hard man." And she turned and left.

"Why, Catherine," says he to me, "would you take money from an honest farmer's wife, who has so little?"

"I would have done," says I, "if you had not been so hasty slapping my wrist."

He shook his head, and we went to buy beef, and when Yorek

chose a piece, I poked him in the back and whispered, "Don't be such a fool, Edward, that is not fresh butchered, it's been dead for a week."

Yorek turned to me, "Well," he says, "well . . ." and he looked at the dealer. "Well, daughter, which shall I take?"

"That one," says I, pointing.

"You have a rare youngster," says the dealer as Yorek paid him.

"Aye," says Yorek, "aye, that I have, if she be not too sharp."

"What?" says the dealer, laughing, "would you have a dullard for a daughter, and never get her married off?"

"Nay," says Yorek, "there are spinsters about who owe their state to being sharp."

"Ho!" laughs the dealer, digging his thumb in my ribs, "this one won't live to be a spinster."

"Aye," says Yorek, serious, "mark them words well, my girl, mark them words well, Catherine."

The dealer looked at him oddly, and we moved on to buy vegetables.

Laden with supplies and in good spirits we left in late afternoon and arrived at the mill just before dark.

Fabian sat astride a bench by the fire, jingling his spurs on the hearth and tossing his knife in the air, catching it by the hilt as it fell.

"Ah!" says he, springing to his feet as we walked in. "Ah, Yorek and the Pippin." He put his knife in its sheath. "So you have come safely back, and what a fine tanned and rosy pair you are. And I trust, Edward, that you brought us some decent victuals?"

He patted my head, then lifted the packs from Edward's shoulders. "Oho!" says he, "beef! We shall dine well this night!"

Taking a crowbar as a spit, he put the roast over the fire and bade me peel the vegetables for the pot. As I prepared the carrots and onions, he sat beside me watching.

"Pippin," says he finally, in a wondrous soft voice, "do you know what I know?"

"No, Max," says I.

"Why," says he, "I know that the moon is not made of green cheese, and I'll wager you know that too, my darling."

He drew me closer when I did not answer.

"Catherine, my pet, my Pippin, how can you be so cruel to Fabian, when you've had naught but tenderness from him?"

"Fabian!" shouted Yorek from the other end of the room. "Stop fondling that girl!"

Fabian raised his eyebrows in mock surprise and pushed me away from him, but he winked, whispering, "We shall have a small discussion on a certain matter later, my darling."

After our diet of porridge, the meal seemed like a feast and we all ate heartily and drank port until our cheeks were rosy in the firelight.

Suddenly the Dozer raised his head from the table and says, "Where's my rum?"

"Here," says Fabian, handing him the bottle. Dozer pulled the cork out with his teeth, spat it on the floor and drank deep.

"Steady," says Yorek. "But three tots, Dozer."

But the Dozer paid him no heed and drank deeper.

"Why, we may let you have a bit more, for you have been a good boy, Dozer," says Fabian, slapping Dozer's back.

"You said yourself, Fabian . . ." says Yorek, but Fabian says, "Tut, tut, Edward, a drop extra won't hurt him."

"Aye, shut your gaff, Yorek, or I'll shut it for you," growled the Dozer, raising the bottle to his lips again.

"Odd's blood, Dozer," says Fabian, "I meant for you to have an extra drink to round out your meal. Do not, I pray you, finish the bottle in one swallow."

But the Dozer did not seem to hear him, so Fabian took Yorek and me by the arms and led us to a corner, saying, " 'Twill be wise if we keep out of his way this night."

But we had only been seated the space of a few minutes when the Dozer roars, "Send that gel here, and fast!"

Yorek and Fabian looked at each other, and then at me, and I hid behind them. "Do not, I beg you, I pray you, do not let him near me," I quavered.

Neither spoke, and the Dozer got to his feet and started toward us.

"Get out of my way, you two," and he threw down the bottle, which was three quarters empty, and then, his voice hoarse, like an animal's growl, "I wants to have a little talk with this brat, I does."

And he stood before Yorek and Fabian, his terrible head lowered, and then he shook it from side to side and whispered, "Aye, it's comin' back to me now, it is . . . Fabian and you, sittin' next to the fire, and what was it he says?"

Fabian turned his head to me, and the dimple was deeper than I had ever seen it. His whole cheek twitched.

"Aye," grunts the Dozer, "I remembers now. He was asking you what Davy said as he lay a-dyin'. . . . Yes, and tellin' you how you should spend the money."

Yorek turned his head and says, "Child, you knew something, and yet you did not speak?"

"Yorek," says I, clinging to his arm, "don't let the Dozer touch me, Yorek, I beg you."

Yorek looked at me, and then at Dozer and says, "Stand back, Dozer."

The Dozer did not move, and Fabian's face went very white, and he says, "Stand back, leave the girl be."

"What," says Dozer, "so you can learn the cipher before me, and run with the loot?"

Fabian turned to me. "For God's sake, girl, speak the truth now, for I cannot answer for this man if you do not. I told you before to tell me. If you had, you would not be in peril now."

"Aye," says Dozer, "how true, for you would have killed her and been far away by now, eh, Fabian? You're a smooth one, ain't you? What a fool I was, not to suspeck your soft ways with the gel."

"I know nothing," says I, trembling all over and clinging to Fabian now.

"Catherine," says he, "do not be more foolish than you have already been. Speak up, and I swear the Dozer will not hurt you. Will you, Dozer?"

But the Dozer did not answer him. Instead he went to the fire, drew his knife and shoved it in the coals.

"Jesus!" breathed Yorek, going as white as Fabian.

Fabian took me by the shoulders and shook me hard. "Dear God, girl, speak! Don't you know what will happen to you?"

But much as I wanted to, I could say nothing; my tongue was a piece of lead in my mouth, and I could not have spoken my own name for every piece of gold in the world, and all I could do was to stand shaking all over, clinging to Fabian and looking from him to Yorek.

And then the Dozer drew his knife from the coals, and the blade glowed cherry red, and he walked slow as a big cat toward the three of us, saying, "You'll talk, gel, for first I'll burn your eyes out, and then I'll notch your ears and your nose like a pig's, and then it'll be your fingers, one by one, and if you don't talk by then, why, there's all your toes, and if you be silent still, you may keep your secret, for I'll cut your tongue out."

But still I could not speak, for my throat seemed froze. The Dozer stood before Yorek and Fabian.

"Stand back, you two; you know when the Dozer means business."

"No," says Yorek, and I saw he trembled too.

"Stand back, you puppets," says the Dozer, his voice no more nor a whisper. "Why, I'll break the two of you like dolls. Give me that gel."

Yorek suddenly struck Dozer with the full force of his fist, the blow catching the Dozer between the eyes, and the Dozer stepped back a pace, shaking his head, and then his fist shot out and Yorek went down like a felled ox. Then the Dozer turned to Fabian.

"You too, Fabian?"

"Do not raise your hand to me," says Fabian, his voice as quiet as the Dozer's, and I saw his knife was drawn.

"Hand me that gel," says the Dozer.

"You fool," says Fabian, "can't you see you've frightened the child witless, and she cannot speak?"

The Dozer suddenly lurched forward, pushing Fabian aside as if he were a stick, and grappled me to him, and then I began to scream, and I screamed and screamed and screamed, until the Dozer dropped his knife and clapped his hand over my mouth.

"Shut the brat up," he said to Fabian. "Get her to talk plain."

Yorek got to his knees, holding his head, still dazed, and then stood, rubbing his throat, where the Dozer's blow had caught him.

Fabian pulled me away from the Dozer and as soon as the Dozer's hand was off my mouth I began to scream again, and Fabian started to lead me to a bench by the fire, but the Dozer roars, "Not so quick, Fabian, there'll be no more secrets between you two from now on."

"Get some wine," shouts Fabian to Yorek, and indeed, they all had to shout to be heard above the sound of my screaming.

Fabian sat on the bench and pulled me roughly to his knee, and put his hand over my mouth. Yorek brought a cup of wine to him, and the Dozer leaned over close to hear.

"Now," says Fabian to me, his hand still over my mouth, "you are going to drink some wine, Catherine, but first you are going to stop screaming. And when you are done with screaming, and begin to drink, why, you are going to sit very quiet on Fabian's knee while he sings you a song, and when Fabian's song is done, miss, you are going to tell us all, all three of us, in very plain English, exactly what Jenkin Davy said before he died. And no harm shall come to you."

But still he did not take his hand from my mouth, and his face was as white as a corpse.

Then he says, "Put the wine on the bench beside me, Edward."

Yorek did so and Fabian took his hand from my mouth and picked up the cup, holding it before my lips. And then he began to sing a strange song, called "Binori, Oh, Binori," as I drank the wine. It was a very long song and I do not remember much about it, except there were two sisters.

And when I had drunk the wine, he says, "Fabian's song has ended, miss."

An awful dread was upon me that I could not remember Davy's words, but finally I says, slow, with all three hung over me, "He said, 'Tell Max our plans is changed. Tell him things is backwards. Tell him to turn the mill upside down.'"

They were all motionless, looking at me for a long moment, then their faces faded away, and there was a great roaring in my ears, and when I opened my eyes I was lying on the floor and Fabian was bathing my forehead with cold water, and the Dozer sat on the bench staring at me, and Yorek stood behind him.

Fabian lifted me up and kissed my cheek.

"Well, gentlemen," he says, "you heard Pippin's words. What do you make of them?"

"Nowt," says Dozer. "Do you think the brat is lying?"

Fabian gave his rare smile.

"No," says he, "I think for the first time in her life, my darling has told the truth. That is such a message as Davy would have given. She could not have made it up of whole cloth."

"And then what makes you of it?" asks Dozer.

"I do not know," says Fabian, slow. "In truth, I do not." And he stroked my hair absently and gazed unseeing into the flames.

"What of you, Yorek?" asks Dozer.

But Yorek only shook his head.

"Well," says Fabian, "I must sleep on it. Perhaps by morning Davy's words will make more sense."

He arose and put his hand on my shoulder.

"And now, Dozer, the child has told us what we would of her, and I must warn you, there will be no more heated knives or threats, for I spoke the truth when I said I was fond of her. Since you have not the wits to understand the cipher, you must trust me, and do as I say, and I say this much, Dozer, if harm comes to her, I will kill you."

And he led me to the corner and wrapped his coat about me and we lay down together. "Sleep soundly, Pippin," he said. "You shall not be disturbed."

I closed my eyes and slept, but not sound, for my muscles kept twitching with such great jerks that they woke me, but Fabian put my head on his shoulder and his arm about me, and his voice was gentle: "Sleep, my darling, sleep; morning will soon be here, and you will have hardly a memory of this night."

But when dawn came and I opened my eyes, the first thing I remembered was that in my fright I had not told them the last part of the cipher, which was to change the eye to an ee, and I lay in a sweat of fear that this secret should prove my undoing.

At the beginning of the morning, naught was said of the happenings of the night before.

Fabian bade me prepare breakfast and then took the other two to a corner out of my earshot. I guessed they were discussing the cipher, for once I heard Fabian's voice, raising in anger: "We shall continue as we were, for I can make naught of the bloody thing, and for all I can see, why, we must turn the place upside down as Davy said, which is precisely what we have been doing."

And I prepared a fine breakfast, for we were well stocked with eggs and bacon and fresh bread which we ate with sweet butter and honey. But I had little appetite.

"More bacon," says Dozer, pointing his knife at me.

"Cook it yourself," says Fabian.

"What?" says the Dozer, rising.

"Leave the girl be," says Yorek.

"She's for to cook," says the Dozer, squinting his eyes.

Fabian tossed him a hunk of bread. "Fill your ugly mouth with that and shut up."

"What are ye wroth with me for?" says the Dozer. "What did I do to you? Was it not Yorek here I floored?"

"Aye, it was," says Yorek, rubbing his throat, "and yours is not such a face as improves any man's appetite over the breakfast table, so kindly shut it, Master Dozer."

Dozer laughed and slapped Fabian across the back, but Fabian drew back, snarling, "Keep your hands off me, you whoreson, or I'll tickle your slats with my knife."

"What, Fabian," says the Dozer, scratching his poll, "now what have I done?"

Fabian's dimple twitched but he said nothing. Then he turned to me.

"Eat your food, Catherine."

"I'm not hungry."

"You see?" says Fabian, pulling me to his side. "You see what you have done? You've frighted the roses from my pretty's cheeks, you have. Do not be afraid, sweetheart, for he shall not harm you. Eat hearty, the food is tasty."

"To hell with the pack of you," says the Dozer amiably and continued to eat. Yorek turned to Fabian.

"What is to be done with this one," and he nodded his head to me, "when the loot's found, Fabian?"

"Have you any suggestions, honest Edward?" says Fabian, mocking.

"Aye, she may come with me and live with my missus and little ones, like one of our own," says Yorek.

Fabian threw back his head and roared. "Aye," says he, "she'd love that, wouldn't you, my pretty? On Yorek's farm, up to your knees in cow dung?"

But for all of Fabian's laughter, after the happenings of the night before the suggestion did not strike me as so dismal, as long as I trod that farm with my head firmly set on my neck in the right direction.

"Nay," says Fabian, offering me a tidbit of his own food, "this one stays with Fabian, for she's Fabian's darling, she is, and in two or three years time, when she's filled out a bit and grown half a head, why she shall be Fabian's true-love, for I'd search many a league to find a fairer face or a cleverer mind. And when Max Fabian wants something, be it women, horses or gold, he gets it."

"Your words are pretty, Fabian," says Yorek, slow. "I wish I knew if your sentiments was so."

Fabian laughed again, and indeed it was strange to see him laugh twice in such a short time, and he says, "Catherine has told us the cipher, which was all any of us could ask of her, and I am not such a beast as the Dozer, to molest or hurt a maid for sport, so rest easy, the girl is safe now."

And then he arose. "And now to work again, this time with a purpose. And you, Catherine, go run in the forest and see if you can replace the roses in your cheeks, for this pallor ill becomes you, and since those roses were mine, I want them back."

The three went off to the passage where they were raising mighty blocks of stone and timbers a foot and a half in girth, and after I had done the dishes and cleansed the pot and swept the hearth, I crept close up to them to make sure all were hard at work.

I then went back and boiled the roots the gypsy woman had given me, and I followed her instructions, and put the dye, which was a purplish brown color, in an empty port bottle. Then scrubbed the pot well with sand from the stream-bed, for I had no wish to be poisoned.

It was still early morning when I took the quills and book from the well and went to my bower, where I settled myself down to write. And write I did, for five hours straight, and it was only when my hand was so weary I could no longer form my letters clearly that I stopped. But my mind was so full of what to set down that, apart from fatigue, I could have continued twice as long.

I had hid all my writing materials and was resting when I heard Fabian's voice ring through the forest. He sang,

> "Binori, oh, Binori,
> I'll be true to my love,
> If my love will be true to me,
> Bow ye down, bow ye down."

"Here, Fabian," I called to him, for he was unwittingly passing me by.

"What a pretty spot you have chosen to sit in," says he, throwing himself in the grass by my side and plucking a violet, which he held before my eyes. "What do you think about, Pippin, here by yourself?"

I shrugged and tossed a leaf in the water and we watched it swirl and float and disappear.

"Are you tired of hunting for treasure?" I asked.

Fabian looked at me sharp for a moment, and then laughed. "Aye, lass, I'm a gentleman, and those two beasts of the field will labor for me."

He placed his hands behind his head and gazed up at the sky. At length he said, "Sing me a song, Pippin."

"What song?" asks I.

"Why, I care not, so long as your voice is sweet," says he, leaning on one elbow.

"We have an old song, sung in our parts, which is called 'Fair Margaret and Sweet William,'" says I, and I began to sing it. It told a sad tale of how fair Margaret loved William, and he proved false to her, and she begged him to love her truly, but he was a knave, so she killed herself, and her ghost came to haunt him of the midnight hour.

When I was through, Fabian says, "Your voice is truly pleasing, Kate, like a flute, a light sound with no harsh depth. Sing me another."

So I sang the song of Lady Eleanor and the Elf-Knight, but when I came to the part where the Elf-Knight bids Lady Eleanor to take off her golden dress beside the river, saying,

> "Look down, look down, you fair young maid,
>   Look down look down says he,
>   Six little maidens I've drownded here,
>   And you the seventh shall be!"

Fabian sat up and spat out a piece of grass. "God's teeth, Pippin, do you not know one happy song?"

"Why," says I, "this one ends very happily, for Lady Eleanor was no fool, and she told the Elf-Knight it was not meet for a lady to undress before a man, and he must turn his back, which he did, and then she grabbed him by the waist and pushed him into the water, and as she held his head under the waves, she sang,

> 'Sink down, sink down, you false false knight,
>   Sink down, sink down,' cried she,
>   'Six little maidens you've drownded here,
>   Go! Keep them companee.'"

Fabian laughed and chucked me under the chin. "Indeed, you have a rare idea of a happy ending."

"What? Would you have him drown her?"

"No," says he, "but why could they not kiss and love each other truly and live happily forever beside the riverbank?"

"Because it was not writ that way," says I. "And if it were, why, it would not be the song it is."

"Bah!" says he, getting restless. "Let us go for a walk, Pippin." And he pulled me to my feet. "And do not be silent for one instant, but chirp like a cricket every second, for truth to tell it shocked me when I saw the Dozer had frighted you so that you could not speak. It would be a dull world with you forever silent, Pippin."

We wandered until we came to the well, where Fabian stopped in his tracks.

"Why do you look at the well?" says I, for I feared he might be curious and find my journal.

"Well?" says he. " 'Tis nothing so innocent as a mere well, my child. 'Tis part of this ancient keep, an oubliette, the most terrible structure ever built by man."

"What is it?" I asked.

"Pippin, I have seen many fearsome things, but none so fearsome as one of these, for in ancient days, when men were savage, they lowered their own kind into these pits and kept them there, alone with their own thoughts until they went mad."

"Oubliette?" says I, "I do not know that word, Max, what does it mean?"

His face was very white, and he says, "It comes from the French, 'to forget,' and that is truly what it was designed for. When a man can no longer bear what he sees and thinks, then he forgets."

I felt cold, but I said, "Shall we lift the lid and see if there are dead men's bones below?"

But he caught me in a grip of steel and says, "Nay, do not jest. I looked in one when I was a lad, and it was filled with toads and adders and all manner of slimy horrors, though it had not been used for five hundred years."

Then he pulled me away. "Your curiosity will do you harm, chuck, for we all face the oubliette at some time, whether we seek it or no. So do not be anxious to hurry the moment. Come, my Pippin, it is spring, and the forest is bright with many pleasant things. Let us seek them and leave this place of horror to the Dozer, for if nature ever provided him with a fitting den, then this is it."

And we walked, holding hands, though the forest, Fabian pointing out flowers and telling me stories about them, and describing others he had seen.

"Adder's tongue," says he, "that's for jealousy. Pippin, you and I shall never fear that flower, for we trust each other. Then there is bellwort, which is hopelessness, and monkshood, which is chivalry, and red clover, which is industry and feeds the honeybee, and candytuft, which signifies indifference, and marigold, which means cruelty in love. That one you and I must take care not to wear over our hearts, for we are much alike.

"And there's heartsease, which is for pleasant thoughts, and sweet William, which begs, 'grant me one smile,' and shepherd's purse, which means, 'I offer you all' and the white rose, which is for silence, and the yellow rose, which says, 'let us forget.'"

And he took my face between his hands and studied it long, as if to read something writ in my eyes. At last he went on with his catalog. "And there's night-blooming jasmine, which is for love that never alters, and rue and nightshade, which are wicked plants. But, oh, Catherine, the loveliest of all is rosemary." And he paused and kissed my cheek.

"And do you know what rosemary is for, my Pippin?"

I shook my head.

"Why," says he, "rosemary is for remembrance, my darling."

And when I did not answer him, he went on: "We shall not pluck the white rose, or the yellow, but we shall pick the night-blooming jasmine and above all, we shall seek rosemary for remembrance."

And still I did not answer him, so he says, "Do you not hear me, Catherine? Your eyes have a dreaming look."

"I hear you," says I.

"And which flowers shall we pick, my pretty?"

I stood on my toes and drew his face down to my level and I said, "We shall pick rue and nightshade unless the Dozer meets with an accident, and very soon."

He held me at arm's length and shook his head in wonder. "By God, I admire you, child. What a woman you will be! And what a breed we shall raise, for in truth, Pippin, there's not another like you in the world."

And so we walked back to the mill and I cooked supper, and when the fire was burning low and we all lay down to sleep, Fabian wrapped his coat about me as always, and whispered, "Rosemary is for remembrance, Catherine. Think hard."

But I feigned misunderstanding and whispered back, "Jasmine is for true love."

"Aye," says he, sighing. "So it is, Pippin. Sleep, child."

For the next five days I worked at my Journal every moment I could, and before I realized it I had covered half the pages, and except for the first page I told the truth unsparingly in every detail, and I would have corrected that first page, but I hated to mar my best penmanship with a correction, so I let it stand.

Fabian seemed another man, so different was he to the hard-bitten dandy I had first met at the inn, and whether I would or no, I found myself more and more under his spell. For he has a charm that I have never seen equaled.

Then one morning, after I had finished my chores and was about to head for my bower, I found him staring at me, and when he saw I had observed him, he smiled in his secret way and nodded toward the forest.

We walked together, his hand on my shoulder, as he led me to my bower.

"Catherine," says he, throwing himself in the thick green grass, "what sort of an accident shall befall the Dozer?"

I sat thinking for a while, before I answered him. Then I said, "A mortal accident."

"Mortal it must be, yes, for if it is not mortal to him, I fear it will be to me. He's not a man to tease," says Fabian, looking at me in an amused way. "And where will you find so constant a heart as mine, fair Pippin?"

"Shoot him," says I.

"Would you miss me?" says he, ignoring my suggestion. "Would you weep for me, sweet Kate?"

"Aye, buckets," says I. "What's the matter with shooting him?"

"Not even half a bucket," says he, laughing. "About a cupful, I'll warrant. But that would be a goodly amount, for I doubt if you'd spare so much as a teaspoon for any other man in the world. I cannot shoot him, sweetheart, for I have no powder or shot."

"What!" says I in surprise.

"No, Pippin, I have had none since we came here, and I believe I have honest Edward to thank for that. I suppose he did not trust me, or feared I would shoot him in the back, for the Dozer would not make a secret of taking it from me."

I sank back in the grass, thinking.

"Stab him," says I finally.

"I have thought of that, my darling, but it would be a hazardous thing. If I did not kill him outright, he would—" but here Fabian paused. "By God, Catherine, Yorek and I together could not finish him off by hand. Do you know what I once saw him do? He took a green turnip in his paw and closed his fingers on it and squashed it to pulp. Neither Yorek nor I are weaklings, but when we tried that trick, neither of us left so much as a dent on a turnip. So prithee, my sweet, if you do not mind, I shall not test my strength against Master Dozer's unless there is no other way."

"I know!" says I, jumping up. "Poison him!"

"Bah!" says Fabian. "There is not that much rum in the world."

"Don't act the fool," says I, "for I know you are not one. When I say poison, I mean poison."

"And where's it to be had? I, for all my versatility, have never dealt in that commodity. It is not a gentleman's way."

"Ho!" says I, sneering and pulling a face. "If you will do murder, please to forget your dainty ways. Murder is for men, and I must say, Mr. Fabian, I have never observed your gentle upbringing standing in your path when something you desire is beyond it."

He laughed but did not answer me.

"I have some poison," says I at length.

He sat bolt upright, and his smile vanished. "Where did you get it? Speak the truth, miss."

"Why, I bought it for sixpence from some gypsies at the market when Edward and I were there."

And then I clapped my hand over my mouth.

"Oh, Max, the gypsy man said a curse would befall me if I told where I got it. He said false kisses and pretty words would turn my head."

"Rubbish!" says he. "Your head is already turned, you vain little goose. And how did you purchase poison? Do not lie to me. Who would be fool enough to sell it to a slip of a girl? Speak!"

And though his voice betrayed no anger, there was an urgency in it that made me remember he was accustomed to being obeyed.

"I have spoken the truth," says I, but I had no intention of telling him of my Journal. "I bought it from a Johnny Fah, saying I wished it to poison rats in my father's barn."

"You are a charming liar," says he, kissing me. "But no matter. I doubt not that you have it, and that is the issue. So long as you did not intend to poison Fabian, it is of no account."

"Poison you!" says I, looking straight into his eyes. "No, Max, for if there is one thing in which I speak only the truth, it is this: you said there was not another like me in the world, but neither have you a match, and whether your ways are good or evil, and whether I would or no, you are the only person in my life I have ever loved."

He put his hands over his face, and I sat in the grass staring at his bowed head.

Finally he folded his hands in his lap like a parson, and his voice was strangled when he spoke: "I wish you had not said that, Kate."

"Why? It is the truth."

"Yes, you spoke the truth, and when such ones as you and I speak the truth, it is frightening. And you have frightened me, Pippin."

I did not understand him and arose, but he held my wrist and brought me down beside him again.

"Pippin—," says he, his voice back to its ordinary tone, "that cipher. It is not complete."

"Is it not?" says I.

"No, part is missing. It must be. Think hard, Catherine. What else did Jenkin Davy say?"

But I only shook my head, and Fabian patted my hand and said, "Let it be, child. Do not fret. The Dozer frightened part of it out of your mind, and perhaps when I have put him out of the way, it will come back. In your sleep you still scream and cling to me, thinking he is after you. Do not fret, Pippin, all will be well. I shall rid you of the Dozer, and then . . ."

"And then?" says I.

"Why then, my Pippin will come to Fabian and say, Rosemary is for remembrance, and whisper in his ear."

He arose and pulled me to my feet.

"I am going back to the mill, Kate. Stay here, or where you wish, but do not go near the mill, for I have work to do and you would be better away."

"Do you want the poison?" says I.

He shook his head. "No, not unless all else fails, for if I am squeamish about one thing, it is poison. It would go against me to poison so much as a dog, let alone a man."

"The Dozer is not a man," says I, "he's an animal."

He only smiled and patted my head and walked away. When he had gone a dozen paces, he stopped and turned around.

"Catherine, rosemary is for remembrance." And he raised his hand in farewell and left.

I sat in the grass by myself, wishing I had kept my own counsel about the poison, for thinking back on it, there was something about that gypsy man and his woman, a way they had of laughing when they spoke serious, and looking at each other with their long, tar-black eyes as though they knew something I could never understand. And I had made a bargain with them, and had done ill to trifle with their trust.

Finally I went to the well and got my Journal and wrote until I deemed it time to return to the mill to prepare the evening meal. I felt better for having written in my Journal, for there is something very comforting in writing one's thoughts down in every detail. I have never been one for exchanging confidences, and it was like having a secret and trustworthy friend in my Journal.

I started for the mill, and when I had approached to within twenty paces, I stopped in my tracks and felt my spine chill, for I heard a terrible sound. It was neither a scream nor a cry, but a hoarse, ugly moan, and I ran quickly into the mill, fearing it might be Fabian.

The main room was deserted, so I hurried to the back, where I found Yorek and Fabian standing and staring, and looking down I saw the Dozer, pinned by a huge beam, blood spurting from a great gash on the top of his head.

"It must have been a rotten rope," says Fabian to Yorek, pointing to a rope end that dangled overhead from another beam.

Yorek nodded and bent over the Dozer.

"We'll get you out, Dozer. Are you hurt sore?"

But the Dozer only moaned louder and rolled his eyes.

"Come, Fabian, we must move fast, or he's done. He's got the full weight of that beam on his chest and shoulder."

Fabian nodded, his face as innocent as a babe's, and he and Yorek put their shoulders together over the beam. I looked up at the rope, and I had not been born and raised in a fishing port not to know a sound rope when I saw one. And the one I saw now was white and crisp clean through, the edges not frayed, but neatly severed by a sharp blade. While the two men worked over the Dozer, I jumped as high as I could and caught the end of the rope and pulled myself hand over hand until I reached the beam, which looked up at the empty sky, and there I untied the rope.

I looked down. It was a drop of eight feet to the floor, and I did not want to jump.

"Fabian," I called, "catch me."

He looked up, saw what I had done and winked at me. He held out his arms and I dropped into them.

As he set me on the floor, Yorek cried, "Never mind the girl now, for God's sake, hurry. Catherine, this is no time for dalliance, get out of the way."

I ran to the fire and thrust the rope into it.

When I returned Yorek was saying, "It's no good, Fabian, it would take six men to lift that beam."

"Poor old Dozer," says Fabian. "It looks as if his hour has come, does it not?"

Yorek turned on him in horror. "Surely you are not serious, Max? Even you would not leave an injured man to die by inches?"

"Indeed no," says Fabian. "But you said yourself it would take six men, and where are the other four?"

He picked up a crowbar.

"I shall put him out of his misery now, so he shall suffer no more. I am not such a heartless man, Yorek, and I cannot bear to stand by and watch him die so slowly. Why, he would thank us for it, could he speak."

"Damn you!" says Yorek, striking Fabian across the mouth, then wrenching the crowbar from him. "You are as great a monster as he!"

Fabian's face went ashen and he put his hand to his mouth, giving Yorek a hard, strange look, and I could not help but think this was the second time Yorek had struck Fabian. But then he merely shrugged and said, "Very well, Edward, what do you suggest? Dismembering him by parts to get him out? You are so humane, pray tell me your plans."

Yorek stood thinking.

"We shall bring in one of the horses," says he at last, "and harness it to one end of the beam, and have him pull gently, and when the rope is taut, and he still strains, it will lift this beam a couple of inches, and one of us must slip the Dozer's body out."

"I will get the horse," says Fabian, leaving.

I stood looking down at the groaning Dozer. It was a sickening sight, so I looked away.

Fabian could not have rushed, for it was nigh on five minutes before he returned leading the stallion.

"Not the stallion, you fool!" roared Yorek. "He can't be trusted either to stand or pull. Get the gelding, damn you!"

I saw what he meant, for the stallion was prancing nervously and tossing his head, so that Fabian was sore put even to hold him, for he was highly strung, and the scent of the Dozer's blood made him wild with fear.

Fabian shrugged and led the stallion out.

Looking down at the Dozer again, I saw that the other half of the rope was bound around the beam which pinned him, and that he lay upon the end.

Fabian returned with the gelding and he and Yorek began tying the beast to the beam.

"Catherine," says Yorek to me, "I told you before to get out of the way. Now go and sit by the fire before you get stepped on."

I went willingly, for I had a growing feeling that Fabian would accidentally touch the gelding with his spur and finish off the Dozer for good, and I did not wish to see it. But I was wrong, for five minutes later he and Yorek staggered into the main room with the Dozer slung between them, Yorek holding him under the arms and Fabian lugging his legs.

They laid him upon the hearth, and then both straightened up.

"Lead the horse out and tether him," says Fabian to me, so I did, and I rushed back to hear Fabian say, "Well, what's to be done?" And he rubbed his curly head with the palm of his hand.

Yorek scratched his chin for a second and then turned to me. "Get some water and that vinegar you bought at the market and my kerchief from my coat pocket."

I brought them to him and he knelt by the Dozer and sponged the blood from his crown, then he soaked his kerchief in the vinegar and placed it upon the Dozer's brow. The Dozer groaned and opened his eyes and tried to sit up, but he fell back, biting his lips.

"It's all right, mate," says Yorek. "You are out from under it now. Where are you hurt?"

The Dozer touched his shoulder. "Here," says he. Then his chest. "And here." Then the top of his crown. "And here."

Fabian and Yorek lifted him to a sitting position and Yorek took the Dozer's shirt off and laid him back on the hearth again. Then he began running his fingers back and forth over the Dozer's chest, pressing at certain spots. And what a chest the Dozer had! Pads of muscle an inch thick, so that not a shadow of a rib showed.

Then Yorek lifted the Dozer's arm, and put his hand on the shoulder, which was as big as a strong man's thigh, and he twisted it gently, saying, "Move your fingers." And the Dozer did. "Now your elbow." And he turned the Dozer's arm about, feeling his collarbone and shoulder blade. "Does it hurt you?"

"Nay," says Dozer, "just me shoulder, which feels like it's been kicked by a barge horse. Is it broke, Yorek?"

"Well," says Yorek, shaking his head, "I'm no surgeon, Bully, but damned if I don't think you're only bruised." He turned to Fabian, "That would have killed an ordinary man."

"Aye," says Fabian. "Give him a tot of rum, Yorek," and he walked outside.

I went back to the beam and retrieved the other half of the rope, hiding it under my skirt. I ran and dropped it down the well. Then I went to my bower, where I found Fabian.

"Well," says he, "Master Dozer, it would seem, is still in good health. Blooming like a God-damned milkmaid."

I smiled ruefully. "When I left, he was complaining that his head hurt him, and wanting rum."

"So it should hurt," says Fabian gloomily. "I used a crowbar on it."

"You did not wield it smartly enough," says I.

"Aye, but I feared that fool of a Yorek might surprise me, and I was in too much haste."

"So now you must devise another plan," says I, putting my arm around his waist, but he shuddered and pushed me away.

"Not today, Lady Macbeth, for I fear the Dozer as much as you do. He is a monster, bless me if he isn't. It made my hair stand on end when Yorek said he was naught but bruised. And his skull, why Catherine, it must be an inch thick."

It was my turn to shudder, and he put his arm about me. "Do not fear, sweetheart. I shall kill him yet." And he kissed my cheek. "But not today, I prithee, Catherine, for there is something downright sickening about a man who will not die when he should."

We sat staring at the little brook, which babbled merrily past us, and finally I said, "Do you think, Max, that the Dozer is not mortal, like other men? For he is less like a human being than any man I have ever seen."

"Aye," says he, "he is human, and once, Catherine, when I was a young boy, I watched some laborers digging the foundation for a house, and deep down, in dry sand, they uncovered an ancient Viking burial ground, and from what I remember of the bones in it, the Dozer must be a descendant of those pirates. There was one, Catherine, who must have been their chief, for he was buried with his sword and mail, and I picked up his skull, which was twice as large and thick as it should have been, and his shoulder bones were as heavy as a horse's. And the teeth in that skull, Kate, my God, the smallest was larger than my thumb nail."

"I wonder how he died," says I. "It would profit us to know."

"I wish I knew," says Fabian, "but I'll wager it took six men to down him."

Suddenly he stood up. "Damn my eyes," says he, "I forgot the other end of that rope."

I pulled him down beside me again.

"No, Max. I fixed it."

"What did you do with it?"

"Why I—" but I stopped, for I had nearly said I put it in the well and I did not want him checking and stumbling upon my Journal.

He raised his head quickly and looked at me strange.

"Well, miss?"

"I burned it in the fire," says I.

"What, you little goose, in front of the other two?" says he sharply, grabbing my wrist.

"Well, it was better than leaving it to be tripped over, for the

Dozer is already on his feet. Besides, when I did it Yorck was busy tending the Dozer and neither noticed."

He lay on his back and pulled me across his chest, and taking my face between his hands, he says, very soft, "Catherine, you are lying again. I can always tell. Now, be Fabian's darling and tell him what you did with that rope, for his life may depend on it." And I saw his dimple twitch.

I took a deep breath and says, "I threw it in the well."

"And why did you not say so at once?"

"In truth, Fabian," says I, pushing myself away from him, "I have lied so long it comes to me natural. And if you do not believe it is in the well, why, lower a lantern to the bottom and look for yourself."

"I believe you," says he, "I believe you, Kate." And he pulled me to him again, smiling, and he says, "What a wicked girl you are. Do you know, Pippin, if you were a nice little girl, I should box your chops for daring to lie to me. But then, of course, if you were a nice little girl, you would not tell lies. I hate nice little girls."

"Let me go," says I, for he was looking at me in a way that frighted me, and I felt his heart pounding beneath my hand.

"Nay, Catherine," he whispered, "stay yet awhile."

"No."

"Just one minute, Kate. Stay. You are so pretty, Catherine. Stay."

"Let me up," says I, and I was truly alarmed, for he had never before looked at me with such a strange expression.

"Ah," he sighed. "Well, as you wish, my pet." And he pushed me away and stood up.

"What a fool I was to leave that rope," says he. "I must use more caution. Well, Pippin, we have yet to eat, so on your feet, miss."

As we walked back I looked at him from the corner of my eye, and found him doing the same, and we both burst out laughing, and he put his arm about my shoulder, and I mine about his waist, and he says, "You do not trust me yet, my dear."

I shook my head.

"Nor I you," says he. "What a pair we are."

"But I love you, Max."

"Aye, and I you, and more's the pity."

The next two days were not happy ones, for food was running low again, and the men could not do much work, owing to the Dozer's bruised shoulder, and Fabian never was one to soil his hands, and Yorek refused to work by himself. So they sat around snarling at one another, and I stayed away from the lot of them, spending most of my day writing in my Journal.

Then, the third night after the Dozer's accident, Fabian called me to him.

"Why do you shun me, child? You have not spoken half a dozen words to me in two days. Did I anger or frighten you, that day in the forest? For if I did, I beg you to forgive me, for I meant you no harm, on my honor. It is just that I am a man, and . . . well, there are times when men are not all they should be."

"No," says I. "It is not that. It is this place and the lot of you. The Dozer growls like a beast when he moves, and Yorek goes about with a long face, as if he would preach me a sermon if I sat beside him, and you—why, your dimple twitches even in your sleep now, for I watched you this morning. So I deem it best to stay out of the way of the lot of you."

"It is strange how I have missed your company," says he, putting his arm about me. "A month ago I would have scoffed to think that Fabian would yearn for any woman, let alone a maid who offers him nought, and has, to date, bitten him, kicked him, hit him, teased him, and caused him to lose more sound sleep than any woman who has crossed his path in thirty-three years. But it is so, and all day yesterday I could not fathom what ailed me, I felt so lost and restless. And then—then it came to me: I missed you."

He paused and stared into the flames, and I put my hand on his, and finally he turned and said, "It did not please me, Pippin, when I realized what ailed me. It did not please me one whit. Why, Catherine, it is ridiculous—that I, a man of thirty-three, should pine for the company of a snippet of fifteen. On my soul, you are a witch, and have bewitched me, for damned if I don't love you truly. Catherine, I do not wish to love you. Why do I love you when I do not wish to love you? I tell you it is ridiculous, and I am confused."

"Fabian," says I, putting my hand to his cheek, "let us put our heads together and make plans to get away from this place soon, for I have felt all day we are sitting on a powder keg."

"Well," says he, "only a woman could speak so, for it is yourself that holds us up. But you are right, the food is low and tempers are short."

"Nay," says I. "Not while the Dozer lives and breathes, for I am not such a fool as to think I would live to enjoy the bounty of wealth while he is about."

"True," says he, "true. Both he and Yorek must go."

I raised my head and stared at him till he said, "God's teeth, Pippin, do not look at me so."

"No harm comes to Edward Yorek," says I, "for I've had naught but good from him. Do what you will with the Dozer, but if harm comes to Yorek, you strike your own colors, for there have been few who have treated me with such kindness."

"You judge me ill," says Fabian, "for when I said he must go, why, that's exactly what I meant. For all that I jest and sneer at his weak ways, I would do him no harm neither, and do you know, Catherine, sometimes, in my heart, I feel envy for him."

I slipped my hand into his and we sat gazing into the flames for a long while. At last he says, "Catherine, what has made you as you are? For I admire you as I would a man of my own years and stature."

I laughed and then stopped, for, truth to tell, it was not so amusing when I thought on it.

"Why Max," says I, "have you not guessed? I am a wood-colt, and if you had known others, you would realize that our lot is not a happy one."

"Damn my eyes," says he, his face harsher still, "I should know and understand that state, my darling, for I am a bastard myself."

"You?" says I, wonderingly. "But you are a gentleman, Fabian."

"Yes," says he, tightening his hold around me, "that I be, and do you remember, my love, when we came to this place, how I told you it was part of the estate of a great lord?"

"Yes."

"Well, that lord is my half brother, and my junior by three years."

"Ah," says I, for I was beginning to understand much about him.

"Aye. I was raised as a nobleman's son, and nothing was too good for me, except for the fact that my father, curse his black heart, never troubled to church my mother. And then, when I was twenty-two, the dirty dog died of a sudden. And had he made provision for his bastard? No! Not so much as a penny, Catherine, not one bloody farthing, and do you know what that God-damned, fat-thewed, soft-bellied half brother of mine says to me? He, the legal heir, with his estates and gold and manors, why, he says, 'You are a bastard, Guy, and while my father may have claimed you, I do not, for from what I have heard of your mother, any blade from here to Land's End might have sired you, so do not come about me begging.'"

Fabian sat and gnawed his knuckles with his white teeth.

"God!" says he. "How I could merely look at him and walk away, I do not know. Why I did not rip his heart from his body and trample on it, I cannot fathom, but he still lives and breathes."

"Are you going to kill him?"

"No. It might amuse me to ruin him, but I would be a fool to kill him, for the murder of a lord would not go unnoticed."

"And how did you live, after your father's death?"

"By my wits, sweetheart. For ten years I've lived by my wits, on the fringe of that society to which I belong, and many a dirty deed I've done to stay there. I am a Montrolfe. For I will use my father's name, whether the court of heralds recognizes me or no."

"And your mother?"

Fabian spat in the fire.

"I do not know, Catherine. She died before I reached the age of eight. But this I can say of her, all my memories of her are sweet. So mayhap she was a good woman."

We sat silently again, until he says, "And your mother?"

"I do not know, Max, for she died of the fever when I was born."

"And who was your father?"

"Nor do I know that, Max. There are those in our parts who say it was Mr. Peterson."

"What? The reverend gentleman who taught you your letters and sat you on his knee and kissed you? That's an unnatural way for a father to act."

"Nay," says I, "for his kisses had naught but affection and sadness in them, and he taught me my letters well. And Fabian, I never met a man so concerned for my soul."

I paused, remembering.

"When I was wicked, he prayed for my soul, and sometimes, just looking at me, he would go off weeping and spend all night on his knees, praying."

"Bah!" says Fabian. "Whether he fathered you or not, either way he is a pompous humbug. For parsons have no right to go about fathering bastards, that being a nobleman's license, and if he did not, then parsons have no right to kiss parlormaids. I do not like him. Do you think he was your father?"

I shrugged. "I do not know, Fabian. I hope not, for he looked like an old goat."

Fabian laughed. "Then he was not your sire, my darling, for you are far too fair of face." He paused, then said, "Unless your dam was so uncommon fair it made no difference who she mated."

We sat silent again until Fabian once more burst out laughing, and I turned to him, puzzled.

"No wonder we are so well matched, my darling," says he.

"Yes," says I, laughing myself, "in truth, Fabian, we are a fine pair of bastards." Then I yawned. "I would sleep now, Fabian."

"Wait," he whispered, "I shall speak to Yorek, and I want you by."

So he called Yorek, who had been sleeping, and the three of us sat talking low.

"Yorek," says Fabian, "things have not gone according to plan, and I cannot say if we will ever find the treasure."

He paused and stared at Yorek and then says, "Edward, your heart has never been in this, and I regret it was I who beguiled you into such hapless work. If you wish to pull out, now is the time, for you may only jeopardize your freedom by staying at unprofitable labor."

"I do not understand you," says Yorek, looking straight at him.

"I mean this," says Fabian. "It was I who put you in this situation, and if you now wish to withdraw, I shall try to compensate you."

"How, by cutting my throat? Beware, Fabian, I am a fair match for you, if not for the Dozer." And he flexed his bronze, hairless forearm before Fabian, and the sinews twisted like serpents.

Fabian spat on the floor in disgust.

"Why should I kill you, you fool? As long as you keep your mouth shut, you have naught to fear from Fabian. I made an error in choosing you for the job, Ned, for you are too honest, and your conscience never ceases to torment you, and to be frank, Yorek, it is not a fortune you want, but a stake to stock your farm well, for it must have done poorly, with you away and only a woman to tend it."

"Aye," says Yorek, slow, "and what have you to offer me, Fabian? Gold you have not found?"

"No," says Fabian, "two fine horses, Edward. The stallion alone is worth ten years' profit from your farm, for the Dozer knows horses, and when he steals one, it is the best. I shall give you the name of a certain person in London who will give you a good price for him. Not full, for you cannot expect that, but a good price. And you may do what you wish with the gelding, but if you sell him on your own, he'll fetch a fair price too."

"This is not like you, Fabian," says Yorek.

And Fabian turned his wicked, unhappy, beautiful face to the fire, saying, "Thank me not, Yorek. I do this not for you nor for myself, but for the Pippin. She is fond of you, and if harm befell you, it is me she would hold responsible."

"And why should you care what Catherine wants?" says Yorek, suspicious. "It ain't like you to care about any save yourself."

"Ah, Yorek," says Fabian, sighing. "You may prate of your wife and children, and I cannot understand it, so let me indulge my whimsies, for neither can you understand mine."

By the light of the moon we followed Yorek outside and helped him untether and saddle the horses.

"I have judged you ill, Max," whispered Yorek. "Give me your hand."

They shook hands and Yorek mounted the stallion while I stood holding the horse's head and looking up at him.

"Come here, Catherine, for you have not bid me farewell."

Fabian took the stallion's head and I went to Yorek's side.

"God be with you, Edward," says I, raising my hand to him. He leaned down from the saddle and stroked my cheek.

"Are you sure, Catherine, that you would not come with me? It will not be an easy life, for I am only a farmer, but my missus will be good to you, and I feel I do wrong to leave you here."

"Nay," says I, "but thank you, Edward." And of a sudden I caught his hand and kissed it, for I liked Edward Yorek, and in all the time I had spent with him, I had known nothing but goodness and kindness from him.

"Be good to her, Fabian, for she minds me of my own little one."

"Edward," says I, "before you go, there is something I must tell you."

"Aye?" says he, but Fabian let go of the rein and came to my side, and I felt his hand upon my shoulder, and the stallion began to prance.

"Go, Edward, before you wake the Dozer."

"One minute, Max," says Yorek. "The lass would tell me something."

Fabian's hand tightened on my shoulder, and I said, "Edward, I am not the child you think I am, for I lied to you. I am fifteen."

Fabian's hand relaxed on my shoulder, and I saw Yorek's teeth flash in the moonlight, and he said, "And I am thirty-seven, Catherine, and Fabian here is thirty-five. So you see, you are still a child compared to us graybeards. But mend your ways and stick to the truth, Catherine. And God be with you."

He saluted us with his whip and was gone.

Then Fabian turned to me. "I am not thirty-five, I am thirty-three. Damn it, Pippin, you frightened me. I thought you might, with that awful perversity of women, change your mind and tell him the cipher. Well, off to bed, my dear. There's dirty work ahead of us tomorrow, and I for one will need my sleep."

When morning dawned and Fabian and Dozer and I were up

and stirring, the Dozer did not at first realize that Yorek was not with us. It was not until after we had breakfasted and he had gone out to water the horses that he knew. He came roaring in like a bull.

"They're gone, Fabian! They're gone, the stallion and the gelding!"

"What's this?" says Fabian, rising.

"I tell you they're gone!" He stood there, panting like a bull.

"By God, it's that dirty dog of a Yorek!" says Fabian. "He's cleared out and taken the horses!"

"Max—" says I, but he put his hand over my mouth.

"What, Edward betrayed us?" says the Dozer. "I cannot believe that, Fabian. Yorek would not cheat me. I might cheat him, but *he* would not play false with *me*. Why—why once, when we was doing time together and I had had a hundred and fifty strokes of the cat and was nigh dead, why, Edward Yorek took his own shirt off and soaked it in salt water and put it on my back and give me his rations and held my head on his lap and give me water when I was too weak to hold a cup. And he were the only man on board who raised his hand to help the Dozer, for the rest all thought no man was ever born who could live through such punishment, and little the rest cared whether Dozer lived or died."

He shook his head, puzzled, and then he says, "And six months later, I mind the time that madman, Foggy we called him, a tiny feller he were, no bigger than that there gel, took to saying Yorek was King George and tried to throttle him, so I wrung his little neck and tossed him overboard, and says, 'Yorek, you done me a good turn, so mate, I done you one.' And Yorek sat down on the deck and wept like a baby, he was that touched, saying over and over, 'Dozer, you shouldn't of done it,' and I kept tellin him, 'Why mate, I didn't mind a bit,' for I didn't, it were no more trouble to me than swatting a fly. Why, even the night he hit me, standin' up for that there gel, I did no more than tap him on the throat, for I'd of killed him had I hit him true, but I was fond of that there Yorek. Why, Fabian, he was kind as a mother to me, if I'd ever known one, when that beam fell on me, saying over and over, 'There, Dozer, there,' just the way I treats horses when other folks says, 'Why the beast has the staggers, hit it with a sledge!' But I never does, I nurses 'em quietlike, and they turns them big silent eyes to me like I was God when I'm gentle with them. Fabian, I could cry to think Yorek played me for a fool and run out on me, for he knew I wanted that stallion. Oh, there was a rare beast! An Arab he was, with a chest like bellows, and them withers! Why, he was a horse in a million, by God. And you could only handle him with a whip, Fabian, but he'd come up to me, he would, rollin' his eyes wild and lay his head on my shoulder and kiss me. With all his strength and spirits, why, he'd come up and kiss the Dozer, docile as a kitten. Him what was one of the few things with more strength than me, would come up sweetlike and want Dozer to stroke his head and talk soft and pretty to him in his ear."

"Well," says Fabian disdainfully, "Yorek was a weak one. You know all manner of men, Dozer. What sort of a man sits down like Yorek and weeps like a maid at the slightest provocation? Does the Dozer weep? Nay. Does Fabian weep? Not likely, my lad. Only the cowardly ones like Yorek shed their false tears. He was a weak one, Dozer, and weak men cannot be trusted. Well, lad, it merely means there's that much more for us when the loot's found."

"But I loved them horses," says Dozer. "And that stallion, I had marked him for my own."

I looked up and saw Fabian's cheek twitch, but apart from that he gave no sign.

"What's done is done, mate. Now, how is your shoulder? Can you work today?"

"Aye," says the Dozer, "it pains me sore, but I can work."

"Good lad," says Fabian, slapping him on his sound shoulder. "I shall take my morning walk and then work with you, Dozer. And I give you my word that we'll have that treasure before two more suns have risen, for I have an idea."

"Eh?" says Dozer, taking a step closer to Fabian. "What sort of idea, Max?"

"All in good time, my lad, all in good time," says Fabian, taking my arm and leading me out.

"Fabian," calls Dozer, "you and me is mates, boy. You wouldn't play me false now, would you?"

"Not I," says Fabian over his shoulder. "Indeed, not I, Dozer. I am a gentleman."

"Why did you let him think Yorek stole the horses?" I whispered.

He looked over his shoulder to be sure the Dozer was well out of earshot.

"My God, Pippin, that brute would kill both of us in sheer rage if he thought I had given them to Yorek. And you heard what he said about the stallion; he had marked him for his own, so of course he means to do us in as soon as the money's found."

I shuddered.

"All's well, my pretty. We have nothing to fear unless he stumbles on the loot."

As we walked around the mill, he put his hand on my shoulder. "Can you not feel the age of this place, Pippin? Twenty score years ago my ancestors lorded this same spot we tread now, mailed, hard warriors, giving quarter to none. Pitiless Montrolfes, Normans and conquerors. God, I could spit on that puppet who struts with his title now, for if he is a Montrolfe, on my honor, Dozer is a gentleman. I tell you, Catherine, my father wore the cuckold's horns before he ever spawned that mush-hearted fop."

I looked up at him and he stopped in his tracks. Then he sat on a stone and stood me before him.

"Look at me, Pippin. Have you ever seen such a man as I? Is there another face like mine in the whole world?"

I looked at him closely and indeed, I had never seen a face like his. The cast of it was so strongly molded as to be almost frightening, his forehead low and broad, with his lamb's curled hair growing to a sharp point and his dark eyes widely spaced and his black eyebrows shooting up suddenly. And his lips were firm and unsmiling, only rarely showing his sharp white teeth, and his chin jutted out, cleft slightly, as if a finger had been laid softly upon it. And the deep, terrible dimple in one cheek that no other man had.

"Nay," says I, "I have never seen a man like you, Max."

"What ails you, Pippin? What is it?"

But I would not answer him and turned away. He caught my arm and pulled me back.

"Catherine, I always know when all is not right. What ails you?"

I stood looking at him again, wondering how to say it.

"Fabian," says I finally, "I have no one in the world but you. You would not betray me, would you, Fabian? You do love me?"

He let his breath out in a mighty sigh and pressed me to him.

"You foolish child, you naughty, naughty girl. How can you frighten me so? How can you doubt me? You frightened me sore, Catherine. Do not do so again, for when Catherine Barton's heart ceases to beat, so shall Fabian's. We were not brought together in this ancient realm of my ancestors for naught, my darling. It was no accident of fate that you and I were dealt from the same deck of cards. It had to be. And you, of all women, have no cause to fear Fabian, nor never have, nor never shall. You are the light of my eyes, Catherine. And I am such a man as none save yourself could ever know and understand and still love. So pity me, Catherine, but never fear me. Once I told you I was a lonely man, and I spoke the truth, God save me, for there are not many like us in the world, Catherine, and Fate had her tongue in her cheek and a dagger in her hand when she jestingly tossed us among our fellow men."

He was often given to talking strange and wild like this to me, but I understood him, for what he lacked I lacked—never a mother's soft hand or tender kiss had blessed our brows, and we had both grown like the trees of my own wild coast, twisted by the wind into strange shapes never intended by nature.

I put my hand to his cheek and pressed the dimple, but this time he did not smile, but gazed at me with his sad dark eyes, saying, "Have you no heart, Catherine? Can you doubt me?"

"Aye," says I, smiling, "aye, Fabian, I have a heart."

"Well, hide it well, Pippin, for we must put our heads together to be rid of the Dozer, and from now until he breathes his last there is no place for hearts, my child."

"We *must* poison him," says I, taking Fabian's hand. "Why not, Max? For though his shoulder be injured, he is still more than a match for you, and Max, I could not see you hurt."

"Or killed," says he, looking down at me. "For if I am, I do not care to dwell on what will happen to you."

"Poison him, Max."

But he shook his head, saying, "Think what you will of me, my child, but I do shrink from that. Poison is a woman's way."

"You said yourself that if you tried to knife him and did not kill him the first thrust, he would do you in. Oh, Max, those hands. Think what they could do to you if he grabbed you."

He stood silent for a long time, and finally he said: "Get the poison."

The Dozer was already at work at the pile of stones in the back room when we entered the mill. Fabian took the last bottle of rum, which was about half full, and poured a couple of inches of the dye in it.

I took the dye bottle from him. "Do you want any more of this, Max?"

He smiled. "I do not know. I don't suppose you know how potent this stuff is, do you?"

"It will kill rats," says I.

He nodded, placed the rum bottle on the table and sat staring at it.

"I shall hide this," says I, taking my bottle and leaving. I returned in about two or three minutes, and he was just as I had left him.

"Well?" says I.

He started, then looked at me.

"Fetch the Dozer. Tell him I would speak with him."

I did so and the Dozer followed me in to Fabian.

"Mate," says Fabian, "let us discuss this idea of mine."

"Aye," says Dozer.

"Now, the way I look at it, we have been fools, all of us," says Fabian. "Especially me. For do you know, Dozer, the first thing we did when we came to this place was to light a fire. What if it had been hid in the chimbley?"

He picked up the rum bottle and held it to his lips.

"Bah!" says he, spitting. "This stuff tastes rotten."

Dozer ran over to the fire, but Fabian called him back.

"Nay, Dozer, even if the fire were not burning, what good would it do us? Neither of us could get our shoulders up that flue.

That's where the girl comes in. We shall let her down from the top with a rope."

"Me?" says I, shrinking back.

"Aye, you," growls the Dozer, raising his hand to me.

"Do not strike her, you fool, you could break her spine like a twig."

"Aye," says Dozer, looking at me with new interest, "happen you'll be of some use, gel. And that fireplace is a good idea, Fabian. We shall douse the fire."

Fabian picked up the bottle again, saying, "Let us drink to a mutual trust, Dozer, for we want no quarreling if it's found."

"We splits even, Max," says the Dozer. "Half for you, half for me."

Fabian raised the bottle again, and again he spat on the floor. "Vile stuff, this. Trust Yorek to buy the cheapest."

"Give it here," says the Dozer. "To your health, Fabian," and he tilted the bottle to his lips.

"It do taste strange," says he. "Well, my guts is lined with lead." And he took three huge swallows.

"Here, don't drink it all. I have not drunk your health yet. Give me some."

Dozer handed Fabian the bottle, and again Fabian raised it.

"I salute you, Dozer," says he, putting it to his lips, then he returned it to Dozer, who emptied it in three more great gulps.

"Now to business," says Fabian. "We shall put out the fire, then I climb the roof with the girl and let her down the chimbley, and you shall be watching down here should she dislodge any of the loot if it is there."

"Nay, I lets her down on the rope, and I pulls her up," says the Dozer. "I don't trust that brat, Fabian, and you has been too soft with her. She could push you off the roof when you wasn't lookin', you bein' unsuspectin' of her ways. So, mate, I goes up with her."

"As you will," says Fabian.

The Dozer looked about him strangely.

"It's gettin' dark in here, Max. What is it? It should be daylight, but it's gettin' like night."

"Why, it must be an eclipse," says Fabian, looking hard at the Dozer.

"An eclipse? But the fire has gone out, Max, and I saw it burnin' bright, not two minutes ago."

He staggered and sat on the bench.

"I'm feelin' queer, mate," says he. "I'm feelin' uncommon strange, and I have a fierce pain in my belly."

He suddenly groaned and clutched his hands to his stomach.

"What ails you, Dozer, are you sick?" says Fabian, very soft.

"Aye, mate," says the Dozer, and he ground his teeth. "Aye. I—it's like I—like I been pizened, Max."

"Indeed?" says Fabian. "You poor lad, lie down. Soon you will feel nothing."

I stared at the Dozer and his eyes were very strange, wide open and staring, with no color but the pupils showing next to the whites, all black, not a whit of color, of blue or gray or brown, or whatever color his eyes were, for I had never looked straight into them before.

Suddenly he raised up with a roar.

"You done it, Fabian, you pizened me with that there rum, God damn your black heart."

Fabian stood with his knife drawn, saying nothing, watching the Dozer like a dog with a bear.

The Dozer put his head on one side, and his face, though it was twisted with pain, had a sly look.

"So you thought you'd do in Thomas Parr, did you, my dainty boy? Thought the likes of you could kill me with your pizens? Well, you have a surprise in store for you, me pretty lad, for the likes of the Dozer don't die easy, and before I kicks off, why, I'll kill you like a fly, I will."

Fabian grabbed me and pushed me behind him.

"You are blind, Thomas Parr. You can see nothing." Fabian did not move his head, but he whispered, "Run to your bower, Catherine, and stay there."

"I hears you, Fabian," says Dozer, his head on one side. "And that gel ain't going no place. She don't leave here."

He put his huge arms in front of him, and slowly backed away from us till he was in front of the door, and then, oh merciful God, he swung it shut and bolted it, and stood leaning against it, facing us.

"Stand still," whispered Fabian to me, and he moved ten paces away and stood behind a bench.

"I am here, Dozer, here," says he, kicking the bench so that his spur jingled. "Here, come and get me."

The Dozer took a step toward him and I drew in my breath.

He stopped in his tracks, and though he was ten feet from me, he pointed his finger straight at me, and my heart turned to ice.

"You!" says he, "you, I have you marked, miss. I know your position, and you are next, as soon as I've finished off your pretty lordling."

I glanced at Fabian, and his face showed neither fear nor anger, only its usual, silent look. He caught my eye, and pointed to the poker and then to the fire. I nodded and moved a step, when the Dozer fixed that finger on me again.

"I hears you. Stand still, or I'll kill you first. I hears every little sound, plain as can be, for I have always had ears like a dog. And the darkness don't bother me none, Fabian, for I've done time in solitary, where it's dark all the time, so once I've stepped in a room and marked the fixings, it makes no difference to me."

He swung his arms in a circle, and his shoulder must have pained him sore, for he groaned, and he was, I knew, not one to whine over trifles.

"And Yorek never stole no horses and run away. You hid them, and you done in Yorek, for it's always been in your mind to be the only one to leave here alive. Well, you won't, my lordling."

He was groaning and grunting whether he would or no, and sweat poured from his face, but still he crept toward Fabian, and though he was twice Fabian in bulk, no cat ever stole upon a bird in the garden more lightly.

I saw my chance and, running, shoved the poker into the hot coals.

Fabian leaped for the Dozer so suddenly my eye could scarce follow him, and his knife swung in a flashing arc.

But the Dozer, through some terrible instinct, lowered his head and shoulders and the knife, instead of plunging into his heart, went to the hilt through the top of his good shoulder.

He sank to his knees, his hands hanging loosely, and Fabian pulled on the knife but it must have been imbedded in bone, for though it took only a second, I saw his face suddenly twitch as he tugged at the handle, and I knew he was afraid.

The Dozer swayed on his knees, and Fabian suddenly raised his boot, placed it on the Dozer's shoulder, pulled with his full strength, and the knife came free. And not a moment too soon, for both of the Dozer's arms came up as Fabian leaped backward.

"I ain't dead yet, Max," he grated, and he lurched toward Fabian with his shoulders hunched, his head lowered, and his arms outstretched.

They were both gasping for breath and the Dozer says again, "Do you hear me, Fabian? I ain't dead yet."

"Nay," says Fabian, panting, "nay, you are not, Master Dozer, for I sought to stick you in the heart, and that's a damned hard thing to find in the Dozer. I have been a fool, Thomas Parr, but the next thrust will see if your guts are lined with lead."

But it was a mistake, for the Dozer only taunted him to make sure of his position, and now he changed his tactics. Wheeling, he picked up the huge solid oak bench, hefting it as if it were a toy.

He threw it and Fabian leaped aside, but not quick enough, for the end caught his shoulder and sent him spinning along the floor. He sprang to his feet like a pit mastiff before the bull, but blood was streaming from a cut on his forehead.

They circled each other like two beasts, and then it was the Dozer who leaped, and the two went down, turning and twisting on the floor, and I saw Fabian underneath. His knife flashed again as he curved his arm around the Dozer's body and buried it in the Dozer's back, over a shoulder blade.

Three times the knife sank in, but still the Dozer did not die. One arm was useless, but with the other he had Fabian by the throat, and Fabian thrashed like a landed fish beneath him.

I knew Fabian was done for if I did not act quickly, and grabbing the poker, which was white hot by now, I ran and pressed it against the Dozer's neck.

He sprang back with a roar, but too late to miss Fabian's knife, which this time sank into his belly. The Dozer staggered back and Fabian stabbed him again, and the Dozer fell to the floor like a giant oak.

He put one hand over his blinded eyes and the other on his

stomach. "God curse your eyes, Fabian. God curse your guts!" were his last words as Fabian's flashing knife found his heart at last.

Fabian stood up and looked about him wildly. We both had only one thought. To get out of that cursed spot and away from the dead body of the Dozer.

We raced out to my bower and Fabian threw himself face down in the grass, sobbing for breath. I stood looking at him for a second, then I turned, took half a dozen steps, and began to vomit.

I retched until my stomach ached, but still I heaved. Finally I crawled to the stream and bathed my face and rinsed my mouth.

Fabian, after a time, sat up, still panting like a dog. He came and lay over the water by my side, washing the blood from his face, finally ducking his whole head under the water and shaking it.

I rolled over and lay on my back, my eyes closed, feeling too sick to care for anything.

"What a ghastly thing for you to witness, my poor child. Forget it, Catherine, put it out of your mind entirely."

He was still shuddering himself, but he placed his hand upon my shoulder, and I began to weep.

"Aye, Catherine, weep. Shed tears for Fabian, for he would not do murder again for ten thousand fortunes. Weep, my poor child, and every tear will help to wash away that terrible memory." And taking his knife, he threw it far down stream.

Finally I stopped crying and sat up.

"Well," says I, folding my hands tight on my lap to stop their shaking, "well, do you want the cipher now?"

"No!" He shuddered again. "No! Tell me tomorrow or the next day, or never. But do not tell me now, for I have no stomach to enjoy the thought of gold this day."

We sat for an hour, he silent, and I trembling, then he got up.

"Let us pretend, Catherine, let us pretend that there is no treasure, that there never was a Jenkin Davy, or a Yorek, or most of all a Thomas Parr. Let us pretend that the old mill is a castle, as it once was, and that I am not a penniless bastard, nor you an unwanted fisher's brat, but that we are a goodly knight and lady fair, and we shall make believe this forest is ours. Come, we shall walk and talk of pleasant things."

We walked for ten paces and then he stopped.

"Oh God!"

"What is it?"

"The Dozer's body. I must be rid of it first."

"But where?"

"The well," says he wearily. "Go back to your bower, Catherine." He started back for the mill, and while he was gone, I ran to the well and got my Journal and hid it beneath a pile of ferns.

Fifteen minutes later he came back, dragging something at the end of a rope.

"Close your eyes as I pass by, Catherine," says he, and I did so willingly.

He joined me a few minutes later and sank down beside me.

"Well," says he, "it is done."

I took his hand in mine, and we sat silently, until he says: "Now, Lady Catherine, please to take my arm and we shall walk."

And walk we did, but not sedately, for he had made up his mind that we should forget the awful happenings of the day. And though I was still close to tears, and he still shaking, we played tag and hide-and-seek and I spy. But one game we did not play, and that was blind man's buff.

Finally, when we both felt lighter of heart and were weary from jesting and running, we fell in a heap together and he said, "Once I saw a play in which a man said, 'Let us sit upon the ground, and tell sad stories of the death of kings.' No sad stories of the death of kings for us, Catherine, but I know some fine tales. Hearken to me, Pippin."

The minutes sped like seconds, the sun raced across the sky, and oh, the tales he told! Of lovers and warriors at Tintagel by the sea, of pirates and highwaymen and little princesses. And the little princesses dwelt in faraway lands, in mansions of white marble, waited upon by dusky slaves clad in many-hued silks, with turbans studded with jewels like stars.

And when the last wondrous tale was told, I bowed my head on my hands and wept. Fabian took my chin and raised my head.

"God's truth, child, why do you weep? I told you these tales to make you happy, not sad."

But I could not answer him and wept more, and he says, "For God's sake, I pray you, stop, for I cannot bear this; I have been unmanned enough for one day."

Still I wept, and I said through my tears, "Whatever beauty I have known I found for myself, and I never had none to share it. I have been so lonely until I met you, Max. The beauty of your tales is like the treasure we seek, and gold and jewels are worthless if you must live alone on a desert isle with them! Oh, what have you done, Max Fabian? You have shared the world with me! You have troubled yourself to tell me strange and beautiful tales, and in all the world, none has ever done so before, and I shall live in fear that I must go back to that desert alone!"

There was a silence between us, and still I wept.

Finally he says, "Alone? Oh God! Alone again? Look at me, Catherine."

But I shook my head.

"Once," says he, "once, Catherine, when I had provoked you mightily, you said, 'You have made we weep, and I shall live to see you cry.'"

I did not answer him.

"Will I make you happy, Catherine, if I fulfill your wish? Men do weep, Catherine. Yorek wept, and even Fabian can. Oh, my child, alone again? Have you not guessed? Only you could make me weep! Do you wish to see Fabian weep?"

I shook my head, and when I raised my eyes, his face became as set as granite, with not one whit of emotion, but oh, his eyes, his strange and terrible eyes were sadder yet than ever I had seen them.

"No! Do not weep, Fabian!" I cried. "I could not bear it!"

He brushed my tears away with the back of his hand.

"Then stop your own weeping, Catherine," he said softly. "Stop. You will break my heart!"

Then a wild look came over his face and he touched my hair with shaking hands, whispering, "Your elf-locks, your lovely elf-locks. Catherine! Oh, Catherine, I tell you, you are breaking my heart!"

He pushed me suddenly aside, jumped to his feet and strode back to the mill.

I sat alone for a while, wondering if the murder had unsat his reason. Finally I followed him.

He sat staring straight ahead, and when I approached him he shuddered and put his hands over his face.

"Leave me alone. Leave me alone."

He went to the bed of boughs in the corner and lay face down. I went and knelt beside him, and stretched my hand out over his head but did not touch him. Instead, I drew my hand back, and he seemed to sense it, for he turned his face sideways and said, "Nay, do not fear me, Catherine. Put your hand upon my head."

His face became ashen and he said in a firm, quiet way, "I have not known such peace and joy as we shared in the forest in all my life."

I felt my lips begin to tremble, and I put my hands over my face.

"I told you pretty tales in the forest, did I not, Pippin? Here's another one, and a true one. Once upon a time there was a little lad who knew simple happiness, and roamed the forest as we have done this day, and he picked violets and cowslips, and startled the pheasant from her brood, and ran away laughing, and he fished for the silvery trout and ate warm ripe strawberries and plucked the wild rose from the hedge and flung pebbles at the lurching hare and drank from cool shallow streams. And when he came home weary, his nurse kissed him and blessed him, and he ran laughing and brown to his bed. And when he sank his head on that pillow, he had no dreams, Pippin, only a deep and easy sleep. Isn't that a pretty tale, Catherine? I was that little lad, you know."

His voice broke and he turned from me, and I crept closer to him, but not close enough to touch.

He sat up suddenly. "You fear the Dozer's ghost, don't you, my little Pippin? You fear to lay your hand upon the head of a murderer, and creep close to his bosom, while that monstrous form lurks unseen in the corners of the room."

Shaking from head to foot, I nodded.

"Fear the living, not the dead, you foolish child."

But night was falling, and the shadows deepened, and I was

rooted with fear to his side, afraid to leave him, and fearing at the same time to approach him lest I raise that fearful man in the well.

"There are no ghosts, Catherine," says he.

"Light a candle," I whispered.

"There are no ghosts, Catherine. Those fisherfolk who raised you filled you with foolish tales of newly departed and vengeful spirits come back to fright the living, did they not?"

I nodded.

"There are no ghosts, Catherine. Come, sleep sound, my poor child. God knows we both need rest after this day."

He drew me to his side and wrapped his cloak about me in the familiar way.

"Don't be afraid, Catherine. I shall light a candle and show you that there are no ghosts. Watch me now."

He lit the candle and went from corner to corner, holding it high and then low.

"You see? Nothing, my pretty darling. There are no ghosts. But if there were, rest assured, Pippin, I would fight him off as bloodily in the next world as I did in this."

He lay beside me and seemed to fall soon asleep, but I did not, half drifting into slumber and then jerking awake. Finally I put my arm around him, and at length, listening to the steady beat of his heart, I slept.

He was already shaven and washed when I awoke. After I had bathed in the stream and combed my hair, I took my Journal from the place where I had hid it in the ferns and put it back on the ledge of the well, and spoke a charm Granny Thewitt taught me. I laid the Dozer's ghost that way.

When I returned to the mill, Max and I sat opposite each other over the table, eating silently.

"Max," says I, finally, "about the cipher—"

"No, no, Pippin," says he before I could speak more. "Let us not face that problem yet."

He seemed very pale, or rather, sallow, for his skin was swarthy, and his hand shook as he raised a cup of water to his lips.

I said nothing, and washed the dishes as usual. An hour passed, and still he did not speak, only sitting there unmoving.

"Max," says I again, "you have killed the Dozer for to find the treasure. Don't you want it now?"

He arose, looked down at me with a strange, sad smile and patted my cheek gently.

"I am not yet myself, nor am I so sure I want treasure."

He walked out and I did not see him again until that afternoon, when he returned and threw himself down on the bench by the fire, his legs outstretched, his head leaning against the stones of the fireplace, and his eyes closed.

He seemed so strangely quiet and calm. I went to his side, and kneeling down, I took his hand and said, "What ails you, Max?"

"Nothing, Pippin. Nothing, darling."

"If it's the Dozer, do not fear him, for I laid his ghost."

"Did you now, my dear," says he absently.

"Shall I tell you the cipher now, Max?"

He opened his eyes in almost a dreaming way.

"If it pleases you to, my pet."

I took a deep breath. "It is this, Max. Jenkin Davy said, 'Tell Fabian our plans is changed. Tell him things is backwards. Tell him to turn the mill upside down. Tell him to change an eye to an ee.'"

He closed his eyes again, that strange, quiet look still on his face, as though he was very, very tired. And so he sat for an hour, reaching out and touching my hair gently now and again.

Finally my curiosity got the better of me.

"What does it mean, Max?"

"What does it mean? Why, it means that the treasure is in the well, my child. I should have known it was, and it was my fear of that cursed place which kept me from even considering it. And now, if I want to have it, I must climb down into that most fearsome of places, and see again that most fearsome of men. I'd sooner see a hundred ghosts of Dozer than view his remains in that well."

"But how do you know it is in the well?" says I.

He looked even wearier.

"It is not difficult, Catherine. Turn the mill upside down, and you have the letters w-i-l-l, and change an eye to an ee and you have w-e-l-l. Is it not simple?"

He looked at me sadly and said, "I do not want to go down in that well, Catherine."

"I shall go for you. It is only at night I fear him."

"Nay, my pretty child. If the loot is as much as I think it is, it must be a hundredweight."

He sighed, sat up and covered his eyes with a hand. I stood looking at him, and finally I touched those gray lamb's curls.

"Do not be afraid, Max. I love you truly, Max."

He looked up again, and smiled that odd, weary smile.

"Pretty Pippin. Do you want me to go now and bring it up? Would you like to play with pearls and rubies, diamonds and golden sovereigns?"

"Nay, Max," says I. "If you do not want them, then nor do I. Let us be as we were yesterday in the forest. Neither of us has ever been so happy. I would not spoil it for all the gold in the world."

He leaned his head back against the fireplace, his eyes closed again, and after a long, long time he says, still in that strange, tired way: "What, have I killed the Dozer and planned and schemed and sold my soul for naught? You are right, my child, I must face it." He arose and took a rope. Coiling it, he draped it over his shoulder and started out.

"May I come, Max?"

"If it pleases you, my pretty. If it pleases you."

When we reached the well, he began to shudder. Taking a deep breath, he heaved off the wooden cover, and there on the ledge was my Journal.

"What is this?" says he, turning to me.

"Why, it is my Journal. I hid it there so none could find it, never knowing the gold was there, too."

He took it out and handed it to me.

"No more secrets between us, Pippin?"

"None," says I. "And you may read it if you will."

"Later, sweetheart, later. Now I must climb down into the oubliette. Pray for me, Catherine."

There was an iron ring about a foot below the lip of the well. He tied the rope to it and just as he lowered himself over, he looked up at me and said:

"If I should not come up, do not seek to aid me. Forget about the treasure and return to your own village and pray for me, when you have a mind to. And remember always, whatever else I may have been, however deeply I may have sinned, I loved you. And I never loved another living soul."

He disappeared and I sat on the ground with my arms clasped around my knees. He could not have been gone for more than a few minutes, but it seemed like hours to me before I saw his face, dead white and twitching, appear above the well.

He threw down three large leather bags, crested in gold and with brass buckles.

"There is your treasure, Catherine."

I looked at the bags, and then at him.

"Are you not going to open them, Max?"

He shrugged and said, "Nay, not now. I shall carry them back to the mill."

At the mill he tossed them down on the hearth and sat himself wearily on the bench again.

"Open them, if you wish," he says.

I knelt and worked at the stiff buckle of the first bag. For a moment I thought it was empty, but digging my hand deep down between the scarlet velvet lining, I brought up a handful of unset jewels—pearls, rubies, diamonds. I looked up at him and handed them to him, then I emptied the lot on the floor, and it made a heap six inches high.

Then I unbuckled the second, and from it I took jewelry, rings, brooches, necklaces, chains, and little gold crowns set with jewels I could not even name.

For the first time he smiled, and reaching down, he put a jeweled circlet on my head.

I opened the last bag, which was very heavy, and it was half-filled with gold coins.

He knelt beside me and plunged his hands in it. Then he laughed. "Shall we throw away the gold, Pippin? It is so heavy to carry, and we have a king's ransom without it."

"Nay," says I, smiling and kissing his cheek.

He emptied all the treasure into one leather bag, and threw the second on the fire. I handed him the third to burn, but he looked at it thoughtfully, saying, "Nay, we shall keep this one to carry our supplies."

He seemed to be almost himself again, and asked if there was any port left.

"A bottle, I think," says I, arising and bringing it to him. It had only a few swallows left in it, and he took a couple and handed it to me, but I shook my head, playing with the jewelry in the bag. So he finished it off himself and sat on the bench again.

"Come here," says he finally. "Sit on my knee, Catherine."

I did, and he stroked my hair. "Pretty, pretty Pippin, with her golden, golden hair. Are you really fifteen, Catherine?"

I nodded. "Will you marry me, Max?"

He smiled and nodded.

"When, Max?"

He put his head on one side and looked at me quizzically.

"When I am sixteen, Max? Many girls marry at that age. I am sorry I am so small for my years."

"Aye," says he, kissing my cheek. "When your head has grown past my shoulder, and I can no longer span your waist with my hands, then shall you be Fabian's bride."

"How long will that be?"

"Soon, my darling. You must grow quickly."

"And when we marry, Max, shall I have a striped red and white taffeta petticoat?"

"You shall have a dozen. No, you shall not, you shall have two dozen, of all the hues of the rainbow, and silks and satins and taffetas, all of them, for you are Fabian's dearest treasure, Fabian's prettiest jewel."

"And shall I have shoes of green Spanish leather?"

"Why, Pippin, you shall have shoes of green Spanish leather with golden buckles, and scarlet pumps with diamond buttons, and little slippers of soft white kid, and pretty sandals of cloth of gold."

"And shall I have a carriage, Max?"

"A carriage? You shall have a gilded coach, with eight matched chestnuts to pull it."

"And shall I have a servant to wait upon me, Max?"

"Why, my little beauty, you shall have a servant who shall do nothing but buckle your little shoes, and another who picks up your petticoats as you step out of them, and one who pours perfume in your bath, and one who hands you a golden goblet when you thirst. But you shan't have a servant to comb your pretty golden hair, my darling, for none but Fabian shall do that."

And then he says, "Now finish writing in your Journal, my love, for we leave within the hour."

I left and returned with the Journal and the dye, and sat down at the table and began to write. After a long while, I looked up, and he was watching me, and he seemed sad again.

"Why," says I, looking closely at him. "You have tears in your eyes!"

"Nay, miss," says he, looking sadder still, "you are mistaken."

He took my finger and placed it against his dimple, and I pressed, and he smiled.

"Hurry, my child," says he.

So now I am closing my Journal, for Max tells me we head for a secret cove where he has a fast cutter and crew waiting for us, and when we reach there, we sail with the tide at dawn.

And I love Max Fabian, and he loves me.

And now I, John Montrolfe, must reluctantly continue this narrative. I feel morally obliged to set down this account, and will endeavor, as my darling Pippin said at the start of her journal, to state "as near as true as I can," the facts as they actually occurred. I have also promised that intolerable Forbes that these facts will be published, and so they shall be, if I must learn to set type by hand.

It is distressing for me to relate some of these incidents, which are of a personal nature, but the reader can believe without question that in order to present the truth, I shall spare no one, least of all myself or my antecedents.

As I laid down my dearest little Catherine's journal, a feeling of inexpressible horror overwhelmed me. I knew with certainty that there was a great deal more to be told, events that occurred after she closed her journal, and I had an instinctive unwillingness to know more.

I put the journal back in the secret drawer, and sat on the edge of the bed with my head in my hands. The slow fever that had been gradually destroying my reason ever since I entered Cliff House now flared with unimaginable fury.

Unable to rise, I fell heavily back, sweat pouring from me, while I trembled as though some giant hand shook me. Hours passed.

I tried to call for Nan, but only a thin croak issued from my lips and my lungs felt as though they were on fire.

I was dying. Why, I did not know, but I was sure of it. Waves of nausea, a raging fever and such pain as I had never imagined were the physical symptoms, while spiritually an almost atavistic horror gripped me so fiercely that I longed for death.

God knows how long I lay in this state before Nan found me—probably only six or seven hours, but time has no meaning when one is in extremis, and it seemed like weeks till I saw her bending over me.

Mercifully, I lost consciousness, and when I again opened my eyes, Nan's great-granddaughter, Beatrice, was taking my pulse.

"Good heavens, Gram! Why didn't you call me before? How could you let him get to this stage? Surely even you must have realized how sick he was?"

Nan mumbled something about having fetched Beatrice as quickly as she could, and then she stood wringing her hands and peering down at me. Obviously the poor old soul was frightened out of her wits by my condition.

"Listen," I heard Beatrice say, "I'm going to cycle right down to the village and get Ted. I'll be back as soon as I can. Put a cold cloth on his head, and for God's sake don't leave him alone again."

"Nay," said Nan piteously. "Don't leave me with him. Don't leave me. Poor boy, he's dying just like my poor Mr. Nicholas did. You're a nurse, stay with him, Beatrice."

"Don't be silly!" Beatrice's voice was sharp with irritation. "Nicholas died of a heart attack. God, what a mess. Get out some clean sheets and pillowcases. Now listen, Gram, I'm going to the village to get Ted—Dr. Forbes."

"Aye? Oh, poor boy, look at the color of him, Beatrice, he's yellow as a Chinaman!"

"Listen to me! I'm going to get Dr. Forbes. *Dr. Forbes! Gram,* do you hear me? He's got to have a doctor immediately. I'll be right back. *Do you understand?*"

Again I lost consciousness, this time for a considerable period, because when I next looked around I was no longer in my room but downstairs on a bed in the library.

The room was in perfect order, as neat as a hospital, and standing before the blazing fire, Beatrice was measuring medicine into a spoon.

On the edge of my bed sat Dr. Forbes, the same fellow whom I had seen in the sports car. He was fiddling with an intravenous tube on my arm.

He did not speak when he saw I was conscious. He looked into my eyes, then dropped his own and continued working with the tube.

The pain was as hideous as before and the fever as raging.

Beatrice came over.

"I think he's come to," she said.

Forbes grunted and stood up.

"Hello, Mr. Montrolfe." She placed her cool strong hand on my forehead. "How are you feeling?"

"What's the matter with me?" I croaked.

She looked questioningly at Forbes.

He stood staring at me, that same masked look of distaste I remembered on his face.

"You have double pneumonia and jaundice." He might have been remarking that it was twenty minutes past two.

"Oh, God! Give me something for this pain," I pleaded.

An expression of anxiety flickered over his face, and, quickly fixing a hypodermic, he plunged the needle in my arm.

To someone suffering exquisite pain, there are no words to describe the bliss of its sudden cessation. With a sigh and a prayer of thanks I sank back as I felt the drug begin to take effect. Again I lost consciousness.

In the hellish days that followed, whenever I opened my eyes, Forbes was by my bedside.

Beatrice assisted him, but it was he who did the nursing, day and night. His face remained unshaven and grew haggard with fatigue, but he never left me. He nursed me devotedly, and time and again, almost by sheer force of will, dragged me back from the brink of death.

But I kept escaping him, and I could slowly feel myself slipping away, no longer able to fight, and dying a little more, hour by hour, minute by minute, second by second.

He sensed it, and, strangely, seemed appalled. He took both my hands in his, as if to transmit his own vitality to me, and leaning over me, his own eyes feverish, he rasped, "You are going to live, Montrolfe. You are not going to die. I won't let you die. You are going to live. *You are going to live.*"

Over and over, those words seeped into the oven of my brain. It was a weird battle between us, I loath to leave, but dying nonetheless, and he, hating me, but bent on my salvation.

"Why?" I whispered. "Why? Why don't you let me die?"

He didn't answer.

"Why do you hate me?"

He never spoke to me unless it was necessary; I might as well have been talking to myself. There was never any conversation between us, none of the platitudes and pleasantries that doctors ordinarily indulge in at the bedside.

Finally the fever reached its peak and a horror of delirium settled on me. I recall both Beatrice and Forbes hanging onto my arms like limpets, trying to restrain me as I struggled to get up. I suppose they must have overpowered me, because I was back in bed when I heard Forbes say, "Get some rest, Beatrice. You're exhausted. I'll have you on my hands sick next. He's quiet now. Go upstairs and get some sleep, dear."

I could hardly believe the difference in his tone. He was obviously deeply attached to her, and his voice was gentle, even sweet.

"What about you?"

"You can spell me in about four hours. Go on now, be a good girl and do as I say."

She left and my delirium returned. I thought I saw the Dozer in one corner of the room, pursuing my dearest Pippin, his monstrous hands outstretched.

"Catherine! Catherine!" I screamed. "Look out, Catherine. Can't you hear me? It's the Dozer—he's in that corner. Catherine, run! The Dozer! The Dozer! Catherine!"

"Where's that book?" It was a voice at my ear. "I know there is one. There must be. Where is it?"

The delirium suddenly subsided, leaving me exhausted but with my brain completely calm and my thinking clear, crystal-clear. It was as if, by its very virulence, the fever had burned the sickness out of my mind.

I must now ask the reader to believe implicitly in my honor. On my honor, I swear I was no longer delirious, that I was, for the first time since entering Cliff House, quite cognizant of all the facts, and that my sanity was completely and without question restored.

During the course of this narrative, the reader will have just cause to doubt the word of a Montrolfe, but as God is my witness, and as He spared me in the hour of my death, this is the truth. I must establish this fact in order that you may fully appreciate the remarkable scene that ensued.

My cries to Catherine and the Dozer had had an electric effect on Forbes.

"What do you know about the Dozer?" he shouted. "Where's that book?"

Too weak to answer, I lay back staring at him.

"I heard you!" His voice was venomous. "God damn you Montrolfes! You all know something!"

He lashed his open hand across my face, and I raised an arm weakly to defend myself.

God! Had I been delivered from the bondage of my own madness only to be thrown into the arms of his?

When I still lay only looking helplessly at him, the last bonds of his consciously controlled hatred snapped, and he seized me by the throat like a madman.

"By God, if I can't get the truth out of you any other way, I'll choke it out!"

His hands encircled my throat, he *was* choking me, and I heard my neck crack like a rifle shot.

Frightened by the sharp sound and by his own violence, Forbes let go my throat and staggered away from me to the fireplace, where he stood panting.

And I, for the first time in my life, lifted my head erect.

He suddenly ran from the room, and I fell back into a deep and sound sleep. This time, when I awoke, Beatrice was beside me.

"Hello!" she said cheerfully. "My goodness, you *are* looking better. Whatever did Dr. Forbes do? You're feeling better, too, aren't you?"

I looked at her suspiciously.

"Where's that damned doctor?"

"Getting a little sleep, finally, poor dear. I've been nearly as worried about him as about you. Nobody can stay on their feet that way indefinitely."

"Listen," I said, taking her arm and pulling her down toward me, "listen, he's crazy. He tried to kill me!"

"Now Mr. Montrolfe," she said soothingly, "you've been very, very ill. You've been delirious for days."

"I tell you he's crazy! He tried to strangle me!"

"Now Mr.—"

But the words died on her lips as I pulled down the collar of my pajamas.

She leaned over and carefully inspected my neck.

"There are bruises on it, aren't there?" I insisted.

She nodded and looked at me strangely. Then, being a practical person, she pulled up a chair, took out some knitting, and, frowning with concentration, began working on the sleeve of a jumper.

"Well, Beatrice," I said finally, "what do you have to say?"

She put her knitting down and gazed at me, her face calm.

"It beats me," she said simply. She knitted for a while and then, "I never did understand his interest in this case. Do you know he asked Dr. Lewis to take over his whole practice while he attended you?"

"Why?"

Beatrice shrugged.

"I don't know, but I'll tell you one thing. He's a good doctor. I know. I'm a nurse and I work for him, and I wouldn't if he weren't a good doctor. And you're alive now because of his skill. Why should anyone who worked so hard to keep you alive try to kill you? It doesn't make sense. It must have been some kind of therapy. Besides, I know him well; I'm going to marry him. He has his faults, I know. He's rather a snob, for instance, but really, underneath, he's thoroughly decent."

"Mmm," I said. "Did you ever hear of Catherine or the Dozer?"

She was counting stitches and raised her head. "Forty-eight, forty-nine—no. Are they friends from Canada?"

She knew nothing. I shook my head.

"You really mustn't talk any more now, Mr. Montrolfe. You've been very ill. I expect this business about Ted will clear itself up. He's been without sleep for four days, and he's just overtired. I think we all are. Now lie down and sleep like a good boy."

I was certainly tired, deliciously tired for a change, and I fell back against the pillow.

Imperious shrieks cascaded from the kitchen.

"Oh damn!" Beatrice folded her knitting deliberately. "There's Gram again. She's getting to be absolutely impossible. It's nothing but Beatrice get me this, Beatrice do that, from morn till night. I'll be right back."

CHAPTER FIVE

Apart from his homicidal tendencies, Forbes did appear to be a competent physician, as Beatrice said.

He made no further reference to the book, nor did I. As a scientist I was used to exercising patience, and I knew that Forbes, given time, would prove himself with the stark simplicity of an algebraic problem.

My recuperation was unusually rapid and thoroughly enjoyable, thanks to the ministrations of Beatrice. Beatrice, as lovely and carefree as a wild rose. To my great surprise we felt remarkably at ease with each other, and I soon realized that she regarded me as Nan had Nicholas. I could do no wrong in her eyes, and she was devoted to me, as, oddly, I was to her.

As I recovered, certain things became daily clearer to me. I knew now that I had been on the verge of a complete nervous collapse before I entered Cliff House. Years of relentless overwork, plus my agonizing solitary life were certainly not conducive to a well balanced personality, and the fatal history of Cliff House had provided the proverbial last straw.

Forbes came daily. I could always hear his red sports car come screeching to a halt on the gravel drive. The door would slam, and there he'd be, one of those ridiculous little flat caps perched on his head.

He dressed immaculately and jauntily—short stiff collars, knitted ties and, usually, a yellow Jaeger weskit and a checkered sports jacket with leather elbows.

The procedure was for me to strip to the waist while he carefully sounded my lungs.

Soon I was strong enough to sit up for extended periods, and to take short walks about the place, although Forbes warned me not to overtax my strength.

Two weeks later I had never felt better in my life.

Forbes eyed me up and down, folded his stethoscope and said, "That congestion in the right lung has cleared up nicely. Very nicely indeed."

He has the most irritating manner of repeating himself.

He then gave me a poke in the ribs that would have rocked a lesser man and that was intended to indicate the examination was over.

Beatrice stood by, regarding me strangely.

"Did you get the mail from the village?" She was speaking to him but gazing at me.

Was I losing my mind again? Devoted service is one thing but, had she been looking at anyone but myself, I would have interpreted her expression as unconscious and unmistakable admiration.

"It's in the car, I'll get it now," Forbes replied.

Beatrice and I were left alone.

"Beatrice, what is it?"

She mumbled something about Byron and began straightening my bed in a flustered manner.

"Byron?" I said in amazement. "What are you talking about?"

"I was ... uh," she pointed to Fabian's portrait. "He ... and you, well ... look like Byron."

"Well, Byron and I had one thing in common, anyway."

I was surprised she mentioned Byron and even more surprised she had heard of him. She wasn't the poetry-loving type, and my remark passed unnoticed.

We were interrupted by Nan. When she saw me naked to the waist, she turned suspiciously to Beatrice.

"What have you two been up to?"

Beatrice blushed.

"Just like Hanner. Can't leave the men alone. Where are my teeth, you wicked girl?"

"Now how would I know?"

"Ye hid 'em!"

"Oh, for God's sake! Why would I want to hide your teeth!"

Forbes came in just then with the mail. "Here they are," he said, "on the mantelpiece." He took out his handkerchief and gingerly handed them to her.

Popping them into her mouth, Nan was transformed into a mutinous-looking old bull-dog.

"Well," she clicked, turning to me, "might as well be you as him, don't make no difference to her, I'm sure. As long as it's got pants on—"

"*Gram!*" screamed Beatrice, "that's *enough!*"

"And you!" Nan pinned me with a beady eye. "If you'd stayed in Afriker, where you belonged, there'd never of been none of this trouble. People banging about in my kitchen, day and night. My poor Mr. Nicholas never used me this way. He never come in my kitchen. Now she's always muckin' about there. 'Meat, Gram,' she says, 'a little chop for Mr. Montrolfe,' and 'Gram, you haven't washed that saucepan for two days.' It's Mr. Montrolfe this, Mr. Montrolfe that! 'And ain't he lookin' better today, Gram. And ain't his color nice now, and ain't he handsome, Gram!'"

Beatrice was scarlet.

"Now, Mrs. Beckett," began Forbes, but she cut him short.

"That's enough out of you. I used to wipe your grandfather's nose when he was in petticoats, and you Forbeses weren't no fancy doctors then, neither. Just plain Forbeses who worked in the glass factory. Until your grandfather married the owner's daughter."

It was Forbes's turn to blush furiously now.

Beatrice turned to Forbes. "Take no notice of her."

"Aye? What did you say?"

"You have ears like a damned lynx. You heard me," snapped Beatrice.

Nan snorted. "Just like Hanner. Can't leave the men alone!"

She left in triumph.

Beatrice slammed the tray on the table again.

Forbes put his arm about her shoulder. "Don't worry about her, Beatrice. If she gets too difficult, we can always put her in a home."

Beatrice looked at him in surprise.

"Put Gram in a home? Oh no, I could never do that. She's part of this house, she's lived here for eighty years, and it would kill her to leave. She'll drive me around the bend, I suppose, but as long as I live, I'll have to look after her."

"Amen," I said.

Forbes glared at me and left, slamming the door so loudly that Beatrice and I both jumped.

"Amen indeed!" Now Beatrice turned her ire on me, furious and embarrassed that Nan had repeated her words. "It's all very well for you to sentimentalize! When things get rough around here, you'll fly straight back to Canada like a homing pigeon, and I know who's going to be left to cope with *her!*"

Two minutes later Forbes was back.

"I forgot to give you the mail," he said repressively.

"So you did," said Beatrice.

"There's no need to be unpleasant."

"I am *not* being unpleasant."

And to think that this happy pair were to be joined in holy matrimony!

Forbes handed her a packet of letters, which she busily inspected. She appeared to be ashamed that she had lost her temper with me, and was much more amenable now.

"There's some for you," she said in surprise.

I held out my hand, but she continued examining them.

"But these are addressed to *Dr.* Montrolfe."

My hand remained outstretched. "They're for me," I said.

"But Mr. Montrolfe, you're not a doctor, are you?"

"Not a medical doctor. I'm a nuclear physicist. Beatrice, don't be so damned nosey. Now hand me my mail; you can read it after I have."

Beatrice handed me the letters, an awed look on her face. "You—you're not—you're not *the* Dr. Montrolfe? The one who won the prize?"

Feeling smug for the first time in my life, I nodded modestly.

She turned to Forbes.

"Did you hear that! Just fancy, living right here under our very noses, and he never said a word about it!"

God, how he hated me. He was standing under Fabian's portrait, and suddenly realizing he had his back to a Montrolfe, he moved hastily away, facing the picture and eyeing it malignantly.

"You don't seem to care for Guy Montrolfe," I said.

He glanced at me sharply and back to the picture. Quite obviously Beatrice's look of admiration had not gone unnoticed by him.

"No, I don't," he said. "The only place I've seen an expression like his before was in a mental institution. Schizophrenia, or I miss my guess. But then, the Montrolfes seem to have suffered from some pathological condition for generations. Generations."

It was cruel and he knew it; Fabian and I looked like twins, and furthermore, when it came to mental aberrations, there were a few points I would have liked to have put to Dr. Forbes about himself.

However, because of the nature of my own recent illness, I was hardly in a position to question the sanity of my physician. I contented myself with the thought that Forbes was an exceedingly handsome fellow, and I had yet to see Beatrice look at *him* as she had at me.

Beatrice and I, Beatrice and I, together. Soon we were taking walks together on the beach. We gardened together. We ate our meals together. In the evening we played chess together, or I strummed melodies for her on the delicate little clavichord in the corner of the library.

She woke the place up, but far from becoming a stately country mansion, more and more Cliff House had the air of a den inhabited by a half-tamed pride of lions.

Instead of dropping his daily visits, the more my health improved, the more I saw of Forbes. He didn't trust me and was taking no chances. Consequently, he never came at the same time two days running, and some days he favored us with his presence on two or three different occasions.

My instinctive antipathy, which, I must say, he did nothing to lessen, increased toward him daily, in contrast to the sincere affection I felt deepening for Beatrice.

I knew her faults—her temper, for instance—but as it was seldom directed toward me, I selfishly enjoyed seeing it exercised on Forbes, and she endeared herself to me in a hundred other ways. I found her wholesomeness, honesty and dreadful schoolgirl philosophy refreshing and sweet, and after being so long lonely, I found it very flattering to be worshiped.

Of course, she wanted Forbes and she wanted me too, and that was impossible. But she was honest about it. That was one of Beatrice's charms. She was unscrupulously honest.

It is not merely a cruel whim that makes the victor place the yoke upon the vanquished.

The Romans, those master psychologists, knew that when a man can not hold up his head he loses more than physical stature.

And if the strongest and most intractable of the Gauls were humbled in one triumphal procession, what of the burdened man born under the yoke?

When I held up my head for the first time I felt like a freeman, a frank. My other infirmities were secondary.

And once free, I cast a delighted and no longer jaundiced eye about, and my glance fell on Beatrice.

One of the most delightful experiences of regaining my health was that I discovered I could eat, digest and enjoy ordinary food.

I say I discovered it, but in fact it was Beatrice who did so. She was a good cook and prepared delicious meals, which at first, she insisted on spoon-feeding me. I was too weak to resist at the time, so I yielded and, contrary to my expectations, I did not die writhing in convulsions. Instead, I thrived.

No mother was ever prouder of an infant's progress than Beatrice was with mine, while Forbes looked on my recovery with his usual mixed emotions. He wanted me to get well, and he didn't.

Daily, Beatrice and I explored a gastronomic world that was entirely new to me. Things that other people take for granted—pork chops, oysters, roast beef and Yorkshire pudding, salads, shrimp—they were all new and exciting adventures for me.

I soon stopped having my meals on a tray. Beatrice wheeled a round, pedestal-type mahogany table into the library, and we ate together before the fire.

The first time we dined together, we used an assortment of kitchen cutlery and cracked plates, but, clearing away the table, Beatrice said, "You know, it's ridiculous spoiling a meal by setting a table with this awful stuff. There must be good china and silver in the house."

Long ago, someone at Cliff House had had exquisite taste, for Beatrice uncovered a trove of gold plate, silver tureens and salvers, linen and beautiful candelabra.

Thereafter we dined in style, although Nan's teeth had a disconcerting habit of turning up under elegantly covered platters.

I stood looking out the French doors in the library at Beatrice working in the garden, spading beds and planting bulbs. With her honey-colored hair, straight back and strong golden arms, she looked like a Saxon goddess.

Beyond her, past the cliffs, I could see the fishing boats of Forsham looking like a watercolor seen from a distance. Earlier the sea had been a giant sapphire, but now the sky was overcast and the water a gun-metal hue. One of those sudden electrical storms was in the air.

"Come on in," I called to Beatrice, "it's going to start raining in a minute."

I went to the fire, put the kettle on the hob for tea and limped back to the window. All at once it was almost dark, then a jagged yellow fork of lightning lit the bay.

Beatrice started for the house as I stood watching the storm's fury.

It was just like the night Catherine had first met Fabian. Indeed, since Cliff House was built on the same spot as the inn, she must have stood right here and watched the barque, "with her mizzen rigging fore and aft," anchored in the bay.

Beatrice tossed her gardening gloves on the terrace and stepped out of her muddy shoes before entering the library; she smelled delightfully of fresh earth and salt wind.

"Damn," she said, "I'd hoped to get those glads in before the storm broke. Oh well, I guess I can finish it tomorrow."

She walked to the fire and then turned to me in surprise.

"You've put the kettle on for tea."

I smiled and nodded. I was becoming quite domesticated; I loved being cozy before the blazing fire, sipping tea with Beatrice, especially when the elements raged impotently outside.

She made the tea while I stood watching her.

"You like this house, don't you?"

She nodded.

"You belong here. But tell me, doesn't it frighten you? It's supposed to be haunted."

Beatrice sniffed derisively.

"That's a tale Gram made up to keep people away. She's jealous. She doesn't want to share this place. That's why she adored Mr. Nicholas so; he hardly ever left his room and never entertained. Me, I'd like to see it as it must have been in the old days. Gay parties. Festive. You know, alive."

"Beatrice," I said, "did you ever see Nicholas?"

She shook her head. "Not more than three or four times in all the years I came here. He sort of scuttled around in the background, like a rat in the wainscoting. You could often hear him, but seldom saw him."

I winced at her description of the poor fellow.

"Once, though, I saw him and I'll never forget it if I live to be a million. I was about twelve, and I'd been gathering shells on the beach. I was just starting to climb up the cliff, when he came running toward me, his arms outstretched. He was shouting, 'Catherine, dear little Catherine, you've come back at last.' Then, when he saw it was me, he burst into tears and ran into the house. He scared me. Who was Catherine? Do you know?"

I nodded. "Someday I'll tell you all about her."

Poor, poor Nicholas. What a shock it must have been for him

to have seen a golden-haired girl on the cliffs, feel his heart leap with joy and then find it was merely some great, wholesome child. I felt sorrier than ever for him.

"Do you believe this house is haunted? Do you believe in things like reincarnation, Mr. Montrolfe? Honestly, do you think maybe we had past existences and can be born again?"

"No," I said firmly, "this house is not haunted. And being born once is quite enough, thank you, my dear."

Any statement I made was gospel to Beatrice. "I expect you're quite right. I mean, after all, honestly, what would be the use of it? I mean, we really should learn in this life, shouldn't we? That's what we're here for, don't you think, Mr. Montrolfe?"

"Don't call me Mr. Montrolfe," I said. "Call me Jack, or, if you have to be formal, John."

I took her hand and held it.

Why, why did it sound so familiar? Then I remembered. Fabian. Fabian saying to Catherine, "Bah, don't call me Mr. Fabian, but Max, or Maximilian, if it pleases you to be formal, for I am a lonely man without kith or kin."

A burst of thunder shook the house, making both of us jump. She tried gently to disengage her hand, but I held it tighter.

"Well?" I said.

"I'd like to, but I oughtn't. It would only make Ted more jealous than he is."

"My God, Beatrice, what you see in that idiot is beyond me."

Something made me look up at the French doors, and as another sheet of lightning lit the darkness, my heart turned over: a face was peering into the room.

Forbes. Peeking in the window like one of Dr. Barnardo's bloody waifs.

He had frightened me. Badly. For a minute I thought perhaps the cursed place *was* haunted and Fabian had come back.

I released Beatrice's hand and went to the doors.

Opening them, I reached out and fairly lifted him off his feet.

"Come in, come in!"

He had stopped slamming doors; it was the stealthy approach now—appearing like one of those trap-door tenors. My heart was still pounding, and I felt like striking him.

If he had dropped out of the sky he wouldn't have surprised Beatrice. Nothing surprised Beatrice.

"Tea, Ted? Mr. Montrolfe and I have just been talking about reincarnation. We both think we're here to live just this one life, and for a purpose. What do you think? But on the other hand, Mr. Montrolfe, it's positively uncanny how alike you and Guy Montrolfe look. If it weren't for that beard. I wonder why he wore it? He'd look exactly like you and so much handsomer if he didn't."

Since my recovery from my illness, I realized that my conviction of my own hideousness had been an obsessive neurosis, but still, it was very pleasant to hear Beatrice say I was handsome.

I shouldered Forbes aside and stood before the portrait.

"I know why he wore a beard, Beatrice. He had a scar on his cheek, like a deep dimple. He said he got it dueling."

I started to laugh as I remembered how Pippin had tripped him up on *that* one.

Beatrice suddenly stood up. "What's the matter, Ted?" She went quickly to his side. "What's wrong? You look as if you're about to faint!"

She was not exaggerating. His face was deathly pale and his eyes bulged.

"How do you know?" he said thickly. "How could you possibly know?"

"You'd better sit down," I said. "You look wobbly."

"You know a lot," he whispered. "Well, let me tell you something! He wore that beard so he wouldn't be recognized. He wore that beard so people wouldn't see the scar and identify him as Max Fabian!"

He turned to Beatrice.

"Please leave us alone, Beatrice."

She looked at him, then at me. And, being Beatrice, merely shrugged and left the room.

Forbes stood hesitantly for a few minutes, glaring at me, then his expression changed and he said in an almost pleasant, conversational tone, "What do you think of old Nanny and Beatrice?"

Now I was the one to be surprised.

"Well, I . . . well, I don't know."

"Are you in love with Beatrice?"

I was tempted to tell him it was none of his damned business, but this was the first time he had spoken civilly to me, and I was very much aware that he too knew something. Something I wanted desperately to know.

"I might be," I said finally.

He was looking at me with careful deliberation.

"Do you remember Tillie Barton?"

Of course I did. Catherine's dragon of an aunt. But I was playing my cards close to my chest now.

"Maybe I do."

"She had a grown family when she adopted Catherine Barton." He was watching me very carefully. "Nanny Beckett is her great-great-granddaughter."

I was too surprised to answer. It had never occurred to me that my dearest little Catherine had had even indirect descendants. But it was, I realized, logical in a small village like Forsham.

"Yes," he said slowly. "Catherine, of course, had no children. But you knew that."

He was trying to draw me out.

I said cautiously, "How would I know?"

"You know. And I intend to find out exactly what you do know. Exactly!"

Even when I tried to like him, I couldn't. He was insufferable.

"I am no longer an invalid," I replied. "And as you can see, I'm a great deal stronger than you."

It was my turn to tease him, and I tried a shot in the dark.

"Yes," I continued, "by some strange psychic mutation, I am as large and strong as the Dozer, so don't try choking me, I don't like it. The Dozer, of course, had no descendants at all. He died."

"Not 'died', Montrolfe. He was murdered."

"Well, 'pizened,' I believe, was the word."

He was very white now.

"Put your cards on the table," he said softly. "On the table."

"Why should I?" He seemed to bring out some hidden demon in me.

I had never seen anyone mirror such frustrated rage. But there was nothing he could do. Physically I could overpower him easily now. He couldn't threaten, and he seemed incapable of bargaining. His face was so shockingly white that again I thought he might faint.

"I begged Nicholas to tell me. He wouldn't. He pretended not to know what I meant. I couldn't wring it out of him."

Nicholas, poor Nicholas. Suddenly I was horrified.

"Did you attend Nicholas during his last illness?"

He nodded.

"Forbes!" I was inexpressibly shocked. "You didn't—Forbes, you didn't murder Nicholas because he couldn't tell you what you wanted to know?"

Gentle, sensitive, ignorant Nicholas, who kept to his room for thirty years, waiting for his sweet phantom to return. . . . Only I knew how he had suffered.

Forbes stiffened like a guardsman.

"I beg your pardon!" He spat his words at me. "*I* am not a *Montrolfe*."

"Well, who the hell are you then?"

He took out his wallet and flung his driver's license on the table between us.

I picked it up.

Of course. Why I hadn't guessed, I'll never know.

EDWARD YOREK FORBES, M.D.

"Yes," he said. "Through my mother, I'm a direct descendant of Edward Yorek."

He walked up and down the room in great agitation, and at last I felt genuinely sorry for him.

I began to feel faint myself, and had to sit down.

"Don't you want to know what happened to Catherine?" he asked. "You don't know everything. Don't you want to know?"

Of course I did.

"Yes," I said, gently this time. "I want to know. But why is all this so important to you?"

"Because," he gritted, "because I promised my mother I would clear Edward Yorek's name. I promised her that if it took the rest of my life, I would clear his name."

The algebraic problem was solved. I knew Forbes now. I knew him well. He was of Yorek's blood, and Pippin had taught me, in her journal, to appreciate the niceties of his character. He would never give in and nothing would stop him. He would sermonize and persevere, and in the end he would win. I admit I admired him. His breed had held fast at Waterloo, at Inkerman, at Mafeking, the Somme and Dunkirk. He was steadfast and implacable and, I knew, could be deadly in his purpose.

He was still pacing.

"Sit down," I said. "Now, let us be frank with each other. I have a journal. It was kept by Catherine until the time she and Fabian left the mill."

His eyes were burning.

"That's what I need. Where is it?"

"Not so fast. What do you have for me?"

"You?" He fell into a chair, and leaning back, gazed searchingly at me. "You? How do I know I can trust you?"

I could have strangled him. I clenched my teeth and fought back the impulse.

"Very well," I said, when I was sure I had myself under control. "Forget it. The deal is off." I arose and started for the door.

"Wait!" He got up too. "I have some documents that have been in my family for two hundred years. There is a diary kept by a Reverend Mr. Peterson, and the transcript of a trial."

He sighed, then continued, "I'll turn them over to you—if you turn that journal over to me."

"What then?"

"Then? Then I want them all published—the journal, the diary and the trial documents, regardless of what either of us finds in the contents. *All published.*"

I deliberated a moment. Then said, "Very well."

"Listen," he said softly. "If you double-cross me, I'll kill you."

And he meant it.

Like two duelists, Forbes and I met formally in the middle of the library.

I handed him the slender little black journal and in exchange he gave me a large, brass-bound tome and a sheaf of yellowed parchments.

We eyed each other with hostility, and then, without a word, he turned on his heel and left.

I lit the candles and seated myself at the round mahogany table where Beatrice and I ate, then opened the book he had given me.

After reading the first few pages of the faded copperplate writing, I saw it was a diary, kept daily at times, sometimes skipping a month or two.

It appeared to be written by a clergyman, for there were a great many quotations from the Scriptures, with hasty notes and ideas scribbled beside them, such as might be useful for sermons. Interspersed with these were items of homely gossip, such as prices paid for food and wine and the many small everyday preoccupations of life in an eighteenth century village.

I came upon an item that was underlined and, flipping the pages ahead, I saw there were dozens marked in the same way. Turning back to the first, I began to read them consecutively.

And here, set down in black and white, as I promised, are all the relevant excerpts from the diary of the Reverend Mr. Peterson, followed by the full and terrible account of the trial.

> On this day, Nellie Barton gave birth to a female child. The Lord be with them both.

> *Two days later:* N. B. died at dawn this day. Tillie Barton gave me leave to christen the babe, whom I named Catherine, that being my mother's name, and one that has always pleased me. God rest that dear woman's soul, and look upon her with infinite mercy.
> "What fruit had ye then in those things whereof ye are now ashamed? for the end of those things is death."
> I have spent the night in prayer.

> *Six months later:* T. B. came to me today, saying she found it increasingly difficult to support Nellie's child, custom being very poor at the inn after her husband's death. I have promised to give her a guinea a year for the babe's keep. Tillie vowed I am a good Christian gentleman and will get my reward in heaven for my charity. Alas, if it were but charity.

> *Over two years pass, with no more underlining, and then:* Catherine's third birthday today. She is remarkably like her mother.

Two years later: Came upon the village children teasing Catherine most cruelly today, and calling her foul names. I scolded the rascals soundly and took little Catherine, weeping, back to T. B. at inn.

Nearly three years later: I promised Catherine a penny last Sunday, should she memorize one of the psalms, and she came to my study today and spieled off six, then demanded a silver sixpence, which I could not forbear giving her. She becomes prettier by the day, being seven now, and I cannot help thinking her aunt is excessively strict with her, although that good woman says the child is so hard to manage that softness is lost upon her, harshness being the one thing she respects, although I cannot see it. I do wish, however, that the child would ponder more on her immortal soul, for she is given to laughter when the name of our Redeemer is said, not knowing, in her innocence, the awfulness of God.

Three months later: The village children, and indeed even some of their elders, plague and tease Catherine mightily on her unfortunate position in their society. Yestereve I came upon some boys pelting her with rotten fish, and their mothers standing by, saying nothing to restrain them, and she not yet eight, poor child.

Six months later: Catherine eight years old this day. It does not seem possible that that length of time has passed since poor Nellie's death. Catherine came to my study and asked for her present, saying I had given her one last year. I had purchased nothing for the child, and my conscience smote me, for indeed, no one else will remember her, so I gave her a little silver thimble which had been my mother's.

I have spent the night in prayer, and the words of Joel have given me great comfort.

"Therefore also now, saith the Lord, turn ye even to me with all your heart, and with fasting and with weeping and with mourning.

"And rend your heart, and not your garments, and turn unto the Lord your God, for he is gracious and merciful, slow to anger and of great kindness, and repenteth him of the evil."

Yea, Lord, I have truly repented.

Easter Sunday, a year later. My dear wife and I celebrated our twentieth wedding anniversary this day, and if God had but seen fit to bless us with issue, our wedded union would be complete.

Four years pass with no more mention of Catherine, and then: Tillie Barton came to me today, saying she can no longer manage Catherine, that the child is very naughty, and when she, Tillie, turns her back to Catherine at the inn, finds she has been drinking wine and singing ribald songs with the sailors. She asks that I request Mrs. Peterson to take Catherine in as a scullery or parlor maid, this house having a good influence on the girl, she says. I being hesitant, Tillie wept and begged me to for the child's sake. Catherine's soul is sorely in need of guidance, and I must take a hand in it, or she will be lost entirely to our Lord.

A month later: Catherine came into service in this house today, she being now thirteen years of age, and so very fair of face that none in these parts can match her, being, in truth, only like her mother.

Three weeks later: I began today to teach Catherine her letters in my leisure time, for indeed her mind is so acute it would be a pity if it were neglected.

A month passes: Catherine amazes me with her intelligence, for in this short space she already reads and writes with ease, and I have now started her on Latin and mathematics, which she masters without difficulty.

If only the dear child would apply herself with the same diligence to the Scriptures, but she will give no thought to her salvation.

Two weeks later: Mrs. Peterson says Catherine performs her duties in a slovenly way, that her manner of address is not respectful, and bids me dismiss her, but in truth, the child does so well I cannot find it in my heart to send her back to T. B. now that her mind is opening and absorbing with such speed, and I have told Mrs. Peterson that for the sake of Christian charity and the poor child's unhappy background, Catherine shall stay. Nor can I abandon all hope of her seeing the light.

That was in May. In July: Catherine has a mischievous streak in her that plagues me mightily, delighting to turn all my books upside down in their cases, and to put sand in my ink, and switching the salt to the sugar at the table and professing no knowledge of it.

In December of that year: Catherine today translated four pages of Caesar's commentaries without error, and she is indeed a credit to me.

In January: Catherine has been naughty, extremely naughty, over Christmastide, calling Mrs. Peterson an old Pope's nose behind her back, and only pinching my cheek and laughing when I reprimanded her. Also, cook says she tipples my brandy and port when none are about, and when I asked of this, she swore on her dead mother's honor she had not touched a drop. She is so like her dear mother in face that at times I could weep when I look upon her.

In May of that year: Catherine has asked me to teach her music and French as well as embroidery. I told her I could instruct her in French but I was not gifted in the other arts. "Why cannot Mrs. Peterson teach me them?" says she, and I did not know how to answer the child.

May 28th: Catherine very naughty. Picked Mrs. Peterson's favorite roses without permission.

June 20th: Young Jack Hawkins, now nearly seventeen, has been hanging about to see Catherine, but she treats him with disdain, saying he is a lout and that once he pelted her with fish and now he stinks of it himself. I have told her he is a fine boy, and what more than a fisherman can she expect in her station? "Humble thyself before the Lord," I said, but the naughty girl only tweaked my wig and ran away.

July 10th: I have told Catherine that if she does not mend her ways I will no longer instruct her, and indeed, if there be one way to make the child behave, that is it, for she burst into tears and put her arms about my neck, swearing she would be good.

July 28th: Catherine naughty and extremely careless in her duties, and Mrs. Peterson says she will have no more of her, but I said without explanation that she will stay. Catherine is so fair even at fourteen that all the young fishermen are already casting sheep's eyes at her, but she will have none of them, and in truth, I would have something better for her.

September 8th: Bishop Tennant spent the night here and Catherine told cook she saw him in his bath and that he had a wart on his ——. Wicked girl. As punishment I shall not teach her French and have increased her Scriptures, she knowing well the Bishop did not have a bath here.

November 10th: On this day Mrs. Peterson walked unannounced into my study while I was instructing Catherine and found me with Catherine on my knee, kissing her, for I had just told Catherine if she did not improve her ways with Mrs. Peterson, that good lady would be sure to send her back to her aunt. Catherine seemed genuinely concerned and promised me she would be a good girl and mind my advice and follow the rules our Lord has put down for us, and vowed she would not tell falsehoods, nor filch liquor, nor treat the villagers so haughtily, nor curse coarsely, and she had thrown her arms about my neck and was kissing me to prove her good intentions when Mrs. Peterson entered. Mrs. Peterson has completely misconstrued my interest in the child, and, indeed, what can I say without making the situation even worse?

December 20th: I came upon Catherine on my way back from Granny Thewitt's cottage. She was sitting on top of the cliffs sulking mightily because Tillie Barton was so harsh with her, and begged me to take her back, swearing she would be a different girl if I would, but I had to tell her it was impossible.

January 29th: Catherine gone from my roof three months now, and I miss her sorely, for her merry pranks livened a sober house.

If only there were some way I could provide for the child, or make a provision for her in my will, but the situation is impossible and always has been.

May 22nd: Mea culpa! I have been weighed and found wanting and if Catherine Barton had stayed under this roof I should not be recording this, for last night the inn burned to the ground, Tillie Barton being absent at Rob Thompson's funeral.

Oh God forgive me.

Two days later: The ashes having cooled, we have gone through the ruins of the inn, stone by stone and charred timber by timber, and there is no trace of my poor child. Bones were found, but they were those of a full-grown man. I could weep when I think of it, for while some of the people of the village think she might have escaped, there being no trace of her body, and have run away, being safe somewhere, I know this could not be so, for where would the poor, neglected child run to? I fear that poor Catherine, in a fright, ran out of the inn when it caught fire and fell over the cliff and has been swept out to sea.

The next day: My conscience will never cease to torment me on the account of that poor child, for I had fifteen years to make a right of a wrong, but now all chance of redemption is gone, and I must face my Maker with this sinful and cowardly heart. May God have mercy on me, and if poor Catherine be before His awful presence at this moment may He, in His infinite mercy, think not of her shortcomings or sins, but only that she was a child whom none had the courage to love, and the sins are not be laid at her door.

A week later: No more is known of the fate of Catherine, or the identity of the man found in the ruins, but on the night of the fire three strangers were seen to enter the outskirts of the village, two together and one singly, and we feel that could they be located, some light might be shed on the origin of the fire and the disappearance of Catherine. One stranger is described as being of particularly villainous appearance, huge and muscular to the point of monstrosity, and the other two being either farmers or fishermen, fair and very like our own people in appearance, although completely unknown here.

July 10th: Alas! News has reached here of poor Catherine's death at the hands of that monster, who is shortly to be brought to trial.

I have spent the night on my knees praying for my Redeemer to forgive me, for had I performed my natural duties Catherine

Barton would not have suffered such a hideous fate.

I have prayed earnestly to my God, but He does not hear me, no sign being given that I shall ever receive His forgiveness. Oh, I am as guilty before my Lord as that wicked, wicked murderer.

Oh Lord! I pray you, on bended knee, I pray you, give me a sign, a task, punish me, but do not let me live to die, to burn forever in the wicked fires of *Hell!*

All that is of me but myself is gone.

"So will I break down the wall that ye have daubed with untempered mortar, and bring it down to the ground, so that the foundation thereof shall be discovered, and it shall fall, and ye shall be consumed in the midst thereof, and ye shall know that I AM THE LORD.

"Thus will I accomplish My wrath upon the wall and upon them that have daubed it with untempered mortar, and will say unto you, The wall is no more, neither they that daubed it."

July 15th: Four days I have spent in constant prayer.

Last night I dreamed I saw the murderer swinging from the gallows, oh wicked, wicked man, his head encased in a black cloth.

July 17th: I am much recovered now, my stomach being able to receive food without revolt, and I sleep again, though not soundly.

I cannot bring myself to attend the trial. I cannot hear from that murderer's lips how he killed her.

But oh, do I sin further by assuming his guilt, before he has been tried by his fellow men? I shall write to Giles at Oxford to send me an exact transcript of the trial.

July 25th: My health has failed again. If I thought I were truly forgiven, I should be glad to face my God, but I fear. I fear to die, I fear to burn in hell. When I am gone from this world, what of myself will be left? Nothing. By my sins I leave an empty heritage.

And the high spirits, the mischievousness which I sought to dampen—now, oh how truly and irrevocably they have been put down!

July 30th: No word as yet from Giles.

August 3rd: The mercy of sleep has been taken from me and my body shakes as with the ague.

Then I turned to the sheaf of yellowed parchments. Opening them, I read:

My dear Mr. Peterson:

Through the special kindness of the learned judges, I was able to obtain the proceedings of the trial you requested, and though, through error of the shorthand writer, some of the proceedings were not taken verbatim, their honors have, however, assured me that all matters of major import are included herein.

Your obedient servant,
James Giles, clk.

TRANSCRIPT

OF

TRIAL

Being the proceedings on the special commissions of oyer and terminer and gaol delivery, for the County of Oxford, held at Oxford, on the sixth day of September, 32 George II, A.D. 1758, before the Hon. Heaslop Bolt, esq., and Sir Joshua Rayburn, knt., two of the Barons of His Majesty's court of Exchequer.

About nine o'clock in the morning, the court being sat, the prisoner was brought to the bar.

CLERK OF THE ARRAIGNS: Prisoner, hold up your hand. You stand indicted by the name of Edward Yorek, late of Byford, in the County of Berks, yeoman, for that you, not having the fear of God before your eyes, but being moved and seduced by the instigation of the Devil, on the eleventh day of June, in the thirty-second year of the reign of our sovereign lord, George the Second, now King of Great Britain, with force, at Witbridge, on the estate of Lord Leafield, in the County of Oxford, in and upon one Catherine Barton did make a murderous assault; and that you, the said Edward Yorek, with both your hands then and there held upon the said Catherine Barton, then and there feloniously, willfully and of your malice aforethought did break the neck of Catherine Barton; and that the said Catherine Barton did, on the eleventh day of June, in the year aforesaid at the place aforesaid, in the county aforesaid, of the mortal injury inflicted, die. And so the jurors aforesaid upon their oath aforesaid, do say that you, the said Edward Yorek, the said Catherine Barton, in the manner and form aforesaid, feloniously and willfully and of your malice aforethought, did kill and murder, against the peace of our lord the King, his crown and dignity.

How say you, Edward Yorek: are you guilty of the murder and felony whereof you stand indicted, or not guilty?

PRISONER: I am not guilty, may it please you.

CLERK OF THE ARRAIGNS: Culprit, how will you be tried?

PRISONER: By God and my country.

CLERK: God send you a good deliverance.

PRISONER: Amen. God send me a good deliverance.

The jury were called and sworn, and the court informed the prisoner of his right to challenge any of them for cause but the prisoner declined.

COUNSEL FOR THE KING (MR. HOWARD): Gentlemen of the jury, the prisoner, Edward Yorek, stands indicted before you for the murder of Catherine Barton, late of Forsham, a maid of fifteen years, which crime he, the prisoner, perpetrated and committed on the eleventh day of June last: and it is now my duty, as counsel on behalf of the King, to use my endeavors for the obtaining of that justice and restitution which the law requires for crimes of this horrid nature. To which end it may be necessary that I point out some facts and circumstances both antecedent and consequent to the commission of the murder, which I doubt not we shall be able to prove, and hope you will be satisfied in your consciences that the prisoner did kill and murder Catherine Barton as laid in the indictment, and if so, that you will find him guilty.

Catherine Barton was kidnaped by a band of felons, of which one was the aforesaid Edward Yorek, and taken by force to the Leafield estate. I shall attempt to prove to you that the unfortunate girl whose death you are now to inquire into, was brutally murdered by this man, in outrageous contempt of and rebellion to those laws which have been wisely and happily for us made, for the preservation of the life and security of His Majesty's subjects.

Now this is how the crime was discovered. On the thirteenth

of June, Edward Yorek approached in London a horse dealer by the name of Ephraim Heal and attempted to sell to Ephraim Heal two horses. Now here the prisoner made a grievous error in his career of crime, for of all the dealers in horseflesh in London, none is known more for his honesty than Ephraim Heal, and, added to this, Ephraim Heal was the very dealer who had, a year previously, sold these very same two horses to Lord Portchester.

Ephraim Heal had heard that as well as the valuables which were removed from the vaults of Lord Portchester in that well known robbery, Lord Portchester was also relieved of two of his finest horses, the black Arab stallion, Prince Ahmed, and the great hunter, Thunder Pride, both of which Ephraim Heal had himself sold to his Lordship. Ephraim Heal detained the prisoner until he was placed in the hands of the bailiff, John Teller, to whom the prisoner told a strange and garbled tale. He and two other convicted felons, one Jenkin Davy and one Thomas Parr, known as the Dozer, had conspired with a mysterious stranger, Max Fabian, to steal the horses, rob his Lordship and meet at a deserted mill on the estate of Lord Leafield. The bailiff and his men, journeying to that place in search of Lord Portchester's treasures, found two bodies, one of a very huge man, branded as a felon and brutally knifed to death, and one of a girl. The felon's body was found shoved carelessly down an ancient well, and that of the girl in the mill itself.

They found her laid upon a bench by the fireside, her hands folded upon her breast, her hair neatly combed, and her clothing in good order. They also found, gentlemen of the jury, that her slender little neck had been snapped like a twig, and her head was hideously twisted to one side.

Further investigation revealed that the girl was one Catherine Barton, aged fifteen, who had lived with her aunt by the village of Forsham, where her aunt owned an inn, the Jolly Sailor Boy. On the twenty-first day of May, that inn burned to the ground, and in the ashes were found the bones of a full-grown man.

The prisoner stated that the bones found in the inn were those of a sailor and felon, Jenkin Davy: and that the giant of a man found knifed to death was Thomas Parr, also known as the Dozer; and that the three of them were to meet at the village of Forsham at the bidding of this mysterious stranger, Max Fabian, in order to proceed to the place where Jenkin Davy had hidden loot. Indeed, as we will attempt to prove, three strangers answering the description of Davy and Parr, and of the prisoner, mind you, were seen near the village of Forsham on the evening in question. But no witness has been found who will say he ever saw a fourth man!

According to the statement made by the prisoner, Thomas Parr murdered Jenkin Davy, and then Thomas Parr and the mysterious Max Fabian set fire to the inn, and taking the girl with them, all three—Thomas Parr, Edward Yorek and Max Fabian—traveled to the estate of Lord Leafield, where they spent the interim time between May 23rd and June 11th.

I shall try to show you, gentlemen, that there never was a Max Fabian, that he is a scapegoat invented by the prisoner, and that this man, Edward Yorek, murdered first Jenkin Davy, then Thomas Parr, and finally, Catherine Barton.

I must ask you to remember, gentlemen, as the evidence is being presented, that Edward Yorek is being tried in this court this day not for the robbery of Lord Portchester's vaults, nor for the theft of his horses, nor the murders of Jenkin Davy or Thomas Parr, both felons and men of unsavory character, and both, from all indications, men of terrible physical strength. Edward Yorek is being tried before man and God today for the murder of a helpless, innocent maid, as little capable of defending her life before him as a lamb before a tiger.

I must ask you, gentlemen, to remember only this, that Edward Yorek is being tried in this court for the willful, unprovoked and monstrously unnatural act of murdering a defenseless child.

We who are counsel for the King shall now proceed to examine the witnesses in support of the indictment, and doubt not but we shall be able to make out the case as I have stated it; and if so, you will find the prisoner guilty, that he may receive the punishment justly inflicted by the law upon those who shall be guilty of the horrid crime of murder.

The Court Crier called Ephraim Heal, who was duly sworn.

COUNSEL FOR THE KING: Have you seen the prisoner before?

WITNESS: Yes, sir.

COUNSEL: Pray tell when and where.

WITNESS: He came to me on the twelfth of June, at my establishment in Pond Street.

COUNSEL: And what was the nature of his business?

WITNESS: Why, he wanted to sell me two horses, Prince Ahmed and Thunder Pride.

COUNSEL: And what did you do?

WITNESS: I sent for the bailiff straight off, for I knew they was stolen from Lord Portchester's stables.

COUNSEL: And how did you know this?

WITNESS: Why, I sold them to his Lordship myself, and I'd know the Prince anywhere, for it was me who brought him to England and sold him at auction, and I remember still how his Lordship and young Mr. Lester Gray tried to outbid each other for him. And as for Thunder Pride, why, his sire was Summer Storm from my own stables and his dam was Sir Alfred Somerston's Lady Belle, and I marked the blaze on his forehead when he was born.

COURT: Prisoner, will you ask this witness any questions?

PRISONER: Thank you, Your Honor, I have no questions.

COUNSEL: You may step down, Mr. Heal.

The Crier then called the bailiff, John Teller, and he was sworn.

COUNSEL: Mr. Teller, do you recognize the prisoner?

WITNESS: Yes, sir. It is the same man Mr. Heal called upon me to apprehend at his place of business on the thirteenth of June last.

COUNSEL: Mention in what manner the prisoner acted when you went to apprehend him.

WITNESS: He seemed very calm, as though relieved to be caught, as though he was glad to make a clean breast of it.

COUNSEL: And did he make a statement?

WITNESS: Yes, sir. He confessed to robbing Lord Portchester of his jewels and other valuables, and claimed that the crime was planned by a man named Fabian, whom he described as a gentleman, but about whose background he was vague. He said the other two accomplices were two felons named Jenkin Davy and Thomas Parr, and confessed that he himself and those two gained employment with Lord Portchester in order to commit the robbery.

Then he directed me to the mill on the estate of Lord Leafield, where he claimed the loot was hidden.

COUNSEL: And did he give you any warning of what else you would find there?

WITNESS: Well, I don't recall his exact words, mind you, but he said that no good could ever come from the lot of it, and perhaps he could sleep sound if the truth were known, before more harm could come from his foolhardiness.

COUNSEL: Foolhardiness! A tender word for Edward Yorek's misdemeaners!

PRISONER: Would ye presume my guilt before it is proved?

COURT: The jury will disregard the last comment of the learned counsel. Mr. Howard, kindly confine yourself to pertinent questions.

COUNSEL: To proceed, Mr. Teller, please tell what you found at the estate of Lord Leafield.

WITNESS: First we were only looking for Lord Portchester's treasures, and his Lordship had sent five of his men along, as well as being present himself to trace his goods; but we found nothing except two bodies, one in the well and one in the mill.

Counsel: We shall return to the bodies later in the questioning. But now, Mr. Teller, will you tell whether you made any further effort to find the Portchester treasure?

Witness: I journeyed to the farm of the prisoner at Byford in Berkshire, and there discovered in a cowshed an empty leather case bearing the arms of Lord Portchester.

Prisoner: Fabian put it there! He must have found the treasure after he killed the girl! I swear I never saw a penny of the loot! Fabian *must* have put the bag there!

Court: Silence! The jury will ignore this outburst. The prisoner will have his opportunity later to present any evidence he may have in his defense.

Counsel for the king, having no further questions to ask the witness, the court informed the prisoner of his right to cross-examine, but the prisoner replied in the negative.

Court: Mr. Teller, you say that prisoner seemed relieved to tell you of his part in the robbery, and willingly gave you information. Would you say he knowingly directed you, of his own free will, to the two dead bodies?

Witness: Truth to tell, Your Honor, he seemed like a man in a dream the whole time. No, not so much a man in a dream as a man just awakening from a nightmare.

Court: And how did he take the news that two dead bodies had been found at the place to which he directed you?

Witness: Why, he professed to be shocked and surprised.

Counsel for the King: You say "professed." You had the impression he was not in fact shocked?

Witness: Yes, sir, I would say he was not, for, as I have stated, he had a dreaming way about him, as though awakened in the course of a nightmare.

Counsel: Thank you, Mr. Teller.

Lord Portchester was called as the next witness.

Counsel for the King: My Lord, I know that you, robbed of nearly a hundred thousand pounds, have been a most unfortunate participant in this drama; but I must ask you, in the evidence you are to present to the court, to kindly refrain from dwelling on your losses and to concern yourself solely with justice being dealt to the murderer. The whereabouts of your monies must be dealt with at another time and in another place. For the present I must ask you to tell the jury what you saw at the estate of Lord Leafield.

Witness: What? You going to tell me, sir, my fortune—gold, silver and jewels—ain't important? That's impertinence, sir.

Court: You will kindly answer the questions put to you, sir.

Witness: Bah! Girls are killed every day. Where's my money?

Mr. Baron Bolt: My Lord, the purpose of this sitting is to determine the innocence or guilt of Edward Yorek in the murder of Catherine Barton. The matter of your purloined fortune must wait its turn in the due course of justice. In English law a human life is of sovereign importance, transcending even that of your lordship's treasure. And now pray answer the questions.

Counsel: You saw the bodies found on Lord Leafield's estate?

Witness: I did.

Counsel: Will you describe them?

Witness: One, in the well, was a giant of a man, stabbed many times.

Counsel: And the other? Will you be so kind as to describe this?

Witness: Well, I and Porritt, my steward, entered the mill with that bailiff fellow. And there, before the fire, on the bench, was the prettiest little maid I ever set eyes on. We thought at first she was asleep, but Porritt, who's always been a fool and coward, let out a sort of scream and says, "Milord, her neck's all askew, she's dead, Milord." So I walked over and jerked her head up straight, and had a good look at her, and surely enough, she was.

Counsel: Thank you, my Lord. Now will you look at the man in the dock. Have you seen him before?

Witness: What?

Counsel: Do you recognize the prisoner? He has stated that he and his two accomplices, Jenkin Davy and Thomas Parr, were in your employ at the time of the robbery.

Witness: Oh yes, yes. That fool of a Porritt hired the whole crew of them to rob me.

Counsel: Do you recognize him?

Witness: No, I do not. Porritt hired him to fix some rafters or something in the cellar, but I never set eyes on him.

Counsel: And before you saw the man called Thomas Parr dead in the well, had you seen him on your estate?

Witness: I do believe I noticed some sort of beast prowling about the stables, but I cannot be sure.

Counsel: Thank you, my Lord. We must ask your indulgence for interrupting your hunting to bring you down here today.

The next witness was Joshua Hogg, fisherman, of the village of Forsham, in Dorset.

Counsel for the King: Can you tell the jury of any unusual events you witnessed on May the twenty-first last?

Witness: Well, there were strangers in the village, or about it.

Counsel: Did you see any of these "strangers" in the district?

Witness: Aye, sir. I was out on the Old Road looking for my bitch Trumpet that has a habit of straying when in season, when I saw two strange men crossing the pasture, heading in the direction of the Jolly Sailor Boy.

Counsel: Could you describe these men?

Witness: One was a giant, an ugly-looking fellow, and I had no wish to get in his way.

Counsel: And the other?

Witness: That's him, there in the dock, I swear it.

Counsel: Did you see any other strangers?

Witness: Only one. While I was returning to my cottage I noticed a horse grazing by the wayside, and wondered that I did not recognize it, if it was one of the villagers' animals. When I approached, a tall fair man rose from the grass and took to his heels. It was dusk and I could not see him well, but I know he was very fair and a stranger.

Counsel: And did you see another mysterious stranger? A gentleman by appearance, who, it seems, is called Max Fabian?

Witness: I saw none but the three I said I saw.

Prisoner: Oh, sir! I beg of you think again. Did you not see another stranger? Someone *must* have seen him. I can describe him for you to the last detail, for I would know him in hell!

    He is a man of about thirty-five years, of my height and strongly built. His hair is gray and very curly and cut short, as though he is accustomed to wearing a peruke. His features can be pleasant or not, according to his mood, and he appears at times to be very handsome, his manner being one of great charm when it pleases him.

    He is a gentleman, of that I am sure, for he speaks precisely, and reads and writes and knows all manner of foreign things.

And oh! He has a dimple in his cheek. A deep dimple that no man could mark and forget. It is in his right cheek—nay, let me think—it is his left. Oh God! I cannot remember, but I think it is his left cheek, and he has a way of frowning when he smiles, which is seldom, and of lifting his eyebrows slightly and looking direct at a person when he speaks. And when he is angry, the dimple on his cheek twitches like it was pulled by strings. I entreat you, did you not see such a man?

WITNESS: On my honor, I said I saw none but the three I have told of, and I never saw this fellow you describe or I would have said so. I am an honest man and speak only the truth. Do you doubt my word?

PRISONER: Nay, nay, I would but have you search your memory.

WITNESS: I have never seen this Max Fabian, nor did I hear talk of him.

COUNSEL: Thank you, you may step down. Crier, will you call Mistress Fairchild?

Mistress Fairchild took the oath.

COUNSEL: Mistress Fairchild, have you seen the prisoner before?

WITNESS: Oh, yes, sir.

COUNSEL: Now, Mistress Fairchild, where did you first see the prisoner?

WITNESS: It were on market day, and he come with a little lass, who sat on a stone by my cart.

COUNSEL: Did you speak with either?

WITNESS: Oh, yes. First I spoke to the little one, but she was as frightened as a deer and ran straight away.

COUNSEL: Pray continue, mistress.

WITNESS: Well, later she and him, that one there, was back by my cart, and they bought eggs and cheese from me, and I asked him if he got a good price for his horse, for he had sold one.

COUNSEL: Yes, and what transpired?

WITNESS: Well, I cannot quite recollect all what happened or how it happened, but the little one—and oh, sir, she were the prettiest little maid I ever set eyes on—she were sitting in the grass with him there, and I can't quite remember whether it was before or after they bought my goods, that he told me she had just recently been bereaved of her mother, and was sore upset by it. Why, yes, it must have been after they bought my goods, for I remember her hiding behind him, weeping, when I spoke to her.

COUNSEL: What made her weep?

WITNESS: I do not know sir. She seemed happy, though timid, one minute, and the next she wept as though frightened by the devil.

COUNSEL: And the prisoner, did he intimidate her at this time?

WITNESS: Intimidate? I do not understand, sir.

COUNSEL: Come, come. Did he frighten her in any way?

WITNESS: Well, I can't say. She seemed by nature such a merry little thing, but he was as grave as a judge, begging Your Lordship's pardon.

COUNSEL: Yes, yes. Now, did he use any violence with her?

WITNESS: Oh, that he did! For I remember well, though I could not hear their words. They was sitting on the grass, talking, when all of a sudden, why, that big, girt fellow boxed her ear so painfully she cried.

COUNSEL: Please continue, Mistress Fairchild.

WITNESS: Well, she stopped weeping after a bit, and she seemed happier, and the next time I looked, she was weeping bitterly again, so I climbed down from my cart and went to see what ailed her. He, him there, said he had given her a sixpence, and she had lost it, and now she wanted another. I felt sorry for the poor child and offered her a farthing, but he turned me away and would not let her take it.

COUNSEL: And what was the prisoner's manner during all this?

WITNESS: Why, he struck me as a hard, cruel man to use a child so.

COUNSEL: And would you say the child was afraid of him?

WITNESS: I would say the poor creature had the heart frightened out of her.

COUNSEL: Did you see the child and prisoner on any other occasion?

WITNESS: Not the prisoner. But I did see the girl going into the gypsy camp, and I thought her father would do well to mind his daughter rather than his horse, for we country people know those gypsies to be ruffians.

COUNSEL: Did you view the body of Catherine Barton?

WITNESS: Yes, sir, and a lovely corpse she made. When the poor child's body was found on Lord Leafield's estate, and the news of it reached the village, I went straight away to the constable, for we don't have many strangers in our parts, and the constable would have me view the corpse, which I did.

COUNSEL: And did you recognize the body?

WITNESS: It was the same maid, but dead, oh so dead, poor thing.

COUNSEL: Thank you, Mistress Fairchild.

COURT: Prisoner, have you any questions to ask this witness?

PRISONER: Yes, Your Honor. Mistress, you say you saw me strike the girl, though you could not hear our words.

Could I not have struck the child, not in anger or wanting to harm her, but the way a parent may cuff a naughty child? Have you not seen a father strike a child for trying to pet a vicious dog, or for playing too near the fire?

WITNESS: Nay, for your whole manner showed you was a hard, cruel man, and the child feared abuse from you.

PRISONER: That is not true! The girl had no fear of me!

COUNSEL: Mistress Fairchild, please step down.

The court crier called George Snider, butcher, who was duly sworn.

COUNSEL FOR THE KING: Mark the prisoner well. Have you seen him before?

WITNESS: I have, sir.

COUNSEL: Kindly explain when and where.

WITNESS: On market day at Handley, sir.

COUNSEL: You are positive it is the same fellow?

WITNESS: I am positive.

COUNSEL: Was he alone when you saw him?

WITNESS: No, for he had a little maid with him.

COUNSEL: Describe to us, please, the maid.

WITNESS: She was very fair, with long golden curls, and a face like an angel's.

COUNSEL: Did you hear the prisoner say anything?

Witness: Well, I remarked to him that he had a rare sharp youngster, and he says, "Aye, if she be not too sharp." So I says, "What, would you have a dullard for a daughter and never get her married off?" And he replies, "There are spinsters about who owe their state to being too sharp." And I laughed and says, "This one won't live to be a spinster." Then, he, this fellow, turns to her with a sinister manner and says, "Mark them words well, Catherine."

Counsel: And what was the girl's manner when he made that remark?

Witness: As I recall, she looked frightened.

Counsel: I have no further questions.

Court: Prisoner, do you wish to cross-examine the witness?

Prisoner: I have no questions, Your Honor.

Court: Mr. Snider, you have sworn that you said, "This one won't live to be a spinster," and the prisoner said, "Mark them words well, Catherine," but in a sinister manner. What would you call a sinister manner, Mr. Snider?

Witness: Why, a sinister manner. I marked them at the time as being strange words for a father to use to a daughter unless he meant her harm.

Court: If they struck you as such at the time, why did you not report them to the constable, if you feared he would murder the girl from those words alone?

Witness: Why, I did not think he would murder her, only that they was strange words for a father with any fondness in him to use to a girl.

Court: You may step down.

The crier then called Chollo, a gypsy.

COURT: Are you a Christian?

WITNESS: Yes, my lord.

COURT: Are you prepared to take a Christian oath, solemnly jeopardizing your immortal soul if you speak not the truth?

WITNESS: Yes.

And he was sworn.

COUNSEL FOR THE KING: Your name, fellow?

WITNESS: Chollo.

COUNSEL: What sort of a name is that? Were you baptized a Christian with that heathen name?

WITNESS: Yes, sir.

COUNSEL: And how do you spell this—this Chollo?

WITNESS: I do not know.

COUNSEL: A fine Christian. And how do the country people address you when it pleases them to speak to your sort?

WITNESS: They call me Johnny Fah, as they call all of my race, may it please your Lordship.

COUNSEL: Do not address me as your Lordship, Johnny Fah. Now speak the truth and answer all my questions, do you hear me?

WITNESS: Yes, your Lordship.

COUNSEL: Bah! I lose patience with you! Now speak up! Have you seen the prisoner before?

WITNESS: No, may it please you, sir.

COUNSEL: Do you remember a young girl who visited your camp on market day?

WITNESS: I remember one such.

COUNSEL: Was it Catherine Barton?

WITNESS: I do not know.

JURY: I desire that he may speak a little louder.

COUNSEL: Speak up!

WITNESS: I do not know.

COUNSEL: Describe the girl.

WITNESS: She had yellow hair and white skin and red cheeks.

COUNSEL: And what did she want of your people? Speak up, fellow, and acquaint the jury with what you may know of this matter.

WITNESS: She wanted to buy poison.

COUNSEL: Poison, is it? And why should a maid wish to buy poison?

WITNESS: I do not know.

COUNSEL: And did you sell her poison?

WITNESS: Oh, no, sir, for we do not deal in such things.

The counsel for the King turned to the prisoner, but the prisoner declined to cross-examine.

COUNSEL: Step down, fellow, and begone from here.

The King's counsel submitted it here.
    Mr. Baron Bolt acquainted the prisoner that, the King's counsel

having gone through their evidence, it was now his time to offer what he could in his own defense.

PRISONER: Gentlemen of the jury, I am not a learned man. I do not know the ways of courts, nor can I cite famous cases to prove my innocence. Neither can I pay for counsel to aid in my defense.

I cannot cast doubt upon the words of the good people who have given evidence here today, for they have told the truth; and I can bring forth no witnesses for my defense, for they are all dead, and it was not I, but Fabian who killed them.

My only defense lies in telling the truth, and I beg you, gentlemen, since it is my only defense, believe me, please believe me, when I tell you the story I am about to. It is not a pleasing one, and where I have erred I am truly sorry and will pay the penalty like a man, for I am far from guiltless; but gentlemen, I swear, I swear on my immortal soul, I am not a murderer.

Bailiff Teller says I seemed relieved to be found out in my crime, and so I was, but for the crime of robbery, not murder, for I swear, gentlemen, I have never done murder. It was Fabian who gave me the address of Mr. Heal, the horse dealer, and he only gave me that address to trick me and trap me, him knowing all the while that Heal would know the horses, and it was Fabian who killed the Dozer and Catherine Barton. I can see now how he planned the whole thing.

Gentlemen: If I had killed Dozer and Catherine, would I have led the bailiff and his men straight to the mill? I did not know they were dead, and I would have had the lot of us face the law, rather than see murder done, which was why I was glad to be found out, not, as the bailiff suggests, that the weight of the murder preyed on my mind, for I did not know then that Catherine Barton and the Dozer were dead.

Fabian planned the whole thing very careful from the first day I saw him waiting outside the prison gates, when Dozer and me was set free together. He came to me first, and said he could find me employment.

Gentlemen: I freely confess I have served time as a felon. I was a poacher and I became a felon through it. I do not tell you this to beg sympathy, but only to explain why I accepted Fabian's offer of employment, for, all the time I was in prison, my wife and children tried to run my farm. I owned a bit of land I worked, but in the time that I was gone my wife had to sell all our stock, animal by animal, and I wanted money for to restock my farm. I swear to you it was the only reason I took up with Fabian, and I told him I would take part in his scheme only if there was no bloodshed, and Fabian promised me there would be none.

We was told by Fabian to go to Jenkin Davy, who was a footman for his Lordship, Lord Portchester that is, and Jenkin Davy took us to his Lordship's steward, Mr. Porritt, who hired both of us.

The Dozer was hired as a groom, for he had a way with horses, a way I never seen equaled. Me, I was hired as a carpenter, to replace rotten beams in the cellars of his Lordship's place.

Fabian never went near us at this time. Don't you see, he planned it all, but none but us, who was his tools, ever set eyes on him. It was him who planned the whole robbery, down to the last details.

Two days before the robbery, the Dozer, Thomas Parr, that is, was to steal five horses from his Lordship's stables, four for riding and one as a pack animal. The Dozer was to take the horses to a place known only to him, and to have provisions for the four of us on the pack horse.

Fabian said if we tried to buy horses to escape after the robbery, we would rouse suspicion, and we could not ride the stolen horses right after the robbery in the neighborhood of his Lordship's estate, as they might be recognized, which was why Dozer had to steal them two days before and hide them for us to pick up later. Fabian also said they would be running around in circles looking for the horses at the time of the robbery, and so they were, too.

He said, Fabian said, he had chosen me for I had an honest face, and my part in the job was very important, and I must not be suspected.

I was doing carpentry work, replacing rotten beams in the cellar, as I said, and I was to drug the guard who was kept in the room outside the vault, twenty feet from where I was working. Then, while the guard was drugged, I was to keep watch while Jenkin Davy broke down the door and chiseled through the stone of the vault. While Jenkin Davy was taking the loot to a place known only to him, I was to repair the door so as to delay the discovery of the robbery, and twenty-four hours after the robbery, Dozer and me was to take the guard to the village to Forsham, where he was to be put on board a barque sailing for France.

We had to drug the guard three separate times. Fabian had it all plotted out just how long each dose would last and when another was to be given to him. You may think it strange that he was not discovered drugged in that time, but Fabian had worked that out too. The guard, Simon, had his meals brought to him twice a day, and he was generally sitting in his chair asleep, so that the servant who brought his meals thought nothing of it. Fabian coached me to make a jest of it to the servant, who laughed with me about Simon always napping.

Twenty-four hours after the robbery, when it was still undiscovered, we gave Simon his last dose of drugs, and then at night we left, Dozer carrying Simon over his shoulder. He carried him so all the way to Forsham, and it did not fatigue him at all, for I have never seen a man to equal his strength.

Fabian had purchased a horse for Jenkin Davy before the robbery, for he said timing was very important, and we was all to meet at Forsham at the same time, so, since Davy had to take the loot from his Lordship's place, cache it and return to Forsham to meet us, he must needs be swifter than us, but Fabian bade Davy turn the beast loose a few miles out of Forsham and enter on foot. You may wonder why Fabian trusted Davy so with the loot. Well, I can only tell you Jenkin Davy was his man, and you may laugh at this, but he was an honest man, a good and honest man. I do not know what hold Fabian had over him, but he would do anything Fabian would of him.

At the time I really did not believe that Fabian did not know where the loot was hid, but it seems he did not, and it was the only honest statement I have known him to make.

He said we was a bunch of scoundrels and none of us was to be trusted, including himself, except Davy, who, he said, had not the wits to dispose of the loot, and so Davy should be the only one to know the final hiding place.

He said we must all be dependent on each other, since it took the four of us to do the job. So that was why I knew where we was to meet, but Dozer did not, and I had to take Dozer to Forsham, and Davy and Fabian and I did not know where the horses was hid, only Dozer knowing that, and Fabian knew the approximate location of the loot, but not the exact hiding place, that being Davy's cipher.

Fabian said Davy could be trusted, for he said though Davy had not enough wits to dispose of the loot, he had sense enough to know he would hang if he tried, and don't forget, Davy was his man and trusted him. Fabian wanted all of us to hand him our shares when the loot was found, as he had connections in France and could dispose of the jewels, and have them converted to sovereigns.

At first, Dozer and me refused, not trusting him like Davy and preferring to trust our own luck on that count. Then we decided to let Fabian take the jewels only, us keeping the sovereigns. Anyway, I only wanted enough to buy a few horses and cows and sheep. But Davy accepted Fabian's offer, and Fabian was to buy a vessel in France for Davy, as Davy had once been a seafaring man and wanted to go back to the sea. When we refused Fabian, he said: "Very well, you fools, hang yourselves with it."

And Dozer says: "If one of us hangs, we all hangs," but Fabian says: "Not Fabian, for when this job is done, there will be none except you three who have ever set eyes on Max Fabian, and he will be far away by that time."

Fabian was to meet us at Forsham, for he had gone on board the barque off the Cornish coast, and he landed at Forsham the same night we did.

When Dozer and me arrived at Forsham, we put Simon, the guard, aboard the barque, but Fabian was not there. He had told us, if he was not on board, or if our timing was not perfect, we were to meet at an inn, the Jolly Sailor Boy, so Dozer and I went to the inn.

Just before we got there, I began to suspect Fabian, and decided to go back to the barque to check on him. While I was gone, the Dozer met Jenkin Davy and stabbed him, and threw his body over the cliff.

The girl, Catherine Barton, saw this, and when I got back to the inn I found Fabian and Dozer drinking next to the fire, and when Fabian called the girl down, she said she had seen Dozer kill Davy. Fabian was very angry, for, as I have said, only Davy knew the final hiding place. Fabian and Dozer decided to fire the inn to dispose of Davy's body, and I begged Fabian not to harm the girl, for I have a little lass of my own. So Fabian said he would not hurt her, and she would come with us, so the three of us, with the girl, was led by Dozer to the horses.

When we got to the place the horses was hid, there was only three of them, not five as there should have been. I began to suspect Fabian even more deeply, and while he slept I took all his powder and shot and dropped them in a stream, for I felt if I misjudged him, it would make no difference, and if I had not misjudged him, I stood a fair chance in a knife fight.

Fabian led us all to the mill, where we labored to find the treasure, but we could not.

About six or seven days after, I forget now, we were low on food, so Fabian suggested I take the girl and go to market, and sell the pack horse and buy supplies.

I know I have said in front of witnesses that Catherine was my daughter, and she was not, but it was Fabian's idea to allay suspicion, he said. I put no importance on it at the time, nor on the fact that he wanted the child to go with me. I see now he planned it all so that I should be seen with the girl. He must have been bent even then on murdering her. And Catherine wanted to go. She was a bright, merry little creature, and I felt it was not right for her to be penned in with three grown men, and I thought she might escape from us that day, for I had told her the night the inn was fired that I would help her escape.

The testimony of Mistress Fairchild is quite true. I did strike Catherine, but only because she refused to escape, saying she loved Fabian.

Oh, gentlemen! I did not mean it as violence, I did not wish to hurt her, but have you never seen a man strike a willful child? I did not strike her to hurt her, but to warn her, for I felt she was imperiling her life being near Fabian.

And I did use those exact words that the butcher heard me say, but again, gentlemen, I swear I meant it as a warning! I did not kill Catherine, believe me. I was fond of the child, for it would have been difficult not to like Catherine. She had at times a willful and provoking nature, but there was something about her, she was such a merry companion who took her lot without complaining, that it was only a brute like the Dozer who would not be taken with her ways. Even Fabian, harsh though he was, said he loved her, and I do believe he did.

Gentlemen, the night I left the mill I told her not to stay with Fabian, but to come with me and live with my wife and me like one of our own, and she raised her pretty little head and kissed my hand.

Does that sound like a maiden who was terrified of me? One I had misused? But she would not leave Fabian, for he had a strange charm about him, and just as Davy would do anything Fabian bade him, so Catherine would not be parted from him, saying she loved him. They were a strange pair, make no mistake on that, but I do believe each loved the other truly.

Why, I can hardly believe Fabian was such a villain as to kill her, yet it must have been he, for the Dozer was dead.

Fabian used to look upon her, when she was not aware of it, with the softest expression on his face, and oh, he had a cruel face ordinarily. And I have seen him, while she slept, sit by her side, looking down at her and every so often touching her hair. Then he would look up at me and say, "By God, Yorek, did you ever seen such a pretty trick as the Pippin?"

Certain I am he did not want to kill her, but she had slipped into his plans by error, and Fabian was such a man as plotted things down to the last small detail. I do believe he enjoyed the planning of the robbery as much as the thought of having the loot. He trusted no one and left nothing to chance, and he had no place in his plans for a young girl.

He was the kind of man who could not bear for his plans to go astray, and put great stock in his cunning. Why, I think him capable of killing even himself if through his own foolishness the robbery had gone awry. He could not bear softness or stupidity, and despised it in himself as much as in others.

He must have killed Catherine, for I did not, but if the villain has a heart, and I think he has not, but if he has, he broke it when he killed that girl. If ever he wept tears in his life, they fell from his eyes when he took Catherine Barton by the throat! But knowing him as I do, I know he would not be influenced by softness or pity, and so wreck his hell-sent plots.

Well, after Catherine and I got back from market, the Dozer decided the girl knew something of where the treasure was hid. He thought Jenkin Davy had told her the cipher as he was dying, and the Dozer was going to torture the truth from her, but I stood up for her, and the Dozer knocked me senseless for my trouble, and when I came to, Fabian was beguiling the girl into telling what she had heard.

I could never be sure Dozer had not frightened the girl so much that she made up the cipher to protect herself, for it never did make much sense, and never, while I was there, helped to find treasure.

About five days after that, Fabian suggested that since we could not find the loot, we might as well split up, and he offered me the two horses as compensation. I swear it, gentlemen, I swear it was Fabian who gave me the horses, in the night, and bade me begone before the Dozer awoke. And so I left, leaving them all alive, Catherine Barton, the Dozer and Fabian.

And Fabian had given me the name of the dealer, Mr. Heal, the rotten dog knowing that Mr. Heal would recognize the horses.

And as for the leather bag being found in my cowshed, Fabian placed it there, to convict me, as he had planned all along.

It was Fabian! Fabian did all!

Fabian killed the girl, Fabian killed the Dozer, and Fabian found the treasure after I left and placed that bag in my cowshed.

Gentlemen, you must believe me! I am a man who, God knows, has run afoul of the law, and I admit it. I will pay whatever measure the law demands of me for the crimes I have committed.

But gentlemen, I avow on the souls of my children—and how more deeply could a man perjure himself if he spoke falsely?— I say, though I be guilty of robbery, I am not a murderer!

Hang me for the robbery if you will. I have said I would gladly pay the price the law demands of me. But I did not kill Catherine Barton. I am not a murderer! I did not kill Catherine Barton! I swear it!

Mr. Howard, Counsel for the King, rose to answer the prisoner's defense.

Mr. HOWARD: Gentlemen of the Jury, I charge that this man, Edward Yorek, killed Catherine Barton. And if there ever were a Max Fabian—which I doubt, for I do think he was a product of this villain's degenerate, twisted, murderer's mind—but if, by any strange accident of fate, there were a Max Fabian, you may be sure, gentlemen, that he lies dead and murdered somewhere yet to be discovered, an unfortunate victim of this monster's ungovernable passions, as Jenkin Davy and Thomas Parr and poor little Catherine Barton now lie dead.

Fabian took part in the robbery? Fabian, according to the prisoner's own testimony, was in Cornwall when the robbery was committed.

Fabian was at Forsham? Not one living soul in Forsham or any other place saw Fabian, but Edward Yorek and Thomas Parr and Jenkin Davy were seen.

Fabian! Fabian gave Edward Yorek the horses! Fabian suggested that Edward Yorek drag that terrified child through the market of Handley! Fabian killed Parr and Catherine Barton! Fabian found the treasure! Fabian, with his hands full of diamonds and gold, I suppose, walked leagues out of his way to leave a crested leather bag in Edward Yorek's cowshed.

Nonsense!

Heap not calumny, Edward Yorek, on the head of a man who is not here and never was, but rather on your own wicked pate, for being caught in the terrible web of violence and deceit which you wove about yourself.

There is no Max Fabian, there never was, except in your mind. There was no Max Fabian, but only yourself, that unfortunate girl, Thomas Parr and Jenkin Davy, and you. And you, Edward Yorek, killed Parr and Davy and broke the girl's neck and departed with the horses and the loot!

Gentlemen: notice the inconsistencies in his description of this mysterious Max Fabian:

Max Fabian had a dimple in his cheek—first his right, then his left—nay—he cannot remember!

Max Fabian, the cruelest of men, would stroke Catherine's hair while she slept, his face tender. This man, this murderer, without heart, this Fabian! Why, Yorek says Fabian loved the maid, yet, according to Yorek, it is Fabian, who loved her, and not our innocent Yorek, who killed her!

Does this make sense? It does not to me. Only one thing in Fabian's description strikes a familiar note to me. He minds me very much of Edward Yorek! Why, Yorek even describes him as being of his own height and build. Yorek is minus the dimple, you understand, but then Edward Yorek could never quite make up his mind about that dimple.

Fabian "gave" him the horses, and directed him, out of malice, to Mr. Heal, knowing Heal would recognize the horses.

If one can believe Yorek's inconsistent reports on this Fabian, Fabian, if he existed, was not the sort of man who "gave" anything away.

Nay, gentlemen, Edward Yorek tried to execute a crime of such fiendish proportions that even the laws of nature and chance were swung from their natural courses, for nature does not suffer monsters to flourish. Indeed, if you will think on it, you will see that nature allows little leniency with monsters, and does her best to rid the world speedily of them.

And it was nature, changing her own laws of chance, that led Edward Yorek, with a hand of doom, straight to the one man who would be sure to set the machinery of the law in motion. Such is the justice of God!

Edward Yorek, in his defense, makes no mention of the incident of Catherine Barton attempting to buy poison, and well he might remain silent, for he knows that that maid, the top of whose head scarcely cleared his shoulder, could hardly hope to rid herself of his villainous company by strangling or otherwise using physical violence on him.

Take a good look at him, gentlemen. Is he not a sturdily built, well set up fellow, not yet even in his prime?

Picture that girl, that poor, terrified child, being dragged through the market in the wake of this monster, her tears availing her naught. And in her desperate, confused mind, trying to think of a plan to escape him!

"Poison, poison," she thinks, pitiful creature. "I could slip it in his drink." For well she knew that her pathetic strength could not be pitted against him.

Well, for once we must curse the Johnny Fahs for not dealing in the black arts, for the poor girl found no poison, and Catherine Barton is now very dead, while Edward Yorek, gentlemen, is very much alive!

Edward Yorek says he was fond of the girl, yet, in front of reliable witnesses, he treated her with marked brutality and threatened her life.

Does he challenge the statements of the witnesses? Nay, for he cannot. Instead, he offers us this threadbare excuse of Fabian again.

He struck Catherine Barton and threatened her life, to protect her from our mysterious Mr. Fabian? What nonsense, gentlemen, what utter nonsense. Edward Yorek insults the intelligence of decent men by offering such transparent lies.

Edward Yorek struck that girl because he is, by nature, a brutal man, and he threatened her life because he intended to take it.

He is a consummate scoundrel! A heartless, monstrous imitation of God's noblest creature, man!

Bring forth your Fabian, Edward Yorek, or hang for want of him! For I have counseled many cases for the crown, but never one in which a shade, a ghost, a fable, was used with such transparency!

In the last extremity of your wickedness, and in fear of the fate you so rightly deserve, your brain, that wicked instrument of the Devil, gave birth to this Fabian! And I charge you, Edward Yorek, you killed Catherine Barton because you feared to leave her as a living witness to an already long list of felonies.

There is no Fabian, gentlemen of the jury, there is no Fabian, and there never was one! But there is a Yorek! Yes, behold him, weeping his murderer's tears and pounding his chained murderer's hands!

CRIER: Oyez, my lords the King's justices do strictly charge and command all manner of persons to keep silence, upon pain of imprisonment!

Mr. Baron Bolt opened to the jury the substance of the indictment as before set forth, and told them that whether the prisoner was guilty, in the manner as therein charged, must be left to their consideration, upon the evidence that had been laid before them.

After reviewing the evidence, His Honor continued: A very tragic story it is, gentlemen, that you have heard, and upon which you are now to form your judgment and give your verdict. The killing of a defenseless girl of tender years is a crime so heinous that it must shock human nature, and the law must inflict its penalty upon the villain of so black a dye as to commit such an outrage.

In the present case, which is to be made out by circumstances, a great part of the evidence must rest upon presumption, in which the law makes a distinction:

A slight or probable presumption only, has little or no weight; but a violent presumption amounts, in law, to full proof; that is, where circumstances speak so strongly that to suppose the contrary would be absurd.

From the evidence of the witnesses for the King, and from the free admissions of the prisoner, you may take these facts to have been proved:

That the prisoner took part in the robbery of Lord Portchester's treasure, together with two known accomplices.

That these robbers kidnaped the girl, Catherine Barton, at Forsham, and that one of the accomplices was there killed.

That the girl was subsequently seen one hundred miles away at the market place in Handley, and in the company of the prisoner; and that the prisoner was there seen to strike her.

That the girl and a second robber were killed upon the estate of Lord Leafield.

That the prisoner afterward attempted to sell in London two horses stolen from Lord Portchester; and that an empty leather bag bearing Lord Portchester's arms was found in the cowshed of the prisoner at Byford, in Berkshire.

It must be kept in mind that the prisoner is being tried here only for the murder of the girl, Catherine Barton. It is not enough to prove that the prisoner is guilty of the robbery, or even that he killed his accomplices.

In all cases of murder at common law, as defined by the Lord Coke, it is of a necessity that there should be malice aforethought, either expressed or implied, which is the essence of the offense.

Counsel for the King argue that they have proved malice; to wit, the "sinister" attitude of the prisoner toward the girl at Handley, followed by her attempt to buy poison, and they offer the empty satchel as proof of motive, in that having found the treasure, the prisoner feared to leave the girl as a witness.

Yet the butcher, George Snider, could not explain what he meant by a sinister manner, and admitted he was not so sufficiently alarmed by the prisoner's statements as to seek protection for the girl. And we have only the word of a gypsy that the maid sought poison.

The prisoner has another explanation for the presence of the empty leather bag in his cowshed: that there was a fourth man involved in the robbery, a mysterious "Max Fabian" who was the mastermind of the whole plot; and that this Fabian placed the bag by stealth in order to convict the prisoner of the murders of which he himself was guilty.

Edward Yorek claims to be a victim, a most unfortunate victim, of a monstrous plot, a forged chain of evidence left by a criminal with such a mind as to make decent men shudder with horror.

The prisoner bases his entire defense upon the existence of this Fabian; indeed, he has described the man in detail. Yet by his own admission he can produce not one particle of proof that such a person ever existed.

You must consider, nevertheless, the prisoner's candor in admitting and confessing his part in the robbery, and his leading the bailiff's men straight to the mill where two bodies were found. It is as reasonable to suppose that he did not know the bodies were there as to think that conscience drove him to return to the scene of his crime.

It is for you, gentlemen of the jury, to say whether presumption of guilt in this case is so strong as to prove the prisoner guilty of murder.

Weigh the evidence with infinite care, gentlemen, while Edward Yorek lives and breathes, for once we place the hangman's noose about his neck and draw it tight, we cannot bring life back to his body to beg forgiveness for our error.

Search your consciences and your souls, gentlemen, so that you may rest and sleep without remorse after you reach your verdict.

If you believe Edward Yorek did unlawfully kill Catherine Barton with malice aforethought, in the manner set forth in the indictment, you must find him guilty of murder. If, however, you do not believe this, you must find him not guilty.

The jury consulted together for fifty-five minutes and then turned to the court.

CLERK OF THE ARRAIGNS: Gentlemen, are you agreed on your verdict?

JURY: Yes.

CLERK OF THE ARRAIGNS: Who shall speak for you?

JURY: Our foreman, Isaac Gills.

CLERK OF THE ARRAIGNS: Edward Yorek, hold up thy hand. Gentlemen of the Jury, look upon the prisoner: How say you, is Edward Yorek guilty of the felony and murder whereof he stands indicted, or not guilty?

ISAAC GILLS: Guilty.

CLERK OF THE ARRAIGNS: Edward Yorek, hold up thy hand. You have been indicted of felony and murder. You have thereupon been arraigned, and pleaded thereto Not Guilty, and for your trial have put yourself upon God and your Country, which Country have found you guilty. What have you now to say for yourself, why the court should not proceed to give judgment of death upon you, according to the law?

PRISONER: I did not do it! I did not do it! I swear on my soul I have never committed murder in my life. I am innocent, I tell you, I am innocent! I did not kill that girl!

CRIER: Oyez! My lords the King's Justices do strictly charge and command all manner of persons to keep silence, whilst sentence of death is passing on the prisoner at the bar, upon pain of imprisonment!

MR. BARON BOLT: Edward Yorek, you have been indicted for the murder of Catherine Barton, and for your trial have put upon God and your Country. That Country has found you guilty.

You have had a long and fair trial and it falls my lot to acquaint you that I am now no more at liberty to suppose you innocent than I was before to presume your guilt.

You are convicted of a crime so dreadful, so abhorrent in itself, that human nature rebels at it. The willful murder of a girl, a child that was gentle, loving and tender, by all accounts. May your heavenly Father forgive you.

It is hard to conceive that anything could have induced you to perpetrate an act so vile, so impossible to reconcile to nature or reason. One should have thought your own senses, your own natural instincts as a father, might have secured you from an impulse so barbarous and wicked.

What views you had, or what was your intention, is best known to yourself; with God and your conscience be it. At this bar we can judge only from appearances, and from evidence produced to us.

Deceive yourself not, Edward Yorek. Remember that you are very shortly to appear before a much more awful tribunal, where no subterfuge can avail, where no art nor disguise can screen you from the Searcher of all hearts. "He revealeth the deep and secret things, he knoweth what is in the darkness, and light dwelleth with him."

Let me advise you to make the best and wisest use of the little time you are likely to continue in this world: Apply to the throne of Grace and endeavor to make your peace with that Power whose justice and mercy are infinite.

Nothing now remains but to pronounce the sentence of the law upon you; which is:

Having considered the foregoing verdict against Edward Yorek, and having found Edward Yorek guilty of the murder of the said Catherine Barton, the said Edward Yorek guilty is. I decern and adjudge that the said Edward Yorek be carried from the bar, back to the Gaol, therein to be fed upon bread and water only, in the terms of the Act of Parliament, in the twenty-fifth year of the reign of his Majesty George the Second, entitled, "An Act for Preventing the Horrid Crime of Murder" until Wednesday, the twenty-fifth day of September next to come;

And upon that day to be taken forth of the said place and carried to the common place of execution, and then and there, betwixt the hours of two and four of the clock after noon, of the said day, to be hanged by the neck by the hands of the common hangman, until he be dead;

And his body thereafter to be delivered to Dr. Alexander Munro, professor of Anatomy from Edinburgh, to be by him publicly dissected and anatomized, in the terms of the said act;

And we ordain all his moveable goods and gear to be escheat and inbrought to his Majesty's use; which is pronounced for DOOM.

Sick to my soul, I put the sheaf of papers containing the transcript of the trial on the table, and turned once more to the Reverend Mr. Peterson's diary.

September 8th: The Lord has truly answered my prayers. Oh, merciful God, I see it all now. Oh Lord! You have honored me beyond all measure, for did not the judge admonish that wicked man, in his last hours, to turn to God? I have been chosen. I, most humble of the Lord's servants, I have been chosen to save Edward Yorek's soul.

September 12th: Oh, the Lord is most merciful, and I see it all clearly now, for in redeeming Edward Yorek from the Devil, and turning his soul, repentant, to the Lord, my own salvation is assured.

Oh, Sweet Redeemer, the task you have set me is not an easy one, but I shall not quail before it. Oh Lord, this burden may be a heavy one, to turn the heart, the hard heart of that most wicked of men, but joyfully shall the burden be borne, joyfully shall the light of my Redeemer shine upon me, and with his spear of righteousness I shall pierce the heart of Edward Yorek, though it be as hard as flint. And he shall fall upon his knees, freely confessing his terrible sins, for he must confess and be truly repentant to receive the blood of the Lamb, yea, to enter that fold. Edward Yorek shall confess and open his heart to his Redeemer. I am truly blessed that the Lord has chosen this difficult penance for me, and the light of the Lord is upon me!

September 22nd: I have traveled first to Mr. Heaslop Bolt, for his permission to see the condemned villain, and Mr. Bolt, being a just and righteous man, God-fearing in all things himself, gladly gave me leave to visit Edward Yorek, when I told him I would save Yorek's soul.

What a filthy hole that gaol is! The stench of it is still in my nostrils, but it is no more than those wretches who inhabit it deserve, having sinned against their Lord.

I found the condemned man in a most piteous state, his eyes blackened, his lips gashed, his shirt hardly more than a bloody rag to cover his lacerated chest and shoulders.

"Fall on your knees and pray, Edward Yorek," I cried, "for the

Lord has sent me, his humble servant, to save your soul, your divine, immortal soul, so that it may do service in His garden, rather than serve that wicked master Satan, who has you in his thrall!"

The poor wretch fell on his knees before me, clinging to my hand and kissing it, and saying,

"Who has sent you, sir? Who has sent you to me in the hour of my extremity?"

"God has sent me," I replied, placing my hand on his head. "Are you truly repentant, Edward Yorek?"

"Oh sir," he said, weeping, "I am tortured beyond all manner of thought, so that I long for the gallows. I am starved and they beat me daily, to divulge the hiding place of the treasure, and I do not know it, sir, I do not know it. I beg you, aid me, give me succour, force those beasts who call themselves men to let me at least die soon!"

"Edward Yorek," I replied, "The Lord is punishing you for your horrid crimes, but be of good cheer, for though He tries you sorely, it is only that your redemption may be the sweeter."

The villain jerked his head back.

"What!" he said. "Have you, a man of God, come here only to mock me? Have I not suffered enough?"

"My poor child," I said, "do you not understand? You must suffer every agony, every torture of the damned, so that your soul may be washed free from the terrible crime you committed."

"I am innocent!" he cried, springing to his feet. "Before God and man, I am innocent. Is it not enough that my wife and children starve in the streets and I must die for another man's crime? Am I to be so cruelly mocked as well?"

"Confess your crime, Edward Yorek, and be truly repentant, and you shall be saved!"

"I shall not confess, for I am innocent!"

I realized how hard was the task the Lord had set me, but the Lord was with me and lent me cunning.

"Edward Yorek," said I, bringing my purse from my pocket, "this is filled with gold. If you will confess and repent, your wife and children will not starve, for I shall see to them. But if you persist in damning your immortal soul, they shall be damned with you. Do you not perceive your wickedness?"

But the villain placed his hands over his face, crying, "Oh God,

Oh God, if there be one, this old man must be sent by Fabian, for none but he could be so wondrous cruel."

"I have studied your trial, Edward Yorek," I replied, "and there is no Fabian. You were tried and found guilty. Do not, I pray you, take up our time with protestations of your innocence, but rather let us sink to our knees in prayer, and save you. As His Honor Mr. Bolt said, you will face a far more awful tribunal when you are taken down from the gibbet, and your soul soars—whence? To God? Let us pray so, unfortunate wretch."

"You old devil!" he shouted. "Would you buy my soul for the price of food for my children? Well, I shall not perjure my soul, no, I shall not! Would you bribe me to confess a crime I did not commit, by the cruellest of all means, my wife and children's empty bellies?"

"I would save your soul," I said calmly, "for my own depends upon it."

"Curse your soul!" He spat upon me in his wickedness.

"I fear not rude words, Edward Yorek, nor violence, for the Lord is with me. Have you learned nothing, you unfortunate man? Has this place taught you nothing?"

His terrible weeping ceased and he laughed wildly.

"Why, yes, this place taught me much. It has taught me that they flog and starve lunatics, hang wretches who steal to eat, throw debtors into prison among felons for the crime of being poor, so that the whole festering lot are made into more felons! And felons live in rotten cesspools and are starved and beaten in a manner I would not treat a beast, so that fever and filth may save our Sovereign the trouble of hanging them!"

"Be silent!" I cried. "You speak treason!"

"And in the last agony, is it enough for a man to be wrongly tried and hanged? Nay! He must be publicly dissected, for his guts to hang in public! Well, hearken to me. This professor will rip the heart from my body, and what will that teach him? Let him look at my guts, and he will see they are like those of any man. Let him look at my heart when I am dead, and he cannot tell it from Fabian's. Oh, God! It is this I have not the strength to bear!

"There is no soul! Who can distinguish the newly ripped heart of Fabian from mine but God, if there be one? And what shall it profit me, if there be a God, to have Him judge my heart innocent, while Fabian's still beats, beats, beats, and beats! While he draws breath and eats and knows all manner of pleasure, and my wife starves to death with my innocent children! Oh, Christ!

"Nay, there is no God! I pray you, sir, do not speak to me of God, for I have searched my soul, here, in this unspeakable solitude, and if my soul is lacking, I know not whereof it lacks. I have not mocked God's ways, yet you come to me, offering me salvation. God, yes, offering me gold in exchange for my soul! Well, my soul is not for sale!"

He sank to the filthy floor, weeping so terribly that the tears cascaded down his cheeks.

"God is not mocked, Edward Yorek!" I cried. "Why do you weep?"

"For my children," he said.

"And you will not turn to God?"

"If there be a God, and He can find His way to this hell, my heart is open to Him," cried the wretch, the most cursed wretch.

"Weep!" I cried suddenly, close to tears myself, not for this man's agony, but at the thought of little Catherine's. "Weep, weep tears enough to drown your children, you most vile of men! For your eyes were dry when you killed another man's child."

He wiped his tears away with his broken hands and stood up.

"Begone, old man," he said, "or I shall do a murder to fit the one I am to hang for."

I left him alone, the wicked, wicked man. Oh Lord, I have failed in the task you have set me. And for that both he and I are doomed.

Three days later I attended his hanging, and as the bailiffs brought him forth a great crowd surged forward to see him.

A woman broke through the ranks of the curious and fell at his feet, clasping his knees. He looked down at her, his villain's face soft, and then four little yellow-haired children ran forth. The bailiffs tried to drive them away but they would not be driven away, and despite the blows which were showered upon them, they clung to his legs, weeping.

Finally two more of the King's men appeared, and, grabbing the woman under the arms, they dragged her away. They returned, each picking up two children and carrying them bodily to their sobbing mother. And when I noted the eldest child, my heart felt like a stone in my bosom, for she might have been Catherine's little sister, but of nine or ten years, and being so like

Catherine with her long golden hair and fair face.

Suddenly an angry murmur arose from the mob, and they began to pelt the unfortunate woman and her children with stones and rotten vegetables, and the children hid their faces in their mother's skirts. She stood with her arms about them to protect them.

I rushed over and stood before them, crying to their tormentors, "Desist, for this poor woman has suffered enough, having espoused a monster."

And the crowd turned its attention to the condemned man, heaving stones at him. The bailiffs, who were also being pelted, shouted angrily and waved their swords, which seemed to enrage the mob, for they surged forward on the prisoner.

One fellow, a farmer, I think, for he carried a huge, pointed cattle goad, raised that wicked instrument and pinned one of Edward Yorek's feet to the ground, then another followed suit, while a third began clubbing him.

He stood silently, never letting so much as a whimper pass his lips—oh, he was a hard man—and then he turned to his wife—just in time to see a large stone catch her on the temple and knock her senseless.

Suddenly he became a madman, and, kicking loose the goads which pinned his feet to the ground, he made to overthrow the two bailiffs who held him.

They could not have kept him secure if the two other officers had not joined them, and it took the exertions of all four men to restrain him.

They began to drag him on his broken, clubbed feet, for he could not walk, up to the gallows, and his face worked fiendishly, and then he cried:

"God curse you, Fabian! God curse your heart and your blood! God curse all your line! God curse them till one may feel all, all, that Edward Yorek has suffered! God is not mocked!"

But as he was stood on the gallows, he suddenly became very quiet and subdued, looking down at his wife, still unconscious, and her little children crouched about her, weeping.

And then the executioner came to him and asked his forgiveness, and he answered in a firm, clear voice:

"I freely forgive you, as I do all mankind, save Max Fabian, whom I have cursed."

The executioner then proceeded to do his duty. The prisoner's neckcloth was taken off, his manacles were removed, and his arms secured by a black sash, and then the cord was put about his neck. The cap was drawn over his face, and upon a signal given by the sheriff, that part upon which he stood instantly sank down from beneath his feet, leaving him entirely suspended.

He died unshriven and unrepentant, his soul lost to his blessed Lord.

I turned to his wife, and, handing a stout fellow in the mob a coin, bade him help me carry the poor woman from the dreadful scene.

I shall do what I can for them, his wife and their children. Perhaps in this way I can in part atone for failing in the task the Lord appointed me.

I bowed my head in my hands and wept. Yes, Edward Yorek, your terrible curses have been most bitterly fulfilled by the last of Fabian's line.

It was I, John Montrolfe, who had written that I had never felt pity or remorse. I was grateful to feel both now, for how otherwise could I extend to others what I had never given to myself? My sufferings have not been in vain, and in this step alone, I knew I was on the road to freedom.

I put down the awful documents and began to assess the things I knew I had yet to do to free myself completely.

You can't go back anywhere, that's the tragedy of it. There was really only one way I could settle the debt, but unlike Pippin and Yorek, I must pay *by,* not with my life.

The other things I could do were, of course, only material things, but I have not been given a choice in making amends and I must do the best I can.

That day I walked to Forsham and took the train to London to see my solicitor.

When I returned, I asked both Beatrice and Forbes to meet me in the library, as I had something of importance to tell them.

There we were, the three of us, gathered together for the last act, and none of us out of character.

I explained that I was determined to atone as best I could. I had deeded over the house and all its contents to Beatrice. They were named my joint heirs, and any interest accruing on the enormous fortune I had inherited was theirs during my lifetime.

For a moment they both looked stunned.

Going to the liquor cabinet, I poured drinks and handed them around.

"Well," I said, "shall we drink to a happy Cliff House, rid forever of Montrolfes?"

They didn't answer me, nor did they respond to my toast.

Then Beatrice suddenly clapped her hands.

"Mine? This house, really mine? Do you mean it? *Oh!*"

Before I could answer Forbes stepped forward, his face stiff with hate.

"Don't be taken in! It's another rotten, filthy Montrolfe trick!"

His glass bounced off Guy Montrolfe's portrait onto the carpet, unbroken, but the liquor dripped from those terrible eyes like tears.

"Look—," I began, but he cut me short.

"I don't believe anything you say! Anything!"

I could hardly blame him.

"And I won't believe anything until I see all the facts published in black and white! Black and white!"

"You will," I replied. "Believe me, you will, down to your last word."

"A likely story! Why should you change your spots now? Why change now?"

Why must he keep repeating himself? I could see my way was going to be a thorny one.

"Because," I answered with as much patience as I could muster, "having read Mr. Peterson's diary and the transcript of the trial, I know I can't be free until I am completely quit of this place."

"Oh, you're not going away?" Beatrice came to my side and looked up at me imploringly, and that, of course, enraged Forbes further.

"You're a monster, like Fabian. A monster!"

If he repeated himself once more, I felt I would murder him. I was anxious now to have done with the whole business so I could leave before another blot stained the Montrolfe escutcheon. He had, I knew, every right to doubt and hate me, but this did not make me any fonder of him.

"Beatrice!" he cried. "Don't be taken in by him. You read that journal, and you know about the trial. I warn you, Beatrice, don't be taken in by him!"

Beatrice turned on him irritably. "Oh, stop shouting! It all happened so long ago, I don't know why you have to make such a fuss about it. I wish you weren't going away, Mr. Montrolfe!"

I was walking to the door, hopeful of avoiding further speech with Forbes.

"You're not going now?" Beatrice looked as if she were about to weep.

"Yes, to pack, my dear, and then to leave. Today."

"If you do, it'll be the first decent thing you've done in your life!" Forbes, of course. "Only I don't believe you will!"

"Oh, I wish you weren't going, Mr. Montrolfe!"

Among the many horrors of my inheritance was myself, and now I knew that I alone was completely responsible for me; I could hold no one else accountable from this minute on; only I could shape my destiny.

"Yes, Beatrice, I'm going. I feel and know it is the only thing I can do."

Forbes now found himself in the indefensible position of being in accord with a Montrolfe, and was hurriedly forced to reverse himself.

"You don't have to leave," he said with dignity. "Beatrice and I will."

"*I will not!*" she exploded.

"Then you do believe him! You honestly believe him!"

There he was, repeating himself again. My sympathies began veering to Fabian.

"Listen," I said, trying desperately to be patient, "listen—." Oh God! He had me doing it now. "Beatrice." I turned to her. "Surely you can't be serious about marrying this—this unspeakable booby?"

"Oh, I am." But she didn't sound any too enthusiastic. Dear Beatrice, she is not overendowed with a sense of humor, but at least it broke the tension for me, and I was able to laugh.

"Beatrice, I forbid, I positively *forbid* you to accept anything from this man. You *know* about the journal and the trial! How can you believe him? How *can* you?"

He was thinking about the horses, I suppose, and suspected me of rushing off to the London authorities to report Cliff House stolen.

He wheeled dramatically to Guy Montrolfe's portrait, and then to me. "Look at him, Beatrice! Then look at *him!* I for one—"

"Oh, shut up!" roared Beatrice. "I always wanted this house and now I've got it. If you don't like it, clear out!"

Now Forbes looked as if he might weep.

"Don't you see what he's doing?" he cried. "The same old story! It's the same old story! All the Montrolfes are the same. They never give *anything!* They *take, take, take!* Don't you see what he's doing? He's taking you from me!"

Yes, it was the same old story, and the same old whining and sermonizing. Apart from my very real regard for Beatrice, I would have liked to have taken her from him, just for the sport of it. But that, of course, would have put us all back at the beginning again, and I was one Montrolfe who had learned his lesson only too painfully and too well.

There were no cuckoos in our nest, and the Barton blood obviously still flowed strongly in Beatrice's veins.

"Nobody is taking me from anybody or anything from me. And if you repeat yourself once more, Ted, I swear to God I'll hit you!"

I limped to the door. Yes, I still limp, but I don't mind too much now. It's a small price to pay. And I knew in my heart that if I put my mind to it, I could induce Beatrice to follow me to the ends of the earth.

Forbes took Beatrice's arm. "Beatrice, you will still marry me, won't you?"

She looked questioningly at me, but I only stood at the open door, saying nothing.

"Yes," she said finally.

"And we'll be just like we were before *he* came?"

"Yes, yes, yes, damn it."

I left the devoted couple to themselves and as I limped up the stairs, feeling singularly happy and with my head erect, Nan leaped from her kitchen lair.

"Pick up your feet!" she roared. "A body can't rest around here!"

"You'll be able to soon, as far as I'm concerned," I said. "I'm leaving."

She cocked her head on one side suspiciously.

"Where you going?"

"Back to that there Afriker. And Beatrice is going to marry the detestable Forbes and live here with him. They're going to have dozens of children, Nan, and the house will resound to the tramp of *their* feet."

"Afriker! You said you was a Canadian!"

From the landing, I blew her a kiss. "Nanny, you are a very naughty old lady."

Beatrice came into the hall, carrying the tray of glasses.

"You keep your damned brats out of my kitchen!" Nan shrieked at her, and slammed her door loudly as she retired.

Beatrice put the tray on the bottom step and looked up at me.

"Now what's up with her?" she asked, puzzled.

"She can't find her teeth."

Beatrice opened the kitchen door.

"They're on the library table."

"Aye?"

"Your teeth!"

"Got 'em in me pocket."

"Oh, for God's sake!"

Forbes came into the hall, holding Nan's teeth in his handkerchief as if he expected them to bite him.

"Beatrice, you are not spending another night under the same roof with that man!"

Beatrice brushed past him with the tray.

"Beatrice, I forbid, I positively forbid—"

There was a loud crash of glass.

"He said he was going, and he is. *He* is going, and *I* am staying! And you can damn well do what you like!"

"Oh. Well—if he's really going..." His voice trailed off lamely.

I packed my few belongings in my two suitcases, and when I reached the foot of the stairs I found Beatrice waiting for me, her face flushed and her eyes bright with tears.

"Can we give you a lift to the village?" she asked bravely.

"No, thank you. I'm looking forward to the walk. I'm also looking forward to catching that train."

I leaned down and kissed her cheek.

"Goodbye, my dear."

"Goodbye." She put her hand to her cheek. "I have always—always—liked you very much. I'll never forget you."

"No," I said, standing in the doorway. "I want you to forget me, Beatrice, and I'll forget you."

I turned to Forbes.

"And I want very much indeed to forget *you*. I'll send you a copy of the book as soon as it's published. Goodbye, both of you. Say goodbye to Nan for me, and don't close the door after me for a while. Let all the ghosts out at once."

As I walked down the broad steps, I turned once more.

"Goodbye, Cliff House," I whispered. "Farewell, Fabian, and my dearest little Pippin. Rest well now."

Then I went on, and did not look back.

Milton Keynes UK
Ingram Content Group UK Ltd.
UKHW012352290324
440273UK00004B/28